Please return on or before the latest date above.
You can renew online at *www.kent.gov.uk/libs*
or by telephone 08458 247 200

THE GIRL OF HIS DREAMS

DONNA LEON

**THORNDIKE
WINDSOR
PARAGON**

This Large Print edition is published by Thorndike Press, Waterville, Maine, USA and by BBC Audiobooks Ltd, Bath, England.

Thorndike Press, a part of Gale, Cengage Learning.

Copyright © Donna Leon and Diogenes Verlaz AG Zurich, 2008.

The moral right of the author has been asserted.

A Commissario Guido Brunetti Mystery.

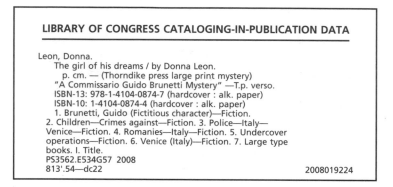

LIBRARY OF CONGRESS CATALOGING-IN-PUBLICATION DATA

Leon, Donna.
  The girl of his dreams / by Donna Leon.
    p. cm. — (Thorndike press large print mystery)
  "A Commissario Guido Brunetti Mystery" —T.p. verso.
  ISBN-13: 978-1-4104-0874-7 (hardcover : alk. paper)
  ISBN-10: 1-4104-0874-4 (hardcover : alk. paper)
  1. Brunetti, Guido (Fictitious character)—Fiction.
  2. Children—Crimes against—Fiction. 3. Police—Italy—
  Venice—Fiction. 4. Romanies—Italy—Fiction. 5. Undercover
  operations—Fiction. 6. Venice (Italy)—Fiction. 7. Large type
  books. I. Title.
  PS3562.E534G57 2008
  813'.54—dc22   2008019224

BRITISH LIBRARY CATALOGUING-IN-PUBLICATION DATA AVAILABLE

Published in 2008 in the U.S. by arrangement with Grove/Atlantic, Inc. Published in 2009 in the U.K. by arrangement with The Random House Group Limited.

U.K. Hardcover: 978 1 405 64993 3 (Windsor Large Print)
U.K. Softcover: 978 1 405 64994 0 (Paragon Large Print)

Printed in the United States of America
1 2 3 4 5 6 7 12 11 10 09 08

For Leonhard Tönz

Der Tod macht mich nicht beben.
Nur meine Mutter dauert mich;
Sie stirbt vor Gram ganz sicherlich.

Death does not make me tremble.
I feel sorry only for my mother.
She will surely die of grief.
Die Zauberflöte
Mozart

1

Brunetti found that counting silently to four and then again and again allowed him to block out most other thoughts. It did not obscure his sight, but it was a day rich with the grace and favour of springtime, so as long as he kept his eyes raised above the heads of the people around him, he could study the tops of the cypress trees, even the cloud-dappled sky, and what he saw he liked. Off in the distance, if only he turned his head a little, he could see the inside of the brick wall and know that beyond it was the tower of San Marco. The counting was a sort of mental contraction, akin to the way he tightened his shoulders in cold weather in the hope that, by decreasing the area exposed to the cold, he would suffer it less. Thus, here, exposing less of his mind to what was going on around him might diminish the pain.

Paola, on his right, slipped her arm

through his, and together they fell into step. On his left were his brother Sergio, Sergio's wife, and two of their children. Raffi and Chiara walked behind him and Paola. He turned and glanced back at the children and smiled: a frail thing, quickly dissipated in the morning air. Chiara smiled back; Raffi lowered his eyes.

Brunetti pressed his arm against Paola's, looking down at the top of her head. He noticed that her hair was tucked behind her left ear and that she was wearing the gold and lapis earrings he had given her for Christmas two years before. The blue of the earring was lighter than her dark blue coat: she had worn that and not the black one. When had it stopped, he wondered, the unspoken demand that black be worn at funerals? He remembered his grandfather's funeral, with everyone in the family, especially the women, draped in black and looking like paid mourners in a Victorian novel, though that had been well before he knew anything about the Victorian novel.

His grandfather's older brother had still been alive then, he remembered, and had walked behind the casket, in this same cemetery, under these same trees, behind a priest who must have been reciting the same prayers. Brunetti remembered that the old

10

man had brought a clod of earth from his farm on the outskirts of Dolo — long gone now and paved over by the autostrada and the factories. He recalled the way his great-uncle had taken his handkerchief from his pocket as they stood silently around the open grave as the coffin was lowered into it. And he remembered the way the old man — he must have been ninety, if a day — had folded back the fabric and taken out a small clod of earth and dropped it on to the top of the coffin.

That gesture remained one of the haunting memories of his childhood, for he never understood why the old man had brought his own soil, nor had anyone in the family ever been able to explain it to him. He wondered, standing there now, whether the whole scene could have been nothing more than the imagination of an overwrought child, struck into silence by the sight of most of the people he knew shrouded in black and by the confusion that had resulted from his mother's attempt to explain to his six-year-old self what death was.

She knew now, he supposed. Or not. Brunetti was prone to believe that the awfulness of death lay precisely in the absence of consciousness, that the dead ceased to know, ceased to understand, ceased to anything. His early life had been filled with myth: the little Lord Jesus asleep in his bed, the resurrection of the flesh, a better world for the good and faithful to go to.

His father, however, had never believed: that had been one of the constants of Brunetti's childhood. He was a silent nonbeliever who made no comment on his wife's evident faith. He never went to church, absented himself when the priest came to bless the house, did not attend his children's baptisms, first communions, or confirmations. When asked about the subject, the elder Brunetti muttered, *'Sciocchezze,'* or *'Roba da donne',* and did not pursue the topic, leaving his two sons to follow him if they wanted in the conviction that religious observation was the foolish business of women, or the business of foolish women. But they'd got him in the end, Brunetti reflected. A priest had gone into his room in the Ospedale Civile and given the dying Brunetti the last rites, and a mass had been said over his body.

Perhaps all of this had been done to console his wife. Brunetti had seen enough of death to know what a great comfort faith can be to those left behind. Perhaps this had been in the back of his mind during one of the last conversations he had with

12

his mother, well, one of the last lucid ones. She had still been living at home, but already her sons had had to hire the daughter of a neighbour to come and spend the days with her, and then the nights.

In that last year, before she had slipped away from them entirely and into the world where she had spent her last years, she had stopped praying. Her rosary, once so treasured, had gone; the crucifix had disappeared from beside her bed; and she had stopped attending Mass, though the young woman from downstairs often asked her if she would like to go.

'Not today,' she always answered, as if leaving open the possibility of going tomorrow, or the next day. She had stuck with this answer until the young woman, and then the Brunetti family, stopped asking. It did not put an end to their curiosity about her state of mind, only to its outward manifestation. As time passed, her behaviour became more alarming: she had days when she did not recognize either of her sons and other days when she did and talked quite happily about her neighbours and their children. Then the proportion shifted, and soon the days when she knew her sons or remembered that she had neighbours grew fewer. On one of those last days, a bitter winter day six years before, Brunetti had gone to see her in the late afternoon, for tea and for the small cakes she had baked that morning. It was by chance that she had baked the cakes; really she had been told three times that he was coming, but she had not remembered.

As they sat and sipped, she described a pair of shoes she had seen in a shop window the day before and had decided she would like to buy. Brunetti, even though he knew she had not been out of her home for six months, offered to go and get them for her, if she would tell him where the shop was. The look she gave him in return was stricken, but she covered it and said that she would prefer to go back herself and try them on to be sure they fitted.

She looked down into her teacup after saying that, pretending not to have noticed her lapse of memory. To relieve the tension of the moment, Brunetti had asked, out of the blue, '*Mamma,* do you believe all that stuff about heaven and living on after?'

She raised her eyes to look at her younger son, and he noticed how clouded the iris had become. 'Heaven?' she asked.

'Yes. And God,' Brunetti answered. 'All that.'

She took a small sip of tea and leaned

forward to set her cup in her saucer. She pushed herself back: she always sat up very straight, right to the end. She smiled then, the smile she always used when Guido asked one of his questions, the ones that were so hard to answer. 'It would be nice, wouldn't it?' she answered and asked him to pour her more tea.

He felt Paola stop beside him, and he came to a halt, pulled back from memory and suddenly attentive to where they were and what was going on. Off in the corner, in the direction of Murano, there was a tree in blossom. Pink. Cherry? Peach? He wasn't sure, didn't know a lot about trees, but he was glad enough of the pink, a colour his mother had always liked, even though it didn't suit her. The dress she wore inside that box was grey, a fine summer wool she had had for years and worn only infrequently, joking that she wanted to keep it to be buried in. Well.

The wind suddenly flipped the ends of the priest's purple stole up into the air; he stopped at the side of the grave and waited while the people following drew up in an unruly oval. This was not the parish priest, the one who had said the Mass, but a classmate of Sergio's who had once been close to the family and who was now a chaplain at the Ospedale Civile. Beside him, a man at least as old as Brunetti's mother held up a brass cup from which the priest took the dripping aspergill. Praying in a voice that only the people nearest to him could hear, he walked around the coffin, sprinkling it with holy water. The priest had to be careful where he placed his feet among the floral wreaths propped against their wooden frames on both sides of the grave, messages of love spelled out in golden letters across the ribbons that draped them.

Brunetti looked past the priest, back towards the tree. Another gust of wind slipped over the wall and ruffled the pink blossoms. A cloud of petals broke loose and danced up into the air, then fell slowly to the earth, surrounding the trunk in a pink areola. A bird started to sing from somewhere inside the remaining blossoms.

Brunetti pulled his arm free from Paola's and wiped his eyes with the inside of the sleeve of his jacket. When he opened them, another blossom cloud was flying up from the tree; his tears doubled it in size until nothing but a pink haze filled the horizon.

Paola grabbed his hand and squeezed it, leaving behind a light blue handkerchief. Brunetti blew his nose and wiped at his eyes, crushed the handkerchief in his right hand and stuffed it into the pocket of his jacket. Chiara moved up on his other side and took his hand. She held on while the words were said, prayers spoken up to the wind, and the workmen stepped forward on either side of the grave to lift the cords and lower the box into the ground. Brunetti had a moment of complete dislocation and found himself looking for the old man from Dolo, but it was the workers, and not the old man, who tossed earth down on to the coffin. It rang hollow at first, but when it had been covered by a thin layer, the sound changed. The spring had been wet, and the heavy clumps fell with a dull thud. And again, and then again.

And then someone on the other side, it might have been Sergio's son, dropped a bouquet of daffodils on to the earth at the bottom of the hole and turned away. The workmen paused, resting on their shovels, and the people standing around the grave took this opportunity to turn away and head back across the newly green grass, towards the exit and the vaporetto stop. Conversation went on by fits and starts as everyone tried to find the right thing to say and, failing that, at least something.

The 42 came and they all boarded. Brunetti and Paola chose to stay outside. It seemed suddenly cold in the shadow of the boat's roof. What had been a breeze within the cemetery walls blew here as wind, and Brunetti closed his eyes and lowered his head to escape it. Paola leaned against him, and, eyes still closed, he put his arm around her shoulder.

The engine changed tone, and he felt the sudden slowing of the boat as they approached Fondamenta Nuove. The vaporetto began the broad curve that would bring it to the dock, and the sun played across Brunetti's back, warming him. He raised his head and opened his eyes and saw the wall of buildings and behind them bell towers popping up here and there.

'Not much more,' he heard Paola say. 'Back to Sergio's and then lunch, and then we can go for a walk.'

He nodded. Back to his brother's to thank the closest friends who had come, and then the family would go for a meal. After that, the two of them — or the four of them if the kids wanted to come — could go for a walk: perhaps over to the Zattere or down to the Giardini to walk in the sun. He wanted it to be a long walk, so he could see the places that made him think of his mother, buy something in one of the shops she liked, perhaps go into the Frari and light a candle in front of the *Assunzione,* a painting she had always loved.

The boat grew closer. 'There's nothing . . .' he started to say but then stopped, not certain what it was he wanted to say.

'There's nothing to remember about her except the good,' Paola finished for him. Yes, that was exactly it.

2

Friends and relatives stood around them as
the boat pulled up to the *imbarcadero,* but
Brunetti kept his attention on the approaching dock and distracted himself with the
thought of the restoration of Sergio's house,
completed only six months before. If talk of
their health was the chief diversion of the
elderly and talking of sports that of men,
then talk of property was the social glue that
held all classes of Venetians together. Few
can resist the lure of the sound of prices
asked and paid, great deals made or lost, or
the recitation of square metres, previous
owners, and the incompetence of the bureaucrats whose task it is to authorize
restorations or modernizations. Brunetti
believed that only food was more often a
topic of conversation at Venetian dinner
tables. Was this the substitute for stories of
what one did in the war: had acumen in the
buying and selling of houses and apartments

been substituted for physical bravery, valour, and patriotism? Given that the only war the country had been involved in for decades was both a disgrace and a failure, perhaps it was better that people talk about houses.

The clock on the wall at Fondamenta Nuove told him that it was only a bit past eleven. His mother had always loved the mornings best: it was probably from her that Brunetti had got his early-morning cheerfulness, the quality of his which drove Paola closest to desperation. People filed off the boat, others filed on, then it took them quickly to the Madonna dell'Orto, where the Brunetti family and their friends got off the vaporetto and started back into the city, the church on their left.

They turned left at the canal, right over the bridge, and then they were at the door. Sergio opened it, and they filed quietly up the stairs and then into the apartment. Paola went towards the kitchen to see if Gloria needed help, and Brunetti walked over to the windows and looked out towards the façade of the church. The corner of a wall allowed him to see only the left hand side and just six of the apostles. The brick dome of the bell tower had always looked like a panettone to him, and so it did now.

He sensed the motion of people behind him, heard voices talking, and was glad that they were not lowered in one of those false genuflections to grief. He kept his back to them and to the talk and looked across at the façade. He had been out of the city that day more than a decade ago when someone had walked into the church and quietly removed the Bellini *Madonna* from the altar at the left and walked out of the church with it. The art theft people had come up from Rome, but Brunetti and his family had remained on holiday in Sicily, and by the time he got home, the art police had gone south again and the newspapers had tired of the case. And that was the end of that. And then nothing: the painting might as well have evaporated.

There was a change in the murmur of voices around him, and Brunetti turned away from the window to see why. Gloria and Paola and Chiara had emerged from the kitchen, the first two with trays of cups and saucers, and Chiara with another one that held three separate plates of home-made biscuits. Brunetti knew that this was a ceremony for friends, who would drink their coffee and soon leave, but he could not stop himself from thinking what a miserable, mean ending it was to a life so filled with food and drink and the warmth they generated.

From the kitchen Sergio appeared with three bottles of prosecco. 'Before the coffee,' he said, 'I think we should say goodbye.'

The trays ended up on the low table in front of the sofa, and Gloria, Paola, and Chiara went back into the kitchen to return a few minutes later, each with six prosecco glasses sprouting out from the fingers of her upraised hands.

Sergio popped the first cork, and at the sound the mood in the room changed, as if by magic. He poured the wine into the glasses, making the round as the bubbles subsided. He opened another bottle and then the last, filling more glasses than there were people. Everyone crowded round the table and picked up a glass, then stood with it half raised, waiting.

Sergio looked across at his brother, but Brunetti raised his glass and nodded towards his elder brother, signalling that the toast, and the family, were now his.

Sergio raised his glass and the room grew suddenly still. He lifted it higher, looked around at the people in the room, and said, 'To Amelia Davanzo Brunetti and to those of us who love her still.' He drank down half the glass. Two or three people repeated his toast in soft voices, and then everyone drank. By the time they lowered their glasses, softness had stolen back into the room, and voices were natural again. The topics of life returned to their conversation, and with them the future tense sneaked back in.

Some glasses were abandoned and a number of people drank coffee, ate a few of the biscuits, and then they began to idle slowly towards the door, each of them pausing to speak to, and then kiss, both of the brothers.

In twenty minutes, there was no one left in the room except Sergio and Guido and their wives and children. Sergio looked at his watch and said, 'I've reserved a table for all of us, so I think we should leave this here and go and have lunch.'

Brunetti emptied his glass and set it beside the still full ones that stood abandoned in a circle on the table. He wanted to thank Sergio for having found something right but undramatic to say, but he didn't know how to do it. He started towards the door, then turned back and embraced his brother. Then he pulled away and went through the door. He went down the steps in silence and outside into the sun to wait for the rest of the Brunettis.

3

The funeral took place on a Saturday, so there was no need for any of them to stay home from work or school the following day. By Monday morning, life had been restored to a normal rhythm, and everyone went off at the usual hour, though in Paola's case, Monday being one of the days when she had no need to present herself at the university, her place of work would be her desk. Brunetti left her sleeping. When he let himself out of the building, he found the day warm and sunny but still faintly damp. He started down towards Rialto, where he could buy a newspaper.

He was relieved to find that he dragged only a slight burden of grief. The relief he felt that his mother had managed to escape from a situation she would have found intolerable had she been aware of it brought him something akin to peace.

The stalls selling scarves, T-shirts, and

tourist kitsch were all open by the time he passed them, but his thoughts kept him blind to their garish colours. He nodded to one or two people he recognized but kept walking at a pace intended to discourage anyone who might want to stop and speak to him. He glanced at the clock on the wall, as he did every time he passed it, then turned towards the bridge. Piero's shop, on his right, was the only one that still sold food: everyone else had switched to junk of one sort or another. He was suddenly assaulted by the smell of chemicals and dyes, as if he had been transported to Marghera or it had come to him. Sharp and cloying, the smell ate at the membranes of his nose and brought tears to his eyes. The soap shop had been there for some time, but until now only the artificial colours had offended him; today it was the stench. Did they expect people to wash their bodies with *this?*

On his way towards Campo San Giacomo he noticed packages of pasta, bottles of *aceto balsamico,* and dried fruit on stalls that had formerly sold fresh fruit. Their lurid colours screeched at him, the visual equivalent of the odours that had forced him to hasten his steps. Gianni and Laura had closed their fruit stand and gone years ago, and so had the guy with the long hair and his wife, though they seemed to have sold it to Indians or Sri Lankans. How long would it be before the fruit market disappeared entirely and Venetians would be forced, like the rest of the world, to buy their fruit in supermarkets?

Before he could dwell on this litany of misery, the memory of Paola's voice overrode his musings, and he heard her telling him that if she wanted to listen to old women complain about how good things had been in the old days and how the whole world was falling apart, she'd go and sit in the doctor's waiting room for an hour some morning: she did not want to have to listen to it from him, in her own home.

Brunetti smiled at the memory, reached the top of the bridge and unwrapped his scarf from his neck before he started down the other side. He cut to the left, past the Ufficio Postale, up and down the bridge, and into Ballarin for a *caffè* and a brioche. He stood, crowded by people on either side, and realized that the memory of Paola's complaint — a complaint about his complaints — had cheered him. He caught his own image in the mirror behind the bar and grinned back at it.

He paid and continued on his way to work, cheered by the warmer weather. As he crossed Campo Santa Maria Formosa, he unbuttoned his jacket. Approaching the Questura, he saw Foa, the pilot, leaning over the side of his launch and gazing up the canal towards the bell tower of the Greek church.

'What's happening, Foa?' he called and stopped beside the boat.

Foa turned and smiled when he saw who it was. 'It's one of those crazy *tuffetti,* Commissario. He's been fishing in there since I got here.'

Brunetti glanced up the canal towards the church tower but saw only the undisturbed surface of the water. 'Where is he?' he asked, walking alongside the boat until he came abreast of the prow.

'He went under just about there,' Foa said, pointing up the canal, 'by the tree on the other side.'

All Brunetti could see was the water of the canal and, at the end, the bridge and the tilting bell tower. 'How long's he been under?' he asked.

'Seems like for ever, but it can't have been even a minute, sir,' Foa said, glancing at Brunetti.

Both men stood silently, staring up the canal, their eyes studying the surface of the water, waiting for the *tuffetto* to appear.

And then there he was, popping up from below like a plastic duck in a bathtub. One moment there was no sign of him, and the next he was sliding along silently, smoothly, tiny waves radiating out on the surface of the water as he paddled forward.

'You think it's good for him to eat those fish?' Foa asked.

Brunetti looked down at the water just beside the boat: grey, motionless, opaque. 'No worse than it is for us, I suppose,' he answered.

When Brunetti looked back, the tiny black bird had disappeared beneath the water again. He left Foa to it, went inside and up to his office.

As he left the house that morning, one of Brunetti's preoccupations had been the imminent return of Vice-Questore Giuseppe Patta. His immediate superior had been absent for two weeks, attending a conference on international police cooperation against the Mafia, held in Berlin. Though the invitation specified that attendees were to hold the rank of commissario or its equivalent, Patta had decided his own attendance was necessary. His absence had been facilitated by his secretary, Signorina Elettra Zorzi, who phoned him in Berlin at least twice a day, often more frequently than that, asking for his instructions about a number of ongoing cases. Since Patta could be counted on never to call the Questura while away, the possibility did not occur to him that Signorina Elettra had been calling him from a hotel in Abano Terme, where she had gone for two weeks of sauna, mud, and massage.

Brunetti went to his office and looked at the papers on his desk. He opened his newspaper and glanced at the front page. When he had read that, he skipped to pages eight and nine, where the existence of countries other than Italy might be acknowledged. Fixed elections in Central Asia, with twelve dead and troops in the streets; Russian businessman and two bodyguards killed in an ambush; mudslides in South America brought on by illegal logging and heavy rains; fear of the imminent bankruptcy of Alitalia.

Did these things happen, Brunetti wondered, with such dismaying regularity, or did the papers simply pull them out and use them when little had happened over a weekend and there was nothing else to write about except sports? He turned another page, but saw nothing he thought he could read with interest. That left culture, entertainment, and sports, but he could not deal with any of those this morning.

His phone rang. He answered with his name and the guard at the front door told him there was a priest there to see him.

'A priest?' Brunetti repeated.

'*Sì*, Commissario.'

'Would you ask him his name, please?'

'Of course.' The officer covered the receiver, and then he was back. 'He says his name is Padre Antonin, Dottore.'

'Ah, you can send him up, then,' Brunetti said. 'Show him the way, and I'll meet him at the top of the steps.' Padre Antonin was the priest who had given the final blessing over his mother's coffin; he was Sergio's friend and not his, and Brunetti could think of no reason that would bring him to the Questura.

Brunetti had known Antonin for decades, since he and Sergio had been schoolboys. Antonin Scallon had come close to being a bully then, always trying to make the boys, especially the younger ones, do what he wanted, name him the leader of the gang. Sergio's friendship with him had never made any sense to Brunetti, though he did notice that Antonin never gave orders to Sergio. After middle school, the brothers had gone to different schools, and so Antonin fell out of Brunetti's orbit. Some years later, Antonin had decided to enter the seminary, and from there he had gone to Africa as a missionary. During the time he spent in a country the name of which Brunetti could never remember, the only news of him Sergio received was contained in a circular letter which came just before Christmas, talking enthusiastically about the work the mission was doing to save souls, and ending with a request for money. Brunetti had no idea whether Sergio had answered the request: out of principle, he had refused to send anything.

And then, about four years ago, Antonin was back in Venice, working as a chaplain in the Ospedale Civile and living with the Dominicans in their mother house beside the Basilica. Sergio had mentioned his return, just as he had occasionally shown him the letters from Africa. The only other time Sergio had mentioned his former friend was to ask Brunetti if he minded if the priest came to the funeral and gave a blessing, a request Brunetti could hardly have refused, even had he been inclined to do so.

He went to the top of the stairs. The priest, dressed in the long skirt of his calling, was just turning into the final flight. He kept his eyes on his feet and one hand on the banister. From above, Brunetti could see how thin the man's hair was, how narrow his shoulders.

The priest stopped a few steps from the top and took two deep breaths, looked up, and saw Brunetti watching him. '*Ciao, Guido,*' he said and smiled. He was Sergio's age, which made him two years older than Brunetti, yet anyone looking at the three men together would assume the priest to be their uncle. He was thin, thin to the point of emaciation, with cheekbones that poked through the skin of his face to create taut dark triangles below.

He slid his hand up the banister, looked back at his feet, and continued up the stairs, and Brunetti could not help noticing the way he pulled on the railing with every step. At the top, the priest paused again, and put out his hand to shake Brunetti's. There was no attempt to embrace him or give him the kiss of peace, and Brunetti was relieved at that.

The priest said, 'I can't seem to get used to stairs again. I didn't see them for twenty years or so, and I suppose I forgot about them. They still seem strange to me. And exhausting.' The voice was still the same, with the exaggerated sibilance common to the Veneto. He had lost the cadence, though, and with it had gone what would once have made him immediately recognizable as being from the province. When the other man still did not move, Brunetti realized that Antonin was talking about the stairs in order to give himself a chance to regain his breath.

'How long were you there?' Brunetti asked, doing his bit to stretch out the moment.

'Twenty-two years.'

'Where were you?' he asked before he remembered he should have known that, if only from the letters Sergio had received.

'In Congo. Well, it was called Zaire when I got there, but then they changed the name back to Congo.' He smiled. 'Same place, but different countries. In a way.'

'Interesting,' Brunetti said neutrally. He held the door open for the other man, closed it behind him, and walked slowly after.

'Sit here,' Brunetti said, angling one of the chairs away from his desk, then turning another to face it, careful to pull it back to leave space between the two chairs. He waited for the priest to sit and then did the same.

'Thank you for coming to give the blessing,' Brunetti said.

'Not the best way to see old friends again

for the first time,' the priest answered with a smile.

Was that meant as a reproach that neither he nor Sergio had made any attempt to contact him in the years since his return to Venice?

'I visited your mother in the nursing home,' Antonin continued. 'A number of the people I knew when they were first in the hospital went out there,' he added, meaning the private nursing home outside the city where Brunetti's mother had spent her last years. 'I know it was very good; the sisters there are very kind.' Brunetti smiled and nodded. 'I'm sorry I was never there when you and Sergio were.' Abruptly the priest got to his feet, but it was only to pull his long skirt out from under him and flick it to one side; then he sat down again and went on. 'The sisters told me you went often, both of you.'

'Not as often as we should have, I suppose,' Brunetti said.

'I don't think there's any "should" in these circumstances, Guido. You go when you can and you go with love.'

'Did she know that we went?' Brunetti found himself asking.

Antonin studied his hands, folded together in his lap. 'I think she might have. Sometimes. I never know what they think or what's going on inside them, these old people.' He raised his hands in an arc of confusion. 'I think that what they do know is feelings. Or that they register them. I think they sense if the person with them is kind and is there because they love them or like them.' He looked at Brunetti and then again at his hands. 'Or pity them.'

Brunetti noticed that Antonin's fingernails covered only half of the bed of the nail, and at first he thought they must have been bitten down, a strange habit in a man of his age. But then he noticed that the nails were brittle and broken off in irregular layers, faintly concave and spotted, and he realized it must be some sort of disease, perhaps brought back from Africa. If so, why did he still have it?

'Do they register all those things the same way?' Brunetti asked.

'You mean the pity?' Antonin asked.

'Yes. It's different from love or liking, isn't it?'

'I suppose so,' the priest said and smiled. 'But the ones I saw were happy to get it: after all, it's much more than most old people get.' Absently, Antonin pinched up the cloth of his robe and ran the fold between the fingers of his other hand to make a long crease. He let it drop, looked at Brunetti and said, 'Your mother was lucky that she still had so many people who came to her with love and liking.'

Brunetti shrugged that away. His mother's luck had run out years ago.

'Why is it you've come?' Brunetti asked, then added 'Antonin' when he heard how harsh his question sounded.

'It's for one of my parishioners,' the priest said, then immediately corrected himself, 'well, if I had a parish, that is. She would be, then. But as it is she's the daughter of one of the men I visit in the hospital: he's been there for months. That's how I've come to know her, you see.'

Brunetti nodded but remained silent, his usual tactic when he wanted to encourage someone to continue speaking.

'It's about her son, actually, you see,' the priest said, looking back down at his skirt.

Because Brunetti had no idea of the ages of the man in the hospital or his daughter, he could have no idea of the age of the woman's son, which meant he could not anticipate the nature of the problem, though the fact that Antonin wanted to speak to him about it suggested it was something at variance with the law.

'His mother is very worried about him,'

Antonin continued.

There were many reasons a mother could worry about her son, Brunetti knew: his own mother had worried about him and Sergio, and Paola worried about Raffi, though he knew that Paola had little reason to worry about what most mothers today feared for their children: drugs. How lucky to live in a city with a small population of young people, Brunetti reflected, not for the first time. If they had to live in a world driven by capitalism, then thank heaven for this fortuitous side-effect: with so small a target population, few would go to the trouble and expense of marketing drugs in Venice.

Into Brunetti's continuing silence, Antonin asked, 'Do you mind if I ask you about this, Guido?'

Brunetti smiled. 'I still don't know what it is you're asking me about, Antonin, so I can't mind,' he said.

The priest at first looked surprised by Brunetti's remark, but then he gave a grin that managed to make him look almost embarrassed and agreed. '*Già, già.* It's hard to talk about.' He paused, then added, 'I suppose I'm not accustomed to the problems of luxury any more.'

'I'm not sure I understand,' Brunetti said.

It was a statement, but it disguised a question.

'Where I was, in Congo, people had different problems: disease, or poverty, or starvation, or soldiers who came and took away their possessions, sometimes their children.' The priest looked across at Brunetti, to see if he was following. 'So I've sort of lost the knack of listening to problems that aren't concerned with survival; to problems that come from wealth, not poverty.'

'Do you miss it?' Brunetti asked.

'What? Africa?'

Brunetti nodded.

Antonin used his hands to make another arc in the air. 'It's hard to say. I miss some of the things about it: the people, the immensity of the place, the sense that I was doing something important.'

'But you came back,' Brunetti observed, saying, not asking. Antonin looked Brunetti in the eyes then and said, 'I didn't have a choice.'

Brunetti asked, 'Your health?' thinking of how thin the man had looked as he came up the steps, how thin he was now, sitting across from him.

'Yes,' the priest said, and then added, 'in part.'

'And the other part?' Brunetti asked because he sensed that he had been led to a point where he was expected to.

'Problems with my superiors,' the priest answered.

Brunetti had little interest in this man's problems with his superiors, but he thought back to what he remembered of Antonin's youthful need to command and found that he was not surprised. 'It was about four years ago that you came back, wasn't it?' Brunetti asked.

'Yes.'

'Is that when the war started?'

Antonin shook his head. 'There's always a war in Congo. At least where I was.'

'War about what?'

Antonin surprised him by asking, 'Are you really interested, or are you just being polite, Guido?'

'I'm interested.'

'All right, then. The war, though there's always more than one, is really many mini wars or robber wars or robber raids — they're all about getting possession of something someone else has that you want. So you wait until you have enough men with guns, and you think you can go and take it away — whatever it is you want — from the other men who are guarding it with their

40

guns. And then there is a fight, or a battle, or a war, and in the end the men who manage to have the most guns or the most men left get to keep or they take over the thing that both sides wanted.'

'What things?

'Copper. Diamonds. Other minerals. Women. Animals. It depends.' Antonin glanced at Brunetti, then went on, 'I'll give you one example. There's a mineral that's found in Congo, well, most of the present supply is found in Congo, and you have to have it to make the chips for *telefonini.* So you can imagine what men will do to get it.'

'No,' Brunetti said with a small shake of his head, 'I don't think I *can* imagine.'

Antonin was silent for a while, then finally said, 'No, I suppose you can't, Guido. I don't think people here, with rules and police and cars and houses, have any idea of what it's like to live entirely without law.' Then, before Brunetti could say it, the priest went on, 'I know, I know, people here talk about the Mafia and how they do whatever they want, but at least they're limited — well, sort of limited — in where they're allowed to work and what they're allowed to do. Maybe what you have to do is imagine what it would be like here if the only power were in the hands of the Mafia.

If there were no government, no police, no army, nothing except roving bands of thugs who thought that having a gun gave them the right to take anything, or anyone, they wanted.'

'And that's how you lived?' Brunetti asked.

'Not at the beginning, no; it got worse towards the end. Before that, we had some protection. And then for a year or so, we had the UN nearby, and they kept things relatively quiet. But then they left.'

'And then you left?' Brunetti asked.

The priest took in a deep breath, as though someone had punched him. 'Yes, then I left,' he said. 'And now I have to busy myself with the problems of luxury.'

'You sound as though you don't like it,' Brunetti observed.

'It's not a question of liking or not liking, Guido. It's a question of seeing the difference and trying to believe that the effects on people are the same and that rich, comfortable people suffer as much as those poor devils who have nothing, and who then have that nothing taken away from them.'

'Without believing that it is the same?'

Antonin smiled and gave an elegant shrug. 'Faith can achieve all things, my son.'

4

Faith or no faith, Brunetti realized he was no closer to knowing what had brought the priest to his office than he had been when the man arrived. He did know, however, that he was being set up by the priest to view him in a sympathetic light because of the way he had just spoken of the plight of the Congolese. But a stone would pity those afflicted people: indeed, Brunetti was curious about a man who seemed to believe that he was displaying some special sensibility by saying such things.

Brunetti made no response. The priest remained motionless and silent, perhaps thinking his last remark — which had sounded like the worst sort of pious platitude to Brunetti — was sufficiently profound to merit only unspoken congratulation.

Brunetti let the silence expand. He had no favours to ask of the priest, and so he let him sit. Finally Antonin said, 'As I told you, I'd like to ask you about my friend's son.'

'Of course,' Brunetti answered neutrally, then, when Antonin did not continue, he asked, 'What has he done?'

The priest pulled his lips together at this and shook his head, as if Brunetti had asked a question too difficult, or impossible, to answer. Finally he said, 'It's not that he's done anything. It's more that he's thinking of doing something.'

Brunetti began to consider possibilities: the young man — he assumed he was young — could be considering a crime of some sort. Or he was involved with people it was dangerous to know. Perhaps he was caught up with drugs or the traffic in drugs.

'What is it he's thinking of doing?' Brunetti finally asked.

'Selling his apartment.'

Brunetti knew his fellow Venetians were considered a house-proud people, but he was not aware that it had been made a crime to sell one. Well, not unless it did not belong to you, that is.

He decided to interrupt Antonin here, or this back and forth could continue for more time than he would have patience for. 'Before we go on with this, perhaps you could tell me if this sale or anything to do

44

with it is criminal?'

Antonin gave this some thought before he answered, 'Not strictly, no.'

'I've no idea what that means.'

'Of course, of course. It's his apartment, so he has the legal right to sell it.'

'Legal?' Brunetti asked, picking up on the priest's emphasis of the word.

'He inherited it from his uncle eight years ago, when he was twenty. He lives there with his companion and their daughter.'

'Is it his or theirs?'

'His. She moved in with him six years ago, but the apartment is in his name.'

'But they're not married?' Brunetti assumed they were not, but it would be better to get this clear.

'No.'

'Does she have residence at the address where they're living?'

'No,' Antonin said reluctantly.

'Why?'

'It's complicated,' the priest said.

'Most things are. Why not?'

'Well, the apartment where she was living with her parents belongs to IRE, and when her parents moved to Brescia, the contract passed to her, and she was allowed to stay there because she was unemployed and had a child.'

'How long ago did her parents move?'

'Two years ago.'

'When she was already living with this man?'

'Yes.'

'I see,' Brunetti said neutrally. The houses and apartments owned and administered by IRE were supposed to be rented to the residents of Venice most in need of financial aid, but over the decades many of those people had turned out to be lawyers, architects, members of the city administration, or people who were related to employees of the public entity itself. Not only that, but many people who rented the apartments, often for derisory rents, managed to sublet them at a considerable profit. 'So she doesn't live there?'

'No,' the priest answered.

'Who does?'

'Some people she knows,' the priest answered.

'But the lease is still in her name?'

'I think so, yes.'

'You think so or you know so?' Brunetti enquired mildly.

Antonin could not disguise his irritation and snapped, 'They're friends, and they needed a place to live.'

Brunetti stopped himself from observing

46

that, though this was a need common to most people, it was not generally answered by the chance to live in an apartment owned by IRE. He chose, instead, to ask more directly, 'Are they paying rent?'

'I think so.'

Brunetti took a deep breath and was careful to make it audible. The priest quickly added, 'Yes, they are.'

What people earned at the expense of the city was not his concern, but it was always useful to know how they did so.

As if sensing a truce, Antonin said, 'But that's not the problem. As I told you, it's that he wants to sell his apartment.'

'Why?'

'That's it, you see,' the priest said. 'He wants to sell it to give the money to someone.'

Brunetti immediately thought of usurers, gambling debts. 'To whom?' he asked.

'To some charlatan from Umbria who's convinced him that he's his father.' Brunetti was about to ask if there were any reason the young man should believe this when the priest added, 'His spiritual father, that is.'

Brunetti lived with a woman whose chief weapons were irony and, when escalation was forced upon her, sarcasm; over the years he had noticed his own increasing tendency

47

to dip into the same arsenal. Thus he consciously restrained himself and asked only, 'Is this man a cleric of some kind?'

Antonin brushed the question aside. 'I don't know, though he presents himself as one. He's a swindler, that's what he is, who's convinced Roberto that he — this swindler — has some sort of direct line to heaven.'

Whatever Geneva Convention still governed this conversation went unviolated by Brunetti, who did not point out that many of Antonin's fellow priests made a similar claim to that same direct line. Brunetti moved back in his chair and crossed his legs. There was something surreal in the scene, Brunetti realized, just as he knew that his sense of the absurd was acute enough to allow him to appreciate it. The priest's moral compass might not register a tremor at fraud committed against the city, but it was sensitive enough to be set atremble by the thought of money going to a belief system different from his own. Brunetti wanted to lean forward and ask the priest just how a person was meant to judge true belief from false, but he thought it wiser to wait and see what Antonin had to say. He worked to keep his face bland and thought that he succeeded.

'He met him about a year ago,' Antonin continued, leaving it to Brunetti to work out the identity of the pronouns. 'He — Roberto, my friend Patrizia's son — was already mixed up with one of those Catecumeni groups.'

'Like the one at Santi Apostoli?' Brunetti asked neutrally, mentioning a church which was used for meetings of a group of particularly unbuttoned Christians: Brunetti, who sometimes walked past as the sound of their evening services emerged, could think of no better adjective.

'In the city, but not that group,' Antonin said.

'Was this other man also a member?' Brunetti asked.

'I don't know,' Antonin said quickly, as though this were an irrelevant detail. 'But what I do know is that, within a month of their meeting, Roberto was already giving him money.'

'Would you tell me how you know this?' Brunetti asked.

'Patrizia told me.'

'And how did she know?'

'Her son's companion, Emanuela, told her.'

'And did she know because there was some sort of decline in the family's finances?' Brunetti asked, wondering why the man couldn't simply tell him what was going on and have done with it. Why did he wait for these repeated, minute questions? The memory flashed into Brunetti's mind of the last confession he had made, when he was about twelve. As he counted out his poor, miserable little-boy sins to the priest, he had become conscious of a mounting eagerness in the priest's voice as he asked Brunetti to explain in detail just what he had done and what he had felt while doing it. And an atavistic warning of the presence of something unhealthy and dangerous had sounded in Brunetti's mind, driving him to excuse himself and leave the confessional, never again to return.

And here he was, decades later, in a parody of that same situation, though this time it was he who was asking the niggling questions. His mind wandered off to a consideration of the concept of sin and the way it forced people to divide action into good or bad, right or wrong, forcing them to live in a black and white universe.

He had not wanted to provide his own children with a list of sins that had to be mindlessly avoided and rules that could never be questioned. Instead, he had tried to explain to them how some actions produced good and some bad, though he had been forced at times to regret that he had not chosen the other option with its easy resolution of every question.

'. . . He's put it on the market. I told you: he says he wants to give the community the money and go and live with them.'

'Yes, I understand that,' Brunetti lied. 'But when? What happens to this woman Emanuela? And their daughter?'

'Patrizia has said that they can go and live with her — she owns her own apartment — but it's small, only three rooms, and four people can't live in it, at least not for very long.'

'Isn't there anywhere else?' Brunetti asked, thinking of the apartment that belonged to IRE and the lease that was now in this woman Emanuela's name.

'No, not without creating terrible problems,' the priest said, offering no explanation.

Brunetti took this to mean the people living in the apartment had some sort of written agreement with her or were the sort who were sure to cause trouble if told to leave.

Brunetti put on his friendliest smile and asked, in his most encouraging tone, 'You said this woman Patrizia's father is in the hospital where you're chaplain.' When An-

51

tonin nodded, he went on. 'What about his home? Is there a chance that they could live there? After all, he's the grandfather,' Brunetti said, as if to name the relationship was to make the offer inevitable.

Antonin shook his head but gave no explanation, forcing Brunetti to ask, 'Why?'

'He married again after his wife — Patrizia's mother — died, and she and Patrizia have never . . . they've never got on.'

'I see,' Brunetti murmured.

To him, it seemed a relatively common story: a family was in danger of losing its home and had to find a place to live. Brunetti saw this as the major problem: a homeless child and her mother, an apartment which they might have to leave and another one to which they could not return. The solution was to find them a home, yet this seemed not to concern Antonin, or if it did concern him, it seemed to do so only because it was related to the sale of the young man's house.

'Where is this apartment he inherited?'

'In Campo Santa Maria Mater Domini. You look straight across at it when you come down the bridge. Top floor.'

'How big is it?'

'Why do you want to know all this?' the priest asked.

'How big is it?'

'About two hundred and fifty square metres.'

Depending on the condition, the state of the roof, the number of windows, the views, when the last restoration had been done, the place could be worth a fortune, just as easily as it could be a pit greatly in need of major work and major expenditure. But still worth a fortune.

'But I have no idea what it could be worth. I don't know that sort of thing,' Antonin said after a long time.

Brunetti nodded in apparent belief and understanding, though the discovery of a Venetian ignorant of the value of a piece of real estate would ordinarily trigger a phone call to *Il Gazzettino.*

'Have you any idea how much money he's already given this man?' Brunetti asked.

'No,' the priest answered instantly, then added, 'Patrizia won't tell me. I think it embarrasses her.'

'I see,' Brunetti said. Then, trying to sound solemn, he went on, 'Too bad. Too bad for all of them.' The priest created two more creases in the cloth of his tunic. 'What is it you'd like me to do, Antonin?' Brunetti asked.

Eyes still lowered, the priest answered, 'I'd

like you to see what you can find out about this man.'

'The one from Umbria?'

'Yes. Only I don't think he is.'

'Where do you think he's from, then?'

'The South. Maybe Calabria. Maybe Sicily.'

'Um-hum,' was all Brunetti was willing to hazard.

The priest looked at him, letting the cloth drop on to his lap. 'It's not that I recognize anything or know the dialects down there, only he sounds like the actors I hear in the films who are *meridionali* or who are playing the parts of men who come from there.' He tried to find a better way to explain this. 'I was out of the country so long, maybe I'm not an accurate judge any more. But that's what he sounds like, though only at times. Most of the time, he speaks standard Italian.' He gave a self-effacing snort and added, 'Probably better than I do.'

'When did you have a chance to listen to him?' Brunetti asked, wondering if he had phrased the question innocuously enough.

'I went to one of their meetings,' the priest answered. 'It was in the apartment of one of them, a woman whose whole family has joined. Over near San Giacomo dell'Orio. It started at seven. People came in. They all seemed to know one another. And then the leader, this man I mentioned, came in and greeted them all.'

'Was your friend's son there?'

'Yes. Of course.'

'Did you go with him?'

'No,' Antonin answered, obviously surprised by the question. 'He didn't know me then.' Antonin paused a moment, then added, 'And I didn't wear my habit when I went.'

'How long ago was this?'

'About three months.'

'No talk of money?'

'Not that night. No.'

'But some other time?'

'The next time I went,' Antonin began, apparently having forgotten saying he had gone to only one meeting, 'he spoke, this Brother Leonardo, about the need to help the less fortunate members of the community. That's what he called them, "less fortunate", as though it would hurt them to be called poor. The people there must have been prepared for this because some of them had envelopes, and when he said this they pulled them out and passed them forward to him.'

'How did he behave when this happened?' Brunetti asked, this time with the real curiosity that was beginning to stir in him.

'He looked surprised, though I don't see why he should have been.'

Brunetti asked, 'Is it like this at all the meetings?'

Antonin raised a hand in the air. 'I went to only one more, and the same thing happened then.'

'I see, I see,' Brunetti muttered and then asked, 'And your friend's son, is he still going to these meetings?'

'Yes. Patrizia complains about it all the time.'

Ignoring the accusatory tone, Brunetti asked, 'Can you tell me anything more about this Brother Leonardo?'

'His surname is Mutti, and the mother house — if that's what it's called, and if there really is one — is somewhere in Umbria.'

'Are they associated with the Church in any way, do you know?'

'You mean the Catholic Church?' Antonin asked.

'Yes.'

'No, they're not.' His response was so absolute that Brunetti didn't pursue it.

After some time, Brunetti asked, 'What is it, precisely, that you'd like me to do?'

'I'd like to know who this man is and

whether he's really a monk or a friar or whatever he says he is.' Brunetti kept to himself his surprise that the priest should want to farm out this research: wouldn't it be easier for a person who was, as it were, in the business to attend to something like this?

'Do they have a name?'

'The Children of Jesus Christ.'

'Exactly where in San Giacomo do they meet?'

'You know that restaurant to the right of the church?'

'The one with the tables outside?'

'Yes. There's a *calle* by the restaurant, first door on the left. The name on the bell is Sambo.'

Brunetti jotted this down on the back of an envelope on his desk. The man had sprinkled water on his mother's casket, and he had also gone to visit her in her last days, and so Brunetti felt himself in the priest's debt. 'I'll see what I can do,' he said and got to his feet.

The priest rose and put out his hand.

Brunetti took it, but the memory of the priest's fingernails made him glad that the handshake was brief and perfunctory. He took the priest to the door, then stood at

the top of the steps and watched him walk
down and out of sight.

5

Brunetti went back to his office, but instead of returning to his chair, he went and stood by the window. After a few minutes, the priest appeared two floors below, at the foot of the bridge leading over to Campo San Lorenzo, easily recognizable even from this acute angle by his long black skirts. As Brunetti watched, he started slowly up the steps of the bridge, lifting his skirts with both hands, reminding Brunetti of the way his grandmother fussed with the apron she sometimes wore. The priest reached the top of the bridge and let the hem of his tunic drop. He put one hand on the parapet and stood there for some time.

Moisture had condensed on the bridge that morning, and the dampness would surely cling to his long skirt. As Brunetti watched him walk down the other side and into the Campo, he recalled an observation Paola had once made, after a train trip from

Padova to Venice when they had sat opposite a long-gowned mullah, busy with his prayer beads for the entire trip. His robes has been whiter than any businessman's shirt Brunetti had ever seen, and even Signorina Elettra would have envied the perfection of the pleats in his skirt.

As they walked down the steps of the station, the mullah moving gracefully off to his left, Paola said, 'If he didn't have a woman to take care of his costume for him, he'd probably have to go out and work for a living.' In response to Brunetti's observation that she was displaying a certain lack of multicultural sensitivity, she replied that half the trouble and most of the violence of the world would be eliminated if men were forced to do their own ironing, 'which word I use as a metonym for all housework, please understand,' she had hastened to add.

And who would disagree with her, he wondered? Brunetti, like most Italian men, had been spared the necessity of housework by the tireless labour of his mother, a background panel of his childhood, seen every day but never noticed. It was only when he did his military service that he had confronted the reality that his bed did not make itself each morning, nor did the bathroom clean itself. He had been lucky enough, after that, to marry a woman much given to what she called 'fair play', who conceded that her paltry hours of teaching allowed her sufficient time to see to some things in the house as well as the hiring of a cleaning woman to do the things she did not care for.

Brunetti gave himself a mental shake, and when the figure of the priest disappeared between the buildings on the other side of the canal, he went back to his desk. He looked at the top sheet of paper there, but soon his gaze drifted off as idly as did the clouds above the church of San Lorenzo. Who would know about this group or about their leader, Leonardo Mutti? He tried to think of anyone in the Questura who was of a religious persuasion, but something in him balked at asking them to make some sort of involuntary betrayal. He tried to summon up the name of anyone he knew who could be considered a believer or who had anything to do with the Church, but could think of no one. Was this a statement about his own lack of faith or of an intolerance he felt towards people who did believe?

He dialled his home number.

'*Pronto,*' Paola responded on the fourth ring.

'Do we know anyone religious?'

'In the business itself or a believer?'

'Either.'

'I know a few who are in the business, but I doubt they'd talk to someone like you,' she said, never one to spare his feelings. 'If you want someone who believes, you might try my mother.'

Paola's parents had been in Hong Kong when Brunetti's mother died; he and Paola had decided not to inform them or summon them home, not wanting to ruin what was said to be a holiday. Somehow, however, the Faliers had learned of Signora Brunetti's death but had succeeded in arriving only the morning after the funeral; Brunetti had seen them both and been warmed by the sincerity of their sympathy and the warmth of its expression.

'Of course,' Brunetti said. 'I'd forgotten.'

'I think she forgets sometimes, too,' Paola said and set the phone down.

From memory, he dialled the home number of Count and Countess Falier and spoke to one of the Count's secretaries. After a few minutes' delay, he heard the Contessa say, 'How lovely to speak to you, Guido. What can I do for you?'

Did everyone in his family, he wondered, think that he could have no interest in them aside from police business? For a moment, he was tempted to lie and tell her he had called simply to say hello and ask how they were adjusting to jet lag, but he feared she would see through that and so he answered, 'I'd like to speak to you.'

He had come, after some years of hesitation and diffidence, to use the familiar *tu* when speaking to her and the Count, but it did not fall trippingly from his tongue. It was certainly less difficult with the Contessa, a fact which reflected his greater ease in dealing with her in every way.

'Whatever for, Guido?' she said, sounding interested.

'Religion,' he answered, hoping to surprise her.

Her answer was long in coming, but when she spoke, it was in an entirely conversational voice. 'Ah, from you, of all people.' And then silence.

'It has to do with an investigation,' he hastened to explain, though really this was not strictly the truth.

She laughed. 'Good heavens, you hardly have to tell me that, Guido.' Her voice disappeared for a moment, as though she had covered the receiver with her palm. Then she was back, saying, 'I've got someone here, but I could see you in an hour, if that's convenient.'

'Of course,' he said, glad of the chance this offered to be out and about. 'I'll be there.'

'Good,' she answered with what sounded like real pleasure and replaced the phone.

He could have stayed and looked at papers, opened files and initialled them, busied himself with the documents that flooded from one side of his desk to the other in a pattern dictated by the tides of crime. Instead, he left the office and walked out to Riva degli Schiavoni and turned right into the midst of glory.

A ferry was passing and he studied the trucks on board, not finding it unusual for a moment that trucks filled with frozen vegetables or mineral water or, for that matter, cheese and milk, were constrained to take a ferryboat in the middle of their delivery route.

A herd of tourists came down the steps of the church, engulfing him briefly before the current of culture carried them down towards the Naval Museum and the Arsenal. Brunetti, who had been becalmed inside their close passage, bobbed in their wake for a few seconds and then set off again up towards the Basilica.

On his left he saw a metal stanchion, used by the boats of those sufficiently wealthy to pay the mooring fees and thus effectively block the view across to San Giorgio of anyone who lived on the lower floors of the buildings on his right. In the absence of a boat, he sat on the stanchion, looking across at the church, the angel, and then the other domes that hopscotched their way up the far side of the Giudecca Canal. He leaned back and wrapped his fingers around the metal edge, enjoying the warmth of it, and studied the way the point of the Salute divided the two canals, watching the boats entering and emerging from them.

His dark grey trousers soon absorbed the rays of the sun and he felt the heat on his thighs. He stood suddenly and brushed the heat away before continuing towards the piazza.

At Florian's, he went into the bar at the back and had a coffee, nodding to one of the barmen whom he recognized but could not place. It was after eleven, so he could have had *un'ombra,* but it was perhaps wiser to arrive at the *palazzo* smelling of coffee rather than wine. He paid and left, pausing for a moment to gear himself for the plunge into the tide of tourists. He thought of the Gulf Stream and his daughter's frequent reminders that it might be coming to a halt. Aside from Paola's worship of Henry James as a household deity, Chiara's interest in ecology was as close to a religion as anyone in the family came.

At times the world's equanimity in the face of the mounting evidence of global warming and its likely consequences alarmed him: after all, he and Paola had had good years, but if even a portion of what Chiara read was true, what sort of future awaited his children? What sort of future awaited them all? And why were so few people alarmed as the grim news kept piling up? But then he glanced to the right, and the façade of the Basilica drove all such thoughts from his mind.

From Vallaresso he took the Number One to Ca'ezzonico and walked down to Campo San Barnaba. His dawdling had consumed the hour. He rang the bell beside the *portone* and soon heard footsteps coming across the courtyard. The immense door swung back and he stepped inside, knowing that Luciana, who had been with the Faliers for longer than he had known them, would have come to answer the door. Could she have grown so short in the time — how long had it been, a bit more than a year — since Brunetti had last seen her? He bent lower than he thought he had the last time and kissed her on both cheeks, took one of her hands and held it between his as they spoke.

She asked her questions about the children, and he answered them as he had been answering them ever since their birth: eating well, learning, happy, growing. What, he wondered, did Luciana know of global warming, and what would she care if she did?

'The Contessa is waiting to see you,' Luciana said, making it sound as if the other woman were waiting for Christmas. Then she quickly returned to the really important things: 'You're sure they're both eating enough?'

'If they ate any more than they do, Luciana, I'd have to take a mortgage on the apartment and Paola would have to start taking in private students to tutor,' Brunetti answered, beginning an exaggerated list of what the kids could eat in one day, which left her laughing out loud with one hand held over her mouth to quiet the sound.

Still laughing, she led him across the courtyard and up into the *palazzo,* and Brunetti made sure the list lasted until they arrived at the corridor that led to the Contessa's study. She stopped there and said, 'I've got to get back to lunch. But I wanted to see you and know that everything's all right.' She patted his arm and turned towards the kitchen, which was at the back of the *palazzo*.

It always took Brunetti a long time to walk down this hallway because of the Goya etchings from the *Disasters of War* series. Here the man, just shot, and still hanging from the pole to which he was tied; the children, faces covered in horror; the priests, looking so much like vultures poised at the point of flight, their long necks similarly featherless. How could things this horrible be so beautiful?

He knocked at the door, then heard footsteps approaching. When it opened, Brunetti found himself looking down at another woman who appeared to have grown shorter overnight.

They kissed. Brunetti must have failed to hide his surprise, for she said, 'It's because I'm wearing low shoes, Guido. No need to worry that I'm turning into a little old lady. Well, littler old lady, that is.'

He looked at the Contessa's feet and saw that she was wearing what looked like a pair of trainers, but the sort on sale in Via XXII Marzo, complete with iridescent silver stripes down the sides. Above them was a pair of what looked like black silk jeans and a red sweater.

Before he could ask, she explained, 'I did

a stretching exercise for my yoga class that must have been beyond me, and it seems I've inflamed a tendon. So it's children's shoes and no yoga for a week.' She gave a conspiratorial smile and added, 'I confess I'm almost glad to be kept away from all that concentration and positive energy. There are times when it's so exhausting I can't wait to get home and have a cup of tea. I'm sure it's all very good for my soul, but it would be so much easier just to sit here and read something like Saint Teresa of Avila, wouldn't it?'

'Nothing serious, is it?' Brunetti asked, nodding towards her foot and choosing to avoid discussion of her soul for the moment.

'No, not at all, but thank you for asking, Guido,' she said, leading him over to the sofa and easy chairs that sat looking across the Grand Canal. She did not limp, but she walked more slowly than was her wont. From behind, she had the form and some-how managed to radiate the energy of a far younger woman, despite her silver hair. To the best of his knowledge, the Contessa had never had cosmetic surgery, or else she had had the best available, for the light wrinkles around her eyes added character, and not years, to her face.

Before they sat, she asked, 'Would you like

anything to drink? Coffee?'

'No, thank you. Nothing at all.'

She did not insist. She patted the sofa where he liked to sit, because of the view, and took her own seat in one of the large chairs, her body all but disappearing between the high armrests. 'You wanted to talk about religion?' she asked.

'Yes,' Brunetti answered, 'in a way.'

'Which way?'

'I spoke to someone this morning who told me he was concerned about a young man who had fallen under the sway — please understand that these are his words, not mine — under the sway of a preacher of some sort, Leonardo Mutti, who is said to be from Umbria.'

Resting her elbows on the arms of the chair, the Contessa brought her latched fingers to just under her chin and rested it on them.

'According to the person who spoke to me, this preacher is a fraud and is interested only in getting money from people, including this young man. The young man owns an apartment and is, I'm told, trying to sell it so as to be able to give the money to this preacher.'

When the Contessa said nothing, he went on, 'Because of your interest in religion and

70

your' — he paused to find the proper word — 'faith, I thought it possible that you would have heard of this man.'

'Leonardo Mutti?' she asked.

'Yes.'

'May I ask what your involvement in all of this is?' she asked politely. 'And if you know either the young man or the preacher?'

'I know the man who reported all of this to me. He was a friend of Sergio's when we were younger. I don't know the young man and I don't know Mutti.'

She nodded and turned her chin aside, as if considering what she had just been told. Finally she looked back at him and asked, 'You don't believe, do you, Guido?'

'In God?'

'Yes.'

In all these years, the only information he had had about the Contessa's beliefs had come from Paola, and all she had said was that her mother believed in God and had often gone to Mass while Paola was growing up. As to why Paola had, if anything, an adversarial relationship with religion, this had never been explained beyond Paola's maintaining that she had had 'good luck and good sense'.

Because it was not a subject he had ever discussed with the Contessa, Brunetti began by saying, 'I don't want to offend you.'

'By saying that you don't believe?'

'Yes.'

'That could hardly offend me, Guido, since I think it's an entirely sensible position.'

When he failed to hide his surprise, she said, her wrinkles contracting in a soft smile, 'I've chosen to believe in God, you see, Guido. In the face of convincing evidence to the contrary and in the complete absence of proof — well, anything a right-thinking person would consider as proof — of God's existence. I find that it makes life more acceptable, and it becomes easier to make certain decisions and endure certain losses. But it's a choice on my part, only that, and so the other choice, the choice not to believe, is entirely sensible to me.'

'I'm not sure I see it as a choice,' Brunetti said.

'Of course it's a choice,' she said with the same smile, as though they were talking about the children, and he'd just repeated one of Chiara's clever remarks. 'We've both been presented with the same evidence, or lack of evidence, and we each choose to interpret it in a particular way. So of course it's a choice.'

'Do you include belief in the Church in

this choice?' Brunetti couldn't stop himself from asking, knowing that the Faliers' social position often put them in contact with members of the hierarchy.

'Good heavens, no. A person would have to be mad to trust them.'

He laughed out loud and shook his head in confusion, encouraging her to say, 'Just look at them, Guido, in their dear little costumes, with their hats and their skirts and their rosaries and their turned around collars. All those things do is demand people's attention, and they often get their respect, as well. I'm sure if all these clerics had to walk around looking just like everyone else and earning respect the way everyone else does — only by the way they act — I'm sure that most of them would have no interest in it, that they'd go out and get jobs and work for a living. If they couldn't use it as a way to make people think they're special, and superior, most of them would have no interest in it at all.' After a long pause, she added, 'Besides, I don't think God profits from the help they offer.'

'That's rather a severe opinion, if I may say so,' Brunetti ventured.

'Is it?' she asked, seeming honestly puzzled. 'I'm sure there are some perfectly nice and decent ones, but I think that, as a group, clerics are best avoided.' Before he could comment, she added, 'Unless, of course, one is forced into their company, in which case they deserve common civility. I suppose.' He waited, familiar with her pauses. 'It's their interest in power, I think, that makes me so dislike them: so many of them are driven by it. I think it distorts their souls.'

'Would you include a man like Leonardo Mutti in what you've just said?' Brunetti asked. He was never sure how to take the Contessa's opinions and wondered if this would prove to have been a long prelude to some sort of revelation about the man.

The glance she gave him was very shrewd but quickly vanished. 'I've heard the name. I just have to remember who it was that mentioned him. When I do, I'll let you know.'

'Is there any way you could . . . ?'

'Refresh my memory?' she asked.

'Yes.'

'I'll ask some of my friends who are given to that sort of association.'

'With the Church?'

She paused for a good while before she answered him. 'No, I was thinking more of — what shall I call it, Guido? The ancillary Church? The non-mainstream Church? You didn't give him a title, and you didn't say what parish he's associated with, so I must assume he's on the fringe somewhere. Involved with . . .' There followed another long pause, which she concluded by asking, 'Religion Lite?'

After her comments, Brunetti was not surprised by the phrase. 'Do you have friends in this fringe?' he asked.

She gave the tiniest of shrugs. 'I know a number of people who are interested in this approach to . . . to God.'

'You sound sceptical,' Brunetti said.

'Guido, it seems to me that the chance for irregularity, to give it a polite name, expands exponentially once you start moving away from the standard churches. There, if nothing else, they have a reputation to preserve, and so they keep an eye on one another and try to stop the worst abuses, even if from no higher motive than self-interest.'

'Not to frighten the horses?' he asked.

'That was about sex, Guido, as we both know,' she said with a certain measure of asperity, as if she had sensed the test he'd set by making the reference. 'I'm talking about fraud. Once a group calling itself a religion has no respectability to lose, no vested interest in preserving the faith and goodwill of its believers, then Pandora's box is opened. And, as you know, people will believe in anything.'

The question was out before Brunetti could think. 'Does any of what you've just said affect the way you and Orazio deal with the clergy?' To temper this open avowal of curiosity, he added, 'I ask because I know you have to meet them socially, and I assume Orazio has got to deal with them professionally.' Brunetti had learned little over the decades about the precise source of the Faliers' wealth. He knew there were houses, apartments, and the leases on shops here in the city and that the Count was often called away to visit companies and factories. But he had no idea if the Church hierarchy was involved in any of his financial dealings.

The Contessa's face took on the look of near-theatrical confusion which he had so often observed. He had never, however, caught her in the act of applying it, as if it were a fresh coat of lipstick, but to see it so easily appear persuaded him that it was just as artificial and as easily put on or removed. 'Orazio has been telling me since I first met him that power is superior to wealth,' she said, smiling. 'If truth be told, it's the same thing the men in my family were always saying.' Again, that bland, almost blank, smile: where had she learned it? 'I'm sure it must mean something.'

When they had first met, Brunetti's initial impression had been that the Contessa failed to understand, not only much of what was said to her, but much of what she said herself. With the glittering penetration of youth, he had dismissed her as a woman given exclusively to society and frivolity, whose one saving grace was her dedication to her husband and her daughter. But over the years, as he watched people outside the family form what was in essence the same opinion, he had paid closer attention to her remarks, and he began to find, camouflaged in the most vapid of clichés and generalizations, observations of such incisive accuracy and insight as to leave him gasping. By now, however, her disguise had become so perfect that few people would think of bothering to penetrate it or even realize that there was anything to penetrate.

'Are you sure you wouldn't like something to drink?' she enquired.

Her words pulled him back and he said, looking at his watch, 'No, thank you, really. I think I'll go home: it's almost time for lunch.'

'How lucky Paola is that you work in the city, Guido, so she always has someone to cook for.' The wistfulness in her voice would lead a listener to believe she longed for nothing beyond spending her days at the stove, cooking for the people she loved, and that she spent her every free hour poring over cookbooks to find new dishes with which to tempt them, when, in fact, Brunetti was sure the Contessa had not been inside the kitchen for decades. Luciana would probably have stopped her at the door, anyway.

He got to his feet, and she did the same. She walked with him to the door of her study, reminding him to give her love to Paola and the children. He bent to kiss her again.

'I'll let you know if I hear anything,' she promised, and he went home to lunch.

6

When Brunetti reached the landing just below their apartment, the air brought no hint of lunch. If Paola had, for some reason, not had time to prepare it, perhaps they could go out. Antico Panificio, not two minutes away, made pizza at lunch, and even though he usually preferred to eat it in the evening, Brunetti thought he would quite like a pizza today. Perhaps with rucola and speck, or that one with *mozzarella di bufala* and *pomodorini.* As he walked up the last steps, he busied himself adding and subtracting toppings from his notional pizza until, as he put his key in the door, he was left with rucola, hot sausage, and mushrooms, though he did not know where those last two had come from.

All thought of pizza fled when he opened the door to the apartment and caught sight of Paola turning into the living room with an enormous bowl of salad in her hands.

That meant one of the children, no doubt in a moment of suicidal optimism, had decided they should have lunch on the terrace. Without even closing the door, Brunetti took three steps down the corridor and, sticking his head into the living room, called out to the three of them, now seated outdoors and waiting for him: 'My chair goes in the sun.' By this time of year, the sun appeared on their large terrace for a few hours each day, the period growing longer as the year advanced. But in these first weeks it fell only on the far end of the terrace and then for just two hours, one on either side of true noon. So only one chair could be placed in the sun, and since Brunetti considered it an act of sovereign madness to eat outside this early in the year, he always claimed that seat as his own.

Having staked his claim once again, he went back and shut the front door. From the terrace, he heard scraping sounds. Here in the living room, the sun had been coming in for much of the morning.

His place, the sun shining on to the back of the chair, was at the head of the table. He walked towards it, patting Chiara's shoulder as he passed her. Chiara wore a light sweater, Raffi only a cotton shirt, though Paola wore both a sweater and a down vest he thought belonged to Raffi. How was it that parents as cold-blooded as he and Paola had produced these two tropical creatures?

He was instantly glad of the warmth on his back. Paola reached for Chiara's plate and, from a large bowl in the centre of the table, spooned up fusilli with black olives and mozzarella: it was a bit early in the season for a dish like this, but Brunetti rejoiced in the sight and scent of it. After setting the plate in front of Chiara, she passed her a small dish of whole basil leaves: Chiara took a few and ripped them into small pieces to sprinkle over the top of the pasta.

Paola then served Raffi and Brunetti, both of whom added torn basil leaves to their pasta, and then she served herself. Before she sat down, she set the spoon aside and covered the bowl of pasta with a plate.

'Buon appetito,' Paola said and began to eat. Brunetti took a few bites, letting his whole body remember the taste. The last time they had eaten this dish had been towards the end of the summer, when he had opened one of the last bottles of the Masi rosato to go with it. Was it too early in the year for rosato? he wondered. Then he saw the bottle on the table and recognized the colour and the label.

'There are *calamari ripieni* after,' Paola declared, no doubt hoping to make it easier for them to decide who wanted to finish the pasta. Chiara, who had the day before added fish and seafood to the list of things she, as a vegetarian, would not eat, opted for more pasta, as did Raffi, who would no doubt go on to pack away his sister's portion of calamari with undiminished appetite and a clear conscience. Brunetti poured himself a glass of wine and assumed the expression of a man who would never think of taking the food from the mouths of his own hungry children.

Chiara helped carry the plates back to the kitchen and returned with a dish of carrots and peas, while Paola brought out a platter of calamari, and he thought he could smell the carrots and leeks — perhaps even chopped shrimp — with which they were filled. Conversation was general: school, school, and school, leaving Brunetti to say he had seen the Contessa that morning and brought her love to all of them. Paola turned her head and gave him a long look when he said this, though the children found it in no way strange.

Seeing Chiara reach for the platter, Paola distracted Raffi by asking him if he and Sara

Paganuzzi were still planning to go to the cinema that evening and, if so, would he like to eat something before they went? He explained that the film had been supplanted by a Greek translation Sara had still to finish, and so he would be going to her home that evening, both for dinner and to help her with the translation.

Paola asked him what the text was, and that led to a discussion of the rashness and folly of the Peloponnesian War, which both found sufficiently interesting to distract them from the sight of Brunetti and Chiara finishing the calamari. Nor did they notice Brunetti lift his empty plate and use it to cover his daughter's.

Athens defeated and the walls destroyed, Raffi finished the vegetables and asked about dessert.

But by then the sun had disappeared, not only from Brunetti's back but from the sky, which was suddenly covered by clouds slipping in from the east. Paola got to her feet and gathered up the plates, saying there was only fruit for dessert, and they could eat it inside. Relieved, Brunetti pushed back his chair, picked up the empty vegetable bowl and the bottle of wine, and went back towards the kitchen.

Long exposure to the vagaries of springtime had chilled him sufficiently to render the thought of fruit unattractive. Paola told him she'd make coffee while doing the dishes and sent him into the living room to read the paper.

She found him there about twenty minutes later. The unopened newspaper lay on his lap, and Brunetti stared off at the rooftops and the sky. That day's headline, giving further details about the recent the capture of one of the chief leaders of the Mafia, looked up at the room, shouting for attention.

She stopped behind the sofa, two cups of coffee in her hands, and asked, 'Reading about your triumph?'

Brunetti closed his eyes. 'Indeed,' he answered. 'A triumph.'

'It's enough to make a person give serious thought to emigration, isn't it?' she asked.

'He's been on the run for forty-three years, and they find him two kilometres from his home.' He raised a hand and let it fall with a helpless slap on the open newspaper. 'Forty-three years, and the politicians fall over themselves praising the police. A triumph.'

'Perhaps what they really mean is that it's a triumph for the power of the Mafia,' Paola suggested. 'It would all be so much easier if the government simply gave them the right to appoint their own minister.' There followed a reflective pause, after which she asked, 'But what to call him? Minister of Alternative Power? Minister of Extortion?'

She placed the coffee on the table and sat beside him.

Knowing he should not say it, Brunetti asked, 'What makes you think they don't?'

'Don't what?'

'Have their own minister.'

Her glance was sudden, alarmed, as she registered that she had just heard something he was not meant to have said.

Her silence grew eloquent until he was forced to speak into it. 'There are voices,' he said and leaned forward to take his coffee.

'Voices?'

Brunetti nodded and sipped at his coffee, keeping his eyes turned away from her.

Paola read this correctly, as a sign that the subject needed to be changed, and so she asked, 'What did my mother have to tell you?'

'That priest friend of Sergio's — the one who came to the funeral: Antonin Scallon — he asked me to find out about someone.'

'You working for Opus Dei now, Guido?' she asked with feigned horror.

85

It took a few minutes for him to explain Antonin's visit and its purpose, and as he spoke he realized how uncomfortable he felt in recounting the story. Something about it did not harmonize either with his memories of Antonin or with his own dramatic instincts: he could not believe in the motives Antonin attributed to anyone in his story, nor, for that matter, in the priest's declared motives for coming to see him.

'Do you think there's something going on between Antonin and the man's mother?' Paola asked when he had repeated everything the priest had told him.

'Trust you to go right for his throat,' he said, not without admiration.

'I don't think it's his throat that's involved here,' Paola observed, taking up her cup of coffee.

Brunetti grinned and considered this, wishing that he had a grappa, or perhaps a cognac, to replace the missing fruit. Then he said, 'I'd thought of that. Certainly it's a possibility. After all, the poor devil spent two decades in Africa.'

Her answer was immediate. 'Does that mean he's bound to have been turned into a sex-crazed maniac by the propensity of the lower races toward sexual excess?'

He laughed, amused at her tendency

86

always to assume that he thought the worst of human nature. Though Paola could now only with difficulty bring herself to vote for the politicians who represented the Left, Brunetti was pleased that her instinct to defend the underdog was still intact. 'Quite the opposite, in fact. My guess is that he saw himself as so superior to Africans that he'd have no real contact with them, and that when he got back here, he'd go after the first European woman who looked at him.'

'And vows of celibacy?' she asked.

As he knew she knew, Brunetti said, 'Celibacy has little to do with chastity, as I have no need to remind you. They have to take a vow not to get married, after which most of them manage to interpret the rule in the way most convenient to them.'

Brunetti leaned back and closed his eyes, and after a time he heard her set her cup down on the table. 'Do you think it's possible that he's telling the truth and he's really worried that this man will be tricked into giving his money and his home away?' she asked.

'What makes you ask that?'

'Because he was good to your mother, Guido.'

He turned, surprised, to look at her. 'How

do you know that?'

'The sisters at the hospital told me. And once, when I went out to visit her, I found him in her room. He was holding her hand, and she looked very happy.'

After a long pause, and not believing his own words, Brunetti said, 'It's possible, I suppose.' Because he had to leave soon, he failed to pursue this possibility. He thought back over the events of the morning and recalled his earlier dismay. 'I couldn't think of anyone I knew who would admit that they believe in God,' he said.

'Boaster,' Paola said, restoring his good spirits.

Though he was tempted to stop for a cognac on the way back to the Questura, Brunetti resisted, feeling more than a bit proud of himself for his self-restraint. His route that day took him through Campo SS. Giovanni e Paolo, so he decided to stop at the rectory and see if Antonin was there. Or better, that Antonin was not there, and he would thus be free to make enquiries about him.

This in fact turned out to be the case, for when he asked the housekeeper who answered the door for Padre Antonin, she said that he was out and asked if he would like to speak to the *parroco,* instead. Brunetti recognized the white-haired woman, then tried to remember why he should do so.

Finally he had it. 'The flower stall at Rialto,' he said.

Her smile threw her wrinkles into confusion. 'Yes. With my grand-niece. I help out on Tuesday and Saturday, when they come in with the flowers.' She placed a hand on his arm and said, 'We've known each other for years, haven't we, Signore?' Then she added, 'And your wife and daughter, too. She's a very pretty girl.'

'So's your great-niece, Signora.'

'We'll have lots of iris this Saturday,' she said, delighting him that she remembered about the flowers.

'Keeps peace in the family if I bring them,' he answered with mock resignation.

'I've seen little need of that over the years, Signore, if you don't mind my saying so.' She stepped back to let him enter, having no doubt assumed that he would want to speak to the pastor.

'I don't mean to disturb the *parroco,*' he lied.

'No, it's no trouble for him, Signore. Believe me. Padre Stefano's just finished lunch, so he's free.' She started towards the steps leading to the upper part of the house, then looked back at him to add in a softer voice, 'He'll be glad of the company, I'm sure.'

While she paused at the top to draw a few deep breaths, Brunetti admired a print of the Sacred Heart on the wall to his right. The long-haired Christ pressed one hand to his chest and held up the other, first finger raised as though trying to get the waiter's attention.

Brunetti was released from contemplation by the sound of the woman's feet moving off down the corridor. He was suddenly aware of how cold it was in the hallway, cold and damp as though the springtime that was busy with the rest of the city had not yet found time to get here. He understood, now, why the woman wore two thick sweaters and heavy brown stockings of the sort he had not seen for decades.

She stopped outside a door on the right and knocked a few times, waited a moment, and then knocked again with force sufficient to do an injury either to her knuckles or the panelling of the door. She must have heard something, for she opened the door and stepped inside, saying loudly, 'Padre Stefano, there's someone to see you.'

Brunetti heard a man's voice answer, but he could not make out the words. The woman appeared at the door and waved him inside. 'Would you like something to drink, Signore? He's had his coffee, but I could easily make you one.'

'That's very kind of you, Signora,' Brunetti said, 'but I just had one in the *campo*.'

She wavered, caught between the demands of hospitality and those of age, so Brunetti insisted, 'Really, Signora, it's as though I'd accepted.'

This seemed to satisfy her. She told him she would be downstairs if he wanted anything and left the room.

Brunetti moved towards where the voice had come from. To the left of the windows that looked out on the *campo,* but facing away from them, an old man sat in a deep armchair, looking as lost between its arms as the Contessa had in hers. Woolly white hair surrounded a natural tonsure that was, like the skin of his face, almost as white as his hair. The eyes of a child looked out of the face of an ascetic. He glanced up at Brunetti, braced his hands on the arms of the chair, and started to push himself to his feet.

'No, Father, please don't bother,' Brunetti said and closed the distance between them before the older man could hoist himself up from the chair.

Brunetti bent over and extended his right hand. 'How nice to see you, my son. How kind of you to come and visit an old man.' He spoke in Veneziano in a sweet, high tenor. Had the old man's hand been made of paper, Brunetti could have been no more frightened of crushing it with his own.

He must have been a tall man once, Brunetti thought. He saw it in the long bones of the priest's wrists and in the length of bone between ankle and knee. The old man wore the long white tunic of his order, his black scapular rusty with age and repeated washing. He wore black leather bedroom slippers, the sole of one of them hanging loose like a cat's mouth.

'Please, please, have a seat,' the priest said, looking about with puzzled eyes, as if suddenly conscious of where he was and concerned about finding a chair for his guest.

Brunetti found a heavy wooden armchair with a tattered embroidery seat and carried it over. He sat and smiled at the older man, who leaned forward, reaching across the narrow distance between them, to pat Brunetti's knee. 'How nice to see you, my son. How nice that you've come to see me.' The old man considered this marvel for some time and then asked, 'Did you come for me to hear your confession, my son?'

Brunetti smiled and shook his head. 'No, Father, thank you.' When Brunetti saw the look he gave at this, he raised his voice and said, 'I've already made my confession, Father. But it's very kind of you to ask.' Well, he had made his confession, hadn't he? And there certainly was no need to tell this old man how many decades ago it had been made.

The priest's expression softened and he asked, 'What may I do for you, then?'

'I'd like to ask you about your guest.'

'Guest?' the old man repeated, as if he weren't sure he had heard the word correctly or, if he had, what the word might mean. He glanced over Brunetti's shoulder and had a look around the room. Guest?

'Yes, Father. About Padre Antonin Scallon.'

The priest's face changed; perhaps it was nothing more than a sudden tightness around the mouth, a fading of the brightness in his eyes. 'Padre Scallon?' he asked in a neutral voice, and Brunetti heard thunder in his failure to refer to his guest by his first name.

'Yes,' Brunetti said, as though unaware of the change in the priest's manner. 'He came to my mother's funeral last week, and I wanted to thank him for it.' As he realized how loud he was speaking and felt almost deafened by it, he watched the priest's reaction to the neutrality in his voice. Just to make the message clear, Brunetti added, 'My wife said I should come and thank him.'

'And without your wife's suggestion?' the priest enquired, and the astuteness with which he asked the question made Brunetti revise his assessment of this man as perhaps feeble of mind as well as hearing.

Brunetti gave something that was meant to resemble a shrug and then, as though suddenly conscious of how rude this might appear, he said, 'It's the correct thing to do, Padre. He was at school with my brother, and so someone from the family should thank him.'

'And your brother?' the old man asked.

Making an attempt to look evasive, Brunetti said, 'My brother couldn't come, so he asked me to.'

'I see, I see,' the priest answered and staring at his own hands, one of which, Brunetti noticed only now, held a rosary. He looked up and asked, 'Was there no time at the funeral?'

'Well, we were all a bit . . . how shall I say this? We were distracted, and so when we got back to Sergio's house we realized that none of us had thought to invite him along with us.'

'But if he said the Mass, wouldn't he have been invited?' the old man asked.

Brunetti did his best to look embarrassed. 'My mother's parish priest said the Mass, Padre. Padre Scallon,' he said, referring to him formally, 'was at the cemetery, and he gave a blessing there.'

'Ah, I understand now,' the priest said. 'So you'd like to thank him for giving the blessing?'

'Yes. But if he's not here, perhaps I could come back,' Brunetti suggested, though he had no intention of doing so.

'You could leave him a note,' the old man said.

'I know, I know. I could have done that. But it was a sign of respect for our mother for him to come, and so . . .' Brunetti let his voice trail off. 'I hope you can understand, Padre.'

'Yes,' he said with a smile that enveloped Brunetti in its sweetness, 'I think I can understand that.' He lowered his head, and Brunetti saw a few of the beads pass through his fingers. Then he looked back at Brunetti and said, 'It's strange, the death of our mothers. It's usually one of the first funerals we go to, and at the time I'm sure we think it's the worst. But if we're lucky, then it turns out to be the best.'

Brunetti let some time pass then said, 'I'm not sure I follow you, Padre.'

'If we were lucky, then all we'll have is good memories and not painful ones. I think it's easier to let someone go when that's true. And we usually have good memories of a mother. If we're luckier still, we were good to them and don't have anything to reproach ourselves with: often, that's so.' When Brunetti did not speak, he asked, 'Were you good to yours?'

Brunetti, having deceived this man about Antonin, owed him the truth at least about this, and so he said, 'Yes. I was good to her. But now that she's gone, I keep thinking that I wasn't good enough.'

The priest smiled again and said, 'Oh, we're never good enough to anyone, are we?'

Brunetti restrained the impulse to put his hand on the old man's arm. Instead, he asked, 'Am I correct in thinking that you have some reservations about Antonin, Padre?' Before the priest could answer, Brunetti said, 'I'm sorry if I put it that way: I don't want to create an awkward situation for you. You don't have to answer: it's none of my business, really.'

The priest thought this over and then surprised Brunetti by saying, 'If I have any reservations, my son, it's about you and why you're trying so hard to disguise this interrogation.' He smiled, as if to sweeten his words, then added, 'You ask questions about him, but it seems to me that you've already made up your mind about him.'

After a brief pause the old man went on. 'You seem like an honest man, so it confuses me that you come here and ask about him in this way, with a suspicion you try to hide.' Almost as if a light had been turned on behind them, the priest's eyes had taken on a new intensity. 'May I ask you one thing, my son?'

'Of course,' Brunetti answered, meeting the old man's eyes but wanting to look away.

'You don't come from Rome, do you?'

Given that they were carrying on the conversation in Veneziano, the question puzzled Brunetti, who replied, 'No, of course not. I'm Venetian. Like you.'

The priest smiled, either at Brunetti's claim or at the intensity of it.

'No, I don't mean that, my son. I hear it in every word you say. I mean do you represent Rome?'

'You mean the government?' Brunetti asked, confused.

It took the priest some time before he said, 'No, the Church.'

'Me?' Brunetti asked, scandalized.

The old priest smiled, gave a snort of laughter, tried to stifle the sound, but then gave in and put his head back and started to laugh. The sound was remarkably deep, like water running in a far-off pipe. He leaned across and patted Brunetti's knee, still laughing, then fought for a moment until he could control himself. 'I'm sorry, I'm sorry, my son,' he said at last, then pulled up the bottom of his scapular and wiped tears from his eyes. 'But you do have the air of a policeman, so I thought you might be from them.'

'I am a policeman,' Brunetti said, 'but a real one.'

For some reason, this set the priest laughing again, and it was some time before he stopped, and more time before Brunetti had explained fully the reason for his curiosity about Antonin. Brunetti realized he was now just as curious about the reason for the old priest's suspicions of him as he was about Antonin.

A comfortable silence fell between them after Brunetti had stopped speaking, until finally the old man said, 'He is a guest in my home, and so I have towards him the obligation of a host.' From the way the priest spoke, Brunetti had no doubt that he

98

would defend his guest with his life, should that be necessary. 'He was sent back from Africa amidst circumstances which were not made clear. The official documents I received telling me that Padre Antonin' — Brunetti was conscious of the warmth with which the old man now used the first name — 'would be my guest made it clear that he is considered to be in disgrace by the people who sent him.'

He paused, as if inviting questions. When Brunetti asked none, he went on. 'He has been with me for some time now, and I have seen nothing that would explain that opinion. He is a decent and kind man. Perhaps he is too convinced of the rightness of his judgements, but that is something that can be said of most of us, I'm afraid. As we get older, some of us become less certain about what we think we know.'

'Apart from the certainty that we're never good enough to anyone?' Brunetti asked.

'That surely.'

Brunetti took this as the admonition it so clearly was and nodded in agreement. He saw that exhaustion had slipped into the room and taken its place in the old man's eyes and mouth.

'I would like to know how much he is to be trusted,' Brunetti suddenly said.

The old man shifted his weight to one side of the chair, and then to the other. He was so frail that it was more a matter of shifting bones and the cloth that covered them. 'I believe he deserves not to be distrusted, my son,' the priest said, and then added, looking secretly gleeful when he said it, 'but at my age that's advice I give about almost everyone, and to almost everyone.'

Brunetti proved incapable of resisting the temptation to ask, 'Unless they come from Rome?'

The old priest's face grew serious and he nodded.

'Then I'll take your advice as given,' Brunetti said, getting to his feet. 'And thank you for giving it to me.'

7

As he continued on the way to the Questura, Brunetti considered what the priest had told him. Decades of exposure, not only to criminality, but to the daily business of life, had worn from Brunetti the capacity for instinctive trust. Perhaps, like the Contessa's faith and in the face of experience, it was something a person had to choose.

Good sense interrupted his reflections to remind him that nothing anyone had told him mentioned any specific action on the part of Antonin that would or could render him suspect in any way. In fact, all Antonin had done was come to give a blessing at the funeral of the mother of an old friend: what prevented Brunetti, then, from viewing this as an act of simple generosity? Decades ago, Antonin had brushed past Brunetti with an abrasive edge, and then he had become a priest.

Despite his mother's faith, anti-clericalism

was part of Brunetti's genetic structure: his father had had only the worst to say about the clergy, an attitude explained by the contempt for power his experience of war had created in him. His mother had never offered opposition to her husband's beliefs just as she had never offered a good word about the clergy, though she was a woman who managed to find something good to say about most people — once even about a politician. These thoughts and memories kept pace with him as he walked back to work.

On his desk at the Questura, as he had feared, Brunetti discovered the fallout from Vice-Questore Giuseppe Patta's attendance at the Berlin conference — no doubt transmitted by phone from his room at the Adlon. Their weekly 'crime alert' would next week be dedicated to the Mafia, no doubt with a view to extirpating it root and branch, something the country had been trying to do, with varying degrees of flaccidity, for more than a century.

He read through the copy of Patta's message, probably emailed to the Questura by Signorina Elettra from her own room in Abano Terme.

- This is a war situation: we must consider ourselves to be at war with the Mafia, which is to be treated as a separate state existing within other states.

- All of our forces to be mobilized.
- Inter-agency cooperation to be maximized.

1. Liaison officer to be named.
2. Ministry of the Interior, Carabinieri, Guardia di Finanza contacts to be created and maintained.
3. Application to be made for special funding under Legge 41 bis.
4. Inter-Cultural dynamics to be stressed.

Brunetti stopped reading here, perplexed by the precise meaning of 'Inter-Cultural dynamics'. He knew from long experience that the people of the Veneto viewed things differently from those of Sicily, but he did not believe it was a gulf that required bridging by 'inter-cultural' anything. But trust Patta to have already seen the advantage to be offered by the possibility of 'special funding'.

Brunetti turned his attention to the growing file of papers and witness statements that had accumulated about a knife-fight that had taken place the week before in front of a bar on the *riva* of the Giudecca. The fight had ended with two men in the hospital, one with a lung that had been punctured by a fish-scaling knife and the other with an eye he was likely to lose, the result of a wound caused by the same knife.

The statements given by four witnesses explained that the knife had been drawn during an exchange of words, after which it had been thrust, then dropped, by one of the men, only to be picked up by the other and used again. Where the statements did not concur was in the attribution of ownership and original use of the knife, and in the chronology of the struggle. The brother and cousin of one man, who had been in the bar at the time the fight broke out, insisted that he had been assaulted, while the brother-in-law and friend of the other said that he had been the victim of unprovoked aggression. On both sides thus was simple truth suppressed. Both men's fingerprints were on the handle, both men's blood on the blade. Six of the other people in the bar, all natives of the Giudecca, could not remember seeing or hearing anything, and two Albanian workers who had stopped for a beer disappeared after the original questioning but before being asked for identity papers.

Brunetti looked up from reading the last papers in the file, struck by just how similar cultural dynamics on the Giudecca were to those said to be current in Sicily.

Vianello appeared at the door to Brunetti's office. 'You hear anything about this fight?' Brunetti asked, using the pages of the report to wave the Inspector to a seat.

'You mean those two idiots who ended up in hospital?'

'Yes.'

'One of them used to work in Porto Marghera, unloading boats, but I heard they had to get rid of him.'

'Why?' Brunetti asked.

'Usual stuff: too much alcohol and too few brains, and too much gone missing from what he was unloading.'

'Which one is he?'

'The one who lost an eye,' Vianello answered. 'Carlo Ruffo. I met him once.'

'You sure?' Brunetti asked. The medical report in the file had said only that the eye was in danger. 'About the eye, I mean.'

'It seems so. He picked up some sort of infection in the hospital, and the last I heard there was no hope they could save the eye. The infection seems to have spread to the other one.'

'So he'll be blind?' Brunetti asked.

'Perhaps. Blind and violent.'

'Odd combination.'

'Didn't stop Samson, did it?' Vianello asked, surprising Brunetti with the reference, before going on, 'I know this guy. Being blind and deaf and dumb wouldn't stop him from being violent.'

'You think he started it?'

Vianello's shrug was eloquent. 'If he didn't, then the other one did. In the end, it's the same thing.'

'Another violent man?'

'So I'm told, only he usually takes it out on his wife and kids.'

Brunetti paused then said, 'You make it sound like it's common knowledge.'

'On the Giudecca, it is.'

'And no one says anything?'

Again, that shrug. 'They figure it's none of their business, which is the way they think, and they also figure we wouldn't be able to do anything about it, and that's probably true.' Vianello crossed his legs and pushed himself back in the chair. 'If I ever raised a hand to Nadia, she'd have me pinned to the wall of the kitchen with the bread knife in two seconds.' After a reflective pause, he added, 'Maybe more women ought to respond like that.'

Brunetti was not in the mood for this sort of discussion and so he asked, 'You got a favourite for the owner of the knife?'

'My guess is that it was Ruffo's. He always carried one, at least that's what I was told.'

'The other one, Bormio?' Brunetti asked, recalling the name from the file.

'Just what people say.'

'Tell me.'

'That he's a troublemaker, especially with his family, as I told you, but that he'd never start anything with someone stronger than he is.' Vianello folded his arms across his chest and said, 'So my money's on Ruffo.'

'Why does it always seem to happen there?' Brunetti asked, not thinking it necessary to name the Giudecca.

Vianello raised his hands in a gesture of incomprehension then let them fall to his lap. 'Beats me. Maybe it's because they're workers, most of them. They do hard physical work, and that makes them less self-conscious about using their bodies to do violent things. Or maybe it's because that's the way things have always been settled: you hit someone or you pull a knife.'

There seemed nothing for Brunetti to add to this. 'You came up about the new orders?' he asked.

Vianello nodded but did not roll his eyes. 'Yes. I wondered what you thought would come of it?'

'You mean, other than finding a soft job for Scarpa?' Brunetti asked with a cynicism that surprised even himself. If Patta was going to take advantage of the current market flurry in the Mafia, then he was sure to see that his assistant and fellow Sicilian, Lieutenant Scarpa, got in on the ground floor.

'Something almost poetic in Scarpa's being assigned to a special unit dealing with the Mafia, don't you think?' Vianello enquired with feigned innocence.

A sense of his position pulled Brunetti back. 'We can't be sure about that,' he answered. Though he was.

'No,' Vianello said, savouring the chance for comment. 'We can't be sure about him at all.' Then, more seriously, 'You think anything will come of this thing in the newspapers?'

'Paola commented on our "triumph",' Brunetti said.

'It is pathetic, isn't it?' Vianello admitted. 'Forty-three years to catch this guy. The papers said today that he went to France for surgery, even sent a claim for the bill to the ULSS office in Palermo.'

'And they paid it, didn't they?' Brunetti asked.

'What do you think he was doing for forty-three years?'

'Well,' Brunetti said, his voice suddenly grown tight, almost as if it wanted to slip beyond his control, 'it seems he was running the Mafia in Sicily. And I assume he was leading a completely undisturbed life, surrounded by his wife and family; helping his kids with their homework, seeing that they received First Communion. And I have no doubt that, when he dies, he will be given a truly moving funeral, again surrounded by his family, and that some bishop, or even a cardinal, will come to say the Mass, and then he will be buried with great pomp and ceremony, and prayers will be said in perpetuity for the peace of his soul.' By the end of his long answer, Brunetti's voice was shaking with something between disgust and despair.

Vianello, voice calm, asked, 'You think he got fingered by one of his own?'

Brunetti nodded. 'It makes sense. Some young boss — well, younger boss — decided he'd like to have a taste of it all — run the whole show — and the old man was an obstacle; inconvenient to have him there. They're running a multi-national corporation, using computers; their own lawyers and accountants. And they've got this old guy, living in what sounds like a glorified chicken coop, writing messages on scraps of paper. Sure, they want to get rid of him. All it would take is a phone call.'

'And now what?' Vianello asked, as if trying to plumb the depths of his superior's cynicism.

'Now, as Lampedusa told us, if we want things to stay as they are, then things will have to appear to change.'

'That's pretty much the history of everything in this country, isn't it?' Vianello asked.

Brunetti nodded, then slapped his palms down on the top of his desk. 'Come on, let's get a coffee.'

As they stood at the bar, drinking their coffee, Brunetti told Vianello about his conversations with the two priests.

When Brunetti had finished, Vianello asked, 'You going to do it?'

'Do what? Try to find out about this Mutti guy?'

'Yes.' Vianello swirled the last of his coffee around and finished it.

'I suppose so.'

'It's interesting, the way you're approaching it,' Vianello observed.

'What do you mean?'

'That this Padre Antonin comes to ask you to find out about Mutti, and all you've done so far — or so it seems to me — is try to find out about Padre Antonin.'

'Why is that so strange?' asked Brunetti.

'Because you're assuming there's something suspicious, or at least strange, in his request. Or in him.'

'Well, I think there is,' Brunetti insisted.

'What? Precisely, that is. Why is it so strange?'

It took Brunetti some time to find an answer to this. At last he said, 'I remember . . .'

'From when you were a kid?' Vianello interrupted, then added, 'I'd hardly want anyone to make judgements about me from the way I was then. I was an idiot.'

The underlying seriousness of what Vianello was trying to tell him prevented Brunetti from making a joke about Vianello's choice of tense. Instead, he said, 'I know this sounds evasive, but it was the way he spoke, more than anything else.' Unsatisfied with that as soon as he said it, he added, 'No, it's more than that. I suppose it was his casual assumption that this other man had to be a thief or a swindler of some sort, but the only evidence he could give me was the fact that the young man was giving him money.'

'Why is that so strange?' Vianello asked.

'Because I had the feeling, all the time Antonin was talking, that if the young man had been giving *him* the money, everything would have been all right.'

'I hope you aren't expecting me to be surprised by the presence of greed in a priest.'

Brunetti smiled and asked, setting down his cup, 'So you think I should be looking at the other one?'

Vianello's shrug was merely the ghost of a gesture. 'You've always told me to follow the money, and it seems that the money here is going in his direction.'

Brunetti reached into his pocket and set some coins on the counter. 'You could be right, Lorenzo,' he said. 'Maybe we could have a look at what goes on at his meetings?'

'This Mutti guy?' asked Vianello in surprise.

'Yes.'

Vianello opened his mouth as if to protest, but then closed it and compressed his lips. 'You're talking about one of these religious meetings?'

'Yes,' Brunetti answered. When Vianello did not respond, Brunetti prodded him,

'Well, what do you think?'

Vianello looked him in the eyes and said, 'If we go, we'd better take our wives.' Before Brunetti could object, the Inspector added, 'Men always look harmless when they're with women.'

Brunetti turned away so that Vianello would not see his smile. Outside the bar, he asked, 'You think you could talk Nadia into doing this?'

'If I hide the bread knife when I ask her.'

8

Discovering information about the meetings of the religious group headed by Leonardo Mutti, however, proved more difficult than Brunetti had foreseen. He did not want Antonin to know what he was doing, there was no listing in the phone book, and his computer skills could find no website for the Children of Jesus Christ. When he asked among the uniformed staff, the best he came up with was Piantoni, who had a cousin who was a member of a different group.

That left Brunetti with no alternative but to go over to Campo San Giacomo dell'Orio and the reported meeting house of the group, a prospect which left him strangely disgruntled, as if the *campo* were located in some other city instead of only ten minutes from his home. How strange, the way some places in the city seemed so far away, while others, actually much farther, seemed but a moment's walk. Just the thought of going to the Giudecca exhausted Brunetti, yet San Pietro di Castello, which took almost half an hour to reach from his home, depending on the boats, seemed right around the corner. Perhaps it had to do with habit and the places he had gone as a boy, or where his friends had lived. With San Giacomo, the police officer in Brunetti had to accept that it could also have to do with the *campo*'s former reputation as a place where drugs were readily available or as a place where the residents had once been perceived as being not only poor but also more at variance with the law than those living in other parts of the city.

The drugs were gone now, or so the police believed. Gone from the area with them, as well, were many of the former residents, replaced by people who were not only not poor, but not Venetian. For two days he delayed going over to have a look but finally decided to go, half amused and half embarrassed at his own insistence on viewing the expedition as a major undertaking.

In Campo San Cassiano, because he felt no need to hurry, he decided to have a look at the Tintoretto *Crucifixion.* Brunetti had always been struck by how bored this Christ looked, stuck artfully up there on his cross, posed in front of the hedge of perpendicular spears that divided the painting in half. Christ seemed finally to have come to accept the truth of those warnings that all this business about becoming human would come to no good; He seemed eager to get back to the job of being God.

Brunetti's eyes moved to the stations of the cross on the far wall, where the dead Christ in the Deposition gave every evidence of being a man pretending to be asleep who would soon jump up and shout, 'Surprise!' How few of these painters seem to have studied the dead carefully or to have seen their terrible vulnerability. Brunetti had always been struck by the helplessness of the dead, their rigid limbs and stiff fingers no longer capable of defending themselves, not even of covering their nakedness.

After some time, he went back outside: the sun fell on his shoulders like a blessing. In Campo Santa Maria Mater Domini he glanced up at the stairway visible through a window and remembered the apartment they had looked at there, first married and frightened by all that space, to say nothing of all that price. Instinct led him on.

Down Ponte del Forner, then past the one remaining place in the city where someone would bother to fix an iron, and then into

Campo San Giacomo dell'Orio. He glanced at his watch and saw that he still had time to slip into the church, where he had not been for years.

Just inside the door, on the right, he found a wooden structure that looked very much like a toll booth in a children's book. Inside sat a young woman with dark hair, head bent over a book. There was a list of what appeared to be prices taped to the right of the window behind which she sat; a red velvet cord isolated the entrance from the rest of the church.

'Two-fifty, please,' she said, glancing up from her book.

'For residents, too?' Brunetti asked, failing to keep indignation from his voice. This was, after all, a church.

'For residents it's free,' she said. 'Can I see your *carta d'identità?*'

Making no attempt to disguise his mounting irritation, Brunetti took out his wallet, opened it, and reached for the document. But then he remembered that it was in the office, being photocopied so that it could be attached to the application for the renewal of his licence to carry a firearm.

He pulled his warrant card from his wallet and passed it under the glass.

'What's this?' she asked. Her voice was

neutral and her face was pleasant, even pretty.

'It's my identification as a policeman. A commissario.'

'I'm sorry,' she said, with what was probably meant to be a smile, 'but you have to have a *carta d'identità*.' She slid the warrant card back towards him, looked at him again, and added, 'A valid one.'

Years of standing in front of Patta's desk had trained Brunetti in the art of reading upside down, so he saw from the title at the top of the page that she was reading *Washington Square.* 'Are you reading that for school?' he asked.

Utterly confused, she glanced at his warrant card, then at the book and, understanding, said, 'Yes. For a class in the American Novel.'

'Ah,' Brunetti said, realizing that she must be one of Paola's students. He picked up the warrant card, slid it back into his wallet, and returned it to his back pocket. A student in his wife's class.

He reached into his pocket and pulled out some change. He sorted through it until he found the right coins and placed them on the counter. She pulled them towards her, peeled off a ticket, and slipped it under the glass.

'*Grazie,*' she said and returned to her book.

'*Prego,*' he answered and walked through the opening in the scarlet cord and into the nave of the church.

He emerged twenty minutes later and walked back around the church to the restaurant. Following Antonin's description, he entered the *calle* to the left and studied the names beside the first door on the left. And there it was: 'Sambo', the second bell from the bottom.

Brunetti hesitated and checked his watch, then he rang the bell. After a moment, a woman's voice answered, '*Sì?*'

Brunetti spoke in Veneziano. 'Signora, could you tell me if this is the place where the friends of Brother Leonardo meet?' There was no disguising the eagerness in his voice, but eagerness could have many causes.

'Yes, it is,' she answered. 'Are you interested in joining us?'

'Very much so, Signora,' he answered.

'We meet on Tuesday,' she said, then quickly added, 'I'm sorry if I don't let you in, but it's time for the children to eat.'

'I'm the one who's sorry, Signora,' he said. 'I know what it's like, so go and feed them. But could you tell me what time the meeting begins?'

'Seven-thirty,' she said. 'That way people can be home for dinner.'

'I understand. Good,' Brunetti answered. 'Go and feed your children now, Signora. Please. I'll see you on Tuesday, then,' he said in his kindest voice.

Brunetti turned away. From behind him, he heard a tinny voice ask, 'What's your name, Signore?'

He made an indecipherable noise, then added '-etti' to the end of it, not wanting to lie. There'd be time enough for that on Tuesday.

9

Vianello and Brunetti met below the clock in front of the Banca di Roma at seven-fifteen on Tuesday evening, accompanied by their wives, who had been, if not delighted, at least curious enough to come along.

After the women exchanged kisses, they turned away from Rialto and started towards San Giacomo dell'Orio. The women lagged behind Vianello and Brunetti, looking into windows and commenting on what they saw and, as all Venetians did, on how the nature of the shops had changed in recent years to suit the tastes of the tourists. 'At least they're still here,' Paola said, stopping to admire the dried fruit in Mascari's window.

Nadia, at least a head shorter than Paola and significantly rounder, said, 'My mother still talks about the way they used to wrap everything up in newspaper when they sold it. She's living with my brother in Dolo now, but she still wants figs from Mascari; won't eat them unless she recognizes the paper.' With a resigned shake of her head, Nadia started off after the men, who had disappeared ahead of them.

As they emerged into Campo San Giacomo dell'Orio, the men paused to await the women then rearranged themselves into couples. Brunetti led them down the narrow *calle* and stopped before the door of the building. He rang the bell for Sambo, and with no questions asked about who they might be, they were buzzed into the building. There was nothing unusual about the entrance: orange and white patterned marble floor, dark wooden panelling a bit the worse for damp, and insufficient lighting.

At the top of the second flight of stairs, the murmur of voices seeped out on to the landing. Uncertain whether to knock on the open door, Brunetti stuck his head inside and called, 'Signora Sambo?' When no one came, he took one step into the apartment and repeated, 'Signora Sambo?'

A short woman with light brown hair appeared through a doorway on the right. She smiled and extended her hand to each of them in turn, encircling their hands with both of hers and leaning forward to kiss them on both cheeks, saying, very formally, 'Welcome to our home.' She made it sound as though her home were somehow theirs, as well.

She had dark brown eyes the outer folds of which tilted sharply down, giving her face a decidedly Oriental cast; her thin nose and fair skin, however, could only be European. 'Come and meet the others.' She smiled again before turning away to lead them into another room, a smile that spoke of her enormous pleasure at their presence.

On the walk over, Brunetti and Vianello had decided it would be best — since they did not know what the legal consequences of their presence here might be — to use their real names, but this woman's unquestioning hospitality had made that decision redundant.

The room into which she led them had a long row of windows that gave out, unfortunately, on to the windows opposite. About twenty people were standing around. On a table against one wall were glasses and a row of bottles of mineral water and fruit juice. A few rows of folding chairs faced away from the windows and towards a single straight-backed chair that stood in front of the far wall. No one smoked.

'May I get you something to drink?' their

hostess asked. In response to their replies, she brought juice for the women and mineral water for the men. As Brunetti glanced around the room, he saw that this was the standard choice.

The men, as did he and Vianello, all wore suits and ties; the women tended to wear trousers or skirts that fell below the knee. No beards, not a tattoo in sight, and no piercing, though some of the people seemed to be still in their twenties. What makeup the women wore was subdued and none of them wore any kind of low-cut blouse or sweater.

Brunetti looked at Paola and found that she was already talking to a middle-aged man and woman. Not far from her, Vianello stood, holding his glass in one hand, while Nadia smiled as she listened to a white-haired woman who had placed one hand familiarly on her arm.

The room was decorated with ceramic plates bearing the names of restaurants and pizzerias. The one closest to him had a folkloristic painting of a man and woman in some sort of traditional costume: long skirt and high shoes for the woman, baggy trousers and broad-brimmed hat for the man. Not far from it was a fuming volcano with

124

'Pizzeria Vesuvio' arching over it in pink letters.

On the far wall, above the chair, hung a large crucifix with crossed olive branches wedged behind it. Through the door at one side of the room, he could see a kitchen where the counter held tall glass jars of pasta, rice, and sugar and more paper containers of fruit juice.

He turned his attention back to Paola and heard the middle-aged woman say, '. . . especially if you have children.'

The man nodded, and Paola said, 'Of course.'

Brunetti was suddenly conscious of a diminution of sound behind him as conversation dropped away. He saw Paola glance towards the silence, and he turned to face it.

A door on the wall opposite the kitchen had opened, and a tall man stood with his back to them, pulling it closed. Brunetti saw grey hair, cut very short, a thin stripe of white above the collar of a black jacket, and very long legs encased in baggy black trousers. The man moved across the room. Brunetti noticed his thick eyebrows, an even paler grey than his hair, and a large nose in the centre of a clean-shaven face. His eyes seemed almost black by contrast, his mouth warm and relaxed into an expression that could very easily become a smile.

As the man crossed the room slowly, he nodded to a few people, pausing once or twice to place his hand on someone's arm as he said something, but never slowing in his progress towards the chair that stood facing the others.

By unspoken agreement, everyone set their glasses on the table and made their way towards the neatly aligned folding chairs. Brunetti, Vianello, and their wives followed and found four seats at the end of the last row. From here, they could see not only the man facing them but the sides of the faces of some of the people sitting in front of them.

The tall man waited for a moment before the people, looking across at them and smiling. He raised his right hand, fingers half cupped and half pointing at them, a gesture Brunetti had seen in countless paintings of Christ newly risen from the grave. The man made no attempt to make the sign of the cross over the heads of his seated audience.

The smile that had been the promise of his mouth broke forth as he began to speak. 'It gives me great joy to be with you again, my friends, because it means that, together, we can examine the idea of doing some good in the world. We live in a time, as you all know, when there isn't a lot of good in evidence where we would most like to see it. Nor do we see much virtue in the people whose duty it is to offer an example.'

The man did not specify, Brunetti noticed, just who these people might be. Politicians? Priests? Doctors? For all Brunetti knew, he could be talking about film producers or television comedians.

'Now, before you ask me who I'm talking about,' the man went on, raising his hands in a gesture that attempted to quell even their unasked questions, 'let me explain that I'm talking about us, about those of us here in this room.' He smiled as though he knew he had just played a joke on them, inviting them to be as amused by it as he was.

'It's too easy to talk about politicians and priests and bishops and I don't know who else, about their duty to set us a good example. But we can't force them to behave in a way we think is good unless we are willing to commit ourselves to the good.' He paused a long moment and then added, 'And, I'm afraid, not even then.

'The only person we can influence in any way to do what we think is good is ourselves. Not our wives or husbands, nor our children, or relatives, or friends or the people we work with, and not the politicians we have elected to act on our behalf. We can tell them, of course, and we can complain about them when they don't do what we think is right. And we can gossip about our neighbours,' and here he gave a complicit smile, as if to suggest he was one of the first to do this, 'but we can't affect their behaviour, not in any positive way.

'The simple fact is that we can't force people to be good; we can't beat them with a stick, the way we can a donkey or a horse. Well, of course we can force them to do some things: we can get children to do their homework, or we can make people give us money and we can give that money to a charity. But what happens when we put the stick away? Do people continue to give money? And do the children continue to do their homework?'

A number of people in front of Brunetti shook their heads or turned aside to whisper. He glanced at Paola and heard her say, 'Clever, isn't he?'

'. . . only ourselves that we can make do good things, because it's only ourselves that we can persuade to *want* to do good things. I know this must sound like an insult to the intelligence of all of you here, and I apologize for that. But it is a truth, at least I think it is a truth, so self-evident that it is easy, too easy, to overlook it. We cannot make people *want* to do things.

'By now, I'm sure most of you are thinking how easy it is for me to *talk* about doing good. And I agree: it's too easy to sit and tell people that they should do good, but it's not at all easy to decide just what good is. I know, I know, those of you who have studied more than I have — and that's probably most of you, I'm afraid —' he said with a proper note of humility, 'you know that philosophers have been arguing about this for millennia, and they're still arguing about it today.

'Yet while philosophers argue about it and write treatises about it, you and I have an instinctive understanding of what good means. We know, in the instant that we see or hear something, that this is good or that is good, or that that other thing is not good.'

He closed his eyes and when he opened them he seemed to be studying the floor in front of his feet. 'It's not my place to tell you what is good and what is not. But I will tell you that goodness usually leaves people who receive it, and those who do it, better in spirit. Not richer, not more wealthy, not with a bigger house or a better car, but simply aware that the sum of goodness in the world has been increased. They can give or they can receive, but afterwards they are richer in spirit and can live more easily in the world.'

He raised his eyes and gazed out at each of the faces in front of him. 'And at the base of this idea of goodness is nothing more complicated than simple human kindness and generosity of spirit. Because we are united here in the Christian spirit, we most often turn to the Gospels for our examples of human kindness and goodness, to the Beatitudes and to the example set by Jesus Christ in His dealings with the world and with the people around Him. He was a well of forgiveness and patience, and His anger, those few times when it was shown, was always directed at offences that we too would see as wrong: turning religion into a business run for profit, corrupting children.'

After some time, he went on, 'People sometimes ask me how they should behave.' He smiled, as though he found the very idea absurd. 'And I have little to tell them, for the example is already there, in the life of Christ and in the examples He has given us. So I think I will do what comes most naturally and most easily to me: I will ask you to speak to my boss.' He laughed, and the others joined him.

'Or perhaps better to say "our boss", for I assume that all of you here tonight believe that He is the one who can tell us and show us by His example how to do good. He never used a stick, never even thought of using a stick. He simply wanted us to learn to see that the good is there for us to choose, and He wanted us to choose it.'

He stopped speaking, raised his hand to the height of his shoulder, and let it fall again.

As the silence lengthened, Brunetti decided that the man had finished, and he turned to Paola, but then the man resumed, though what he said was little different from what had gone before. Citing the Gospels, he gave examples of Christ's charity and goodness and pointed to the spirit of loving kindness that must have animated Him to behave in this fashion. He spoke of Christ's sacrifice, described His suffering, both before and during the Crucifixion, in vivid detail, always explaining that these were things that Christ had chosen to do in order that good would result. Few things, he said, were a greater good than giving mankind the gift of salvation.

He repeated that Christ had not needed to use a stick. The metaphor, so often repeated, could well have sounded hackneyed or absurd if spoken by someone less in harmony with his audience, but it did not. If anything, its clarity and the tone in which he proposed such a ridiculous possibility struck the audience with great force; Brunetti appreciated the rhetorical power of the argument, however absurd he thought it to be.

Another quarter of an hour passed, and Brunetti's attention drifted away from the speaker to what he could see of the audience. He noticed nods and heads turned aside as people whispered; he saw men place their hands on those of the women sitting beside them; one woman reached into her purse and took out a handkerchief and wiped her eyes. After another five minutes the man lowered his head, then brought his hands, palms pressed together, up to touch his lips.

Brunetti waited for the applause, but there was to be none. Instead, Signora Sambo, who had been sitting in the front row, got to her feet. She took a step forward and then turned to face the others. 'I think we've all been given a great deal to think about tonight.' She smiled at them, looked briefly down at her shoes then back at them again. Brunetti realized that speaking like this to a group made her nervous.

She gave a very small smile. 'But we all have families to get back to and things that we must do, and so I think it might be time for us to go back into the world' — here she smiled again, even more nervously — 'and continue with our daily attempt to do good for those around us — family, friends, and strangers.'

It was awkwardly said, and she knew it, but no one in the room seemed to mind, if the expressions on their faces were any indication. They got to their feet; a few went over to speak to her, and some went to speak to the man in the chair, who rose as they approached.

Brunetti and Vianello exchanged a glance, gathered up their wives, and were the first to leave the apartment.

10

Downstairs, they filed outside, none of them saying a word. They walked back to San Giacomo dell'Orio and headed across the *campo.* When they entered the narrow *calle* that would take them back towards Rialto, Brunetti saw Paola, who was walking in front, glance over her shoulder, as if to check that none of the other people who had been at the meeting were behind them. Seeing no one, she stopped, turned and approached Brunetti. She bent and rested her forehead against his chest. Voice muffled by the fabric of his jacket, she said, 'I am the only one who can make myself want to do the good of putting alcohol into my body. I will run screaming mad if I do not have that goodness. I will perish, I will die, if I do not have a drink.'

A deadpan Nadia put her hand on Paola's shoulder and gave it a comforting squeeze. 'I, too, want that goodness,' she said, and then to Brunetti, 'and you can do one good thing by saving this woman's life, and mine, by finding us a drink.'

'Prosecco?' he suggested.

'Heaven will surely be yours,' Nadia agreed.

Brunetti, not to put too fine a point on it, was astonished. He had known Nadia for years, for almost as long as he had known Vianello. But it had been a formal sort of knowing: telephone calls when he was looking for her husband; requests for information about people she might know. But he had never seen her as a person, a separate entity with a spirit and a mind and, it seemed, a sense of humour. She had always been, in a way he was embarrassed to admit even to himself, an appendage to Vianello.

Paola, he knew, spoke to her occasionally, met her now and again for a coffee or a walk, but she never told him what they talked about. Or he had never asked. And so here she was, after all these years, a stranger.

Rather than reflect upon this, Brunetti led them into a bar on the left and asked the barman for four proseccos. When the wine came, they did not bother with toasts or the business of clicking their glasses together: they drank it down and set the glasses back on the counter with relieved sighs.

'Well?' Vianello asked. None of them believed this was a question about the quality of the wine.

'It was all very slick,' Paola said, 'all very "touchy-feely", as the Americans would say.'

'All very positive and heart-warming,' Nadia added. 'He never criticized anyone, never talked about sin or its consequences. All very uplifting.'

'There's a preacher in Dickens,' Paola said. '*Bleak House,* I think.' She closed her eyes in a way long familiar to Brunetti, who could all but see her leafing through the thousands of pages that lay stored in her memory.

She opened her eyes and said, 'I can't remember his name, but he has the wife of Snagsby, the law stationer, in thrall, and so he's a permanent guest at their dinner table, where he spends most of his time spouting platitudes and asking rhetorical questions about virtue and religion. Poor Snagsby wants to drive a stake through his heart, but he's so much a prisoner of his wife that he doesn't even know he wants to do this.'

'And?' Brunetti asked, curious as to why they had all been taken to dinner with this Snagsby, whoever he was.

'And there is a sort of generic resemblance

between him and the man we just listened to — Brother Leonardo — if that's who he was,' Paola answered, reminding Brunetti that Signora Sambo had not bothered to use the man's name, nor had anyone in the room used it during the evening.

'Nothing he said was in any way exceptional, just the same sort of pious platitudes you get in the editorials in *Famiglia Cristiana,*' Paola went on, leaving Brunetti to wonder how on earth she could be familiar with them. 'But it's certainly the sort of thing people like to hear,' she concluded.

'Why?' Vianello asked, then waved to the barman, passing his hand over the four glasses.

'Because they don't have to do anything,' Paola answered. 'All they have to do is *feel* the right things, and that makes them believe they deserve credit for having done something.' Her voice deepened into disgust and she added, 'It's all so terribly American.'

'Why American?' Nadia asked, reaching for one of the fresh glasses the barman set on the counter.

'Because they think it's enough to feel things: they've come to believe it's more important than doing things, or it's the same thing or, at any rate, deserves just as

137

much credit as actually doing something. What is it that poseur of a president of theirs was always saying, "I feel your pain"? As if that made any difference to anything. God, it's enough to choke a pig.' Paola picked up her glass and took a hefty slug.

'All you've got to do is have the proper feelings,' she went on, 'the fashionable sentiments, and make a business about how delicate your sensibility is. And then you don't actually have to *do* anything. All you do is stand there with your precious sentiments hanging out while the world falls over itself applauding you for them and giving you credit for having the same feelings that any sentient being would have.'

Brunetti had seldom seen Paola respond so savagely. 'My, my, my,' he observed and took a sip of his prosecco.

Her head whipped towards him, her eyes startled. But then he watched her play her remarks back and take another hefty swig before saying, 'It was exposure to all that goodness, I think. It goes right to my head and provokes the worst parts of my character.'

They all laughed and the conversation became general.

'I'm always nervous when people don't

use concrete nouns when they speak,' Nadia said.

'It's why she never listens to politicians,' Vianello said, wrapping an arm around her and pulling her closer to him.

'Is that how you keep her in thrall, Lorenzo?' Paola asked. 'You read her a list of nouns every morning?'

Brunetti glanced at Vianello, who said, 'I'm not a big fan of preachers, myself, especially when they make it sound like they aren't preaching.'

'But he wasn't preaching, was he?' Nadia asked. 'Not really.'

'No,' Brunetti said, 'not at all. But I think we should remember that he saw four people there he had never seen before, and it might be that he was keeping things light and general until he found out who we were.'

'And *I'm* the one with the low opinion of human nature?' Paola asked.

'It's only a possibility,' Brunetti said. 'I was told that there is generally a collection, or at least people pass him envelopes, but there was none of that tonight.'

'At least while we were still there,' Nadia said.

'True enough,' Brunetti admitted.

'So what do we do?' Paola asked. Turning

to Brunetti, she said, 'It will put our marriage in serious peril if you ask me to go again.'

'Peril peril, or pretend peril?' he asked.

Brunetti saw her lips draw together as she considered how to answer him. 'Pretend peril, I suppose,' she finally admitted, 'though the thought of having to go again would drive me to drinking the cooking sherry in the afternoon.'

'You already do,' he said, putting an end to the discussion of Brother Leonardo.

11

The next day, Brunetti had barely seated himself at his desk when he received a call from Signorina Elettra, newly returned from Abano, who informed him that the Vice-Questore, himself just back from the crime seminar in Berlin, wanted to have a few words with him. This phrase, 'have a few words with him', struck an odd note: its measured neutrality had none of Patta's usual aggressive bluster, nor did it reflect the patent falsity of Patta's amiability when he felt himself in need of a favour.

Curiosity led Brunetti downstairs and into Signorina Elettra's office. He saw immediately that something was different, but it took him a moment to realize what it was: on her desk, where he had grown accustomed to seeing the large console of her computer, he saw only a thin black screen. The keyboard, bulky and grey, had been replaced by a sleek black rectangle on which flat keys did their best to look invisible.

Signorina Elettra's ensemble for the day of her return complemented the keyboard: a black and grey patterned sweater that he recalled Paola's calling to his attention in Loro Piana's window a week before, and black trousers below which lurked the tips of a pair of black patent leather pumps that were half shoe, half rapier.

'Do you have any idea of just which words he wants to have with me?' Brunetti asked by way of greeting.

Signorina Elettra pulled her attention away from the screen. As Brunetti watched, her smile dissolved and was replaced by a stiff-faced look of great attentiveness. 'I believe the Vice-Questore has taken an interest in the subject of multi-cultural sensitivity, sir,' she explained, choosing to use the English phrase.

'Berlin?' Brunetti asked.

'From the notes the Vice-Questore has given me for his report to the Questore about the conference, I am led to that conclusion.'

' "Multi-cultural sensitivity"?'

'Indeed.'

'Does that have a meaning in Italian?' Brunetti enquired.

She reached absently for a pencil, which

she held by the tip, tapping the eraser against a sheet of paper on her desk. 'From the notes he gave me, I suspect it means that there will be some new directives issued concerning the behaviour of officers in situations involving *extracomunitari*.'

'All foreigners or just *extracomunitari?*' Brunetti asked.

'No, not Europeans or Americans, sir. I think the expressions formerly used were "Third World", or "poor".'

'Now replaced by *"extracomunitari"?*'

'Exactly.'

'I see,' Brunetti said, wondering if the piece of paper beneath the eraser was part of Patta's report. 'Is there a precise form that this sensitivity is meant to take?'

'I think it concerns the way the arresting officer is supposed to speak to the person he's arresting, sir,' she said blandly.

'Ah,' Brunetti returned, his question disguised as a noise.

'It seems the current philosophy,' she began, placing an unduly heavy emphasis on that word, as if she were posting it on a wall, the better to take a few shots at it, 'is that the members of minority groups are the victims of a stance of —' She broke off and pulled the sheet of paper forward. 'Ah yes, here it is,' she continued, using the eraser to point at the centre of the page. ' ". . . a stance of undue verbal aggression on the part of the arresting officers," ' she finished.

'What's a verbal stance?' Brunetti asked.

'Well might you ask, sir,' she said then leaned forward to consult the paper again. ' "The damage caused by the memory of suppression is such that even those who have no active memory of that suppression carry the damage of such treatment in their psychic vocabulary, and thus any reintroduction of oppressive behaviour is bound to damage their sense of self-worth, especially in cases where that self-worth is tied to tribal, religious, racial, or cultural traditions." '

She glanced up. 'Shall I go on, sir?'

'If you think there's any sense in it, please do,' Brunetti said.

'I'm not sure that there is, but there's at least one paragraph you might find interesting.'

'I am attention itself,' Brunetti said.

She lifted the page aside and ran the eraser down the one below it. 'Ah, yes,' she said. " 'Because of the ongoing ethnic and cultural enrichment of our society, it is now doubly important that the forces of order accept with tolerance and patience the cultural diversity of our newest residents. Only by a policy of broadminded acceptance of cultural multiplicity can we demonstrate the sincerity of our willingness to welcome those who have chosen to seek their future among us." ' She looked up and smiled.

'Are you able to translate that?' he asked.

'Well,' she began, 'I've seen all of his notes, so I know how it continues. But I think what it really means that it's soon going to become even more difficult to arrest *extracomunitari*.'

The frankness and clarity of her explanation, two qualities absent from most of the documents that crossed Brunetti's desk, momentarily stunned him. 'I see,' he said. 'Is he in?' he asked, nodding towards Patta's office, though it was, given her recent phone call, hardly necessary to enquire.

'In and waiting,' Signorina Elettra answered, giving no sign of contrition that she had delayed Brunetti from answering his superior's summons.

Brunetti knocked on the door and entered at the sound of Patta's voice. The Vice-Questore sat behind his desk, his pose so monumental that he seemed to have been sculpted there. 'Ah, good morning, Commissario,' Patta said. 'Please, have a seat.'

Seeing that there were some papers in front of Patta, Brunetti chose the chair closest to his desk. Patta had addressed him by his rank: this could be a good thing because of its suggestion of respect; it could just as easily be a bad thing because of its implication of inferior position. Patta's expression seemed cordial enough, though from past experience Brunetti knew this was meaningless: vipers liked to bask on rocks in the sunshine, did they not?

'Did you have a profitable time at the conference, Dottore?' Brunetti asked.

'Ah, yes, Brunetti,' Patta said, sitting back in his chair and extending his legs to cross his ankles. 'Yes, I did. It's a good thing to get out of the office every so often and get in touch with our colleagues from other countries. Get an idea of how they look at things, what their problems are.'

'Were there many interesting presentations?' Brunetti asked, for want of anything else to say.

'It's not the presentations where you learn things, Brunetti: it's from talking to your colleagues in private, listening to what they have to say about what's actually happening in their countries, on the streets.' This said, Patta appeared to grow even more expansive. 'That's how you learn what's going on.

Networking, Brunetti: that's the secret. Networking.'

Brunetti knew that Patta spoke Italian and a particularly impenetrable Palermitano dialect; after that he had a smattering of English words, as well as the odd French phrase, especially those related to food. Beyond that, however, Brunetti was at a loss to understand in what language his superior's networking might have been conducted.

'Indeed, sir. I understand,' Brunetti answered, curious to see where Patta's amiability was going to lead. In the past, it had usually led to ambitious new projects that would produce statistical evidence of increased efficiency on the part of the police.

'I don't have to remind you,' Patta said, his voice leaking affability, 'how important it is that we expand our concern with sectoral issues here.' Brunetti's sensors began to quiver at the sound of 'sectoral issues', which Patta pronounced in something resembling English. 'We need an innovative approach to issues of acculturation, and we have to develop a hands-on methodology that will allow us to implement effective methods of taking our message to the broader community.'

Brunetti nodded and then took his lower lip between thumb and forefinger, a gesture he had observed actors use in films when they wanted to give evidence of deep thought. The gesture, however, seemed not to suffice, for Patta kept his eyes on him and did not resume speaking. Brunetti measured out a very thoughtful, 'Uh-huh.'

This apparently was enough. 'In order to implement this, I'm going to establish a task force to deal with these issues,' Patta declared.

It was natural enough for Brunetti to leap from films to books: he found himself recalling one of the final scenes in *1984,* where Winston Smith screams, in order to spare himself from the final horror, 'Do it to Julia, do it to Julia!' At the thought of being named for this task force, Brunetti too would have fallen to his knees and pleaded, 'Do it to Vianello, do it to Vianello,' had Patta not resumed. 'In this case, I think it's necessary for us to respond in a truly innovative fashion, and so I've decided to appoint someone from the ranks to head this new unit. We need a man who has been on the force for some time and who best represents the city.' Brunetti nodded in full agreement.

'Alvise,' the Vice-Questore proceeded, gazing off at the middle distance, as if seeing the realization of this innovative project, 'fills both of these requirements.' Patta brought his gaze back to Brunetti, who had by then managed to wipe all trace of astonishment from his face. 'As I'm sure you agree, Commissario.'

'Indeed, he does,' Brunetti said, making no reference to intelligence, nor yet to common sense.

'Good,' Patta said with what sounded like real satisfaction, 'I'm glad to hear you agree with me.' So pleased was the Vice-Questore with Brunetti's apparent assent that he failed to add the 'for once,' which Brunetti expected.

'It will, of course, require that Officer Alvise be relieved of his normal duties,' Patta went on, then asked, in a rare moment of camaraderie, 'Do you think he'll need a separate office?'

Brunetti tried to give the appearance of thought, then replied, 'No, Vice-Questore. I think Officer Alvise would prefer to remain with his colleagues.' As if the Vice-Questore was sure to agree, Brunetti added, 'That way, he can profit from their input.'

'I'd thought of that, of course. He's a team player, Alvise, isn't he?' Patta asked.

Brunetti said, 'Yes, he is,' trying to work out where on earth Patta could possibly have got Alvise's name. Why, of all the officers at the Questura, would he have chosen Alvise for this job? Indeed, for any job?

'Has he come highly recommended?' Brunetti asked with real curiosity.

'Yes,' Patta answered. 'The Lieutenant — who will be his overseeing officer in this — thought he would be the ideal choice.'

The mention of Lieutenant Scarpa — for Patta would speak of no other lieutenant with the same easy familiarity — made Brunetti instantly wonder why the Lieutenant wanted to be in command of a dunce like Alvise, but then he realized he had no idea what the project was or, indeed, whether its failure might be the Lieutenant's objective. 'Will the task force be a European project?' he asked.

'Of course,' Patta said. 'These are expansive ideas, expansive projects. It's time this sleepy city joined the rest of Europe, don't you think?'

'Without question,' Brunetti answered with his best smile, remembering a poet who had once said that it was a good thing the causeway existed, or Europe would have been isolated. 'So the funding will be European?' he asked.

'Yes,' Patta said, not without pride. 'It was one of the prizes I was able to bring home from the conference.' He glanced across at

Brunetti, eager for his approval.

This time Brunetti's smile was a real one, the sort that comes with having solved a problem. European money, governmental funds, the golden shower from the coffers of a generous and prodigiously uninterested Brussels, the careless largesse of bureaucrats.

'How very clever,' Brunetti said, in acknowledgement of the Lieutenant's skill. 'And I've no doubt Alvise will turn out to have been the perfect choice.'

Patta's smile, if possible, broadened. 'I'll be sure to tell the Lieutenant you said that,' the Vice-Questore said.

Brunetti's smile could not have been more gracious had it been genuine.

12

Signorina Elettra's consternation, when she heard of Alvise's appointment, was complete; her reaction proved to be the common one as the news spread through the Questura during the next few days. Alvise to head a task force, Alvise to head a task force: those who heard it were as compelled to repeat it as was the boy who first learned that Midas had ass's ears. Yet by the end of the following week, no news was forthcoming about the precise duties, indeed the precise nature, of the task force: the staff stood breathless as Alvise took his first tentative steps up the ladder of success.

Alvise was frequently seen in the company of Lieutenant Scarpa, and he was overheard using the familiar *tu* with his superior, a liberty none of the other members of the uniformed branch was permitted, or would much want. Strangely, the usually verbose Alvise was reticent about his new duties and unwilling — or unable — to discuss the nature or purpose of the task force. He and Scarpa spent a great deal of time in the Lieutenant's tiny private office, where they were observed going over papers, often while the Lieutenant spoke on his *telefonino*. Reticence or discretion were two words not habitually associated with Alvise, and yet they soon came to characterize his behaviour.

Novelty could never long survive at the Questura, and within days most people returned to the habit of paying no attention to Alvise and what he did. Brunetti, however, was tantalized by the thought of that money from Brussels and curious about where it would end up. He did not for a moment — given Scarpa's supervision of the project — doubt that it would be the Lieutenant who decided its destination: he wondered only to whom and for what declared purpose the money would be allocated.

Berlin seemed to have unplugged something in Patta, for memos, reminders, notes, and suggestions flowed from his office. His requests for statistical information regarding crime and those accused of it created entire new waves of reports: because Patta was a man of the old school, none of this

153

was done by email, and so tides of papers ebbed up and down the stairs and into and out of the offices of the Questura. Then, as suddenly as it had come, the tide of words retreated and things went back to normal, though Alvise remained singled out, in charge of his one-man task force.

During this time, Brunetti became complicit in his own forgetting of Don Antonin's request. Indeed, he and Paola had dinner with her parents one evening, the older couple, about to leave for Palermo and Brunetti refrained from asking the Contessa if she had learned anything. Nor did she volunteer any information.

The morning after that dinner, Brunetti arrived at the Questura at eight-thirty. It was a rainy Thursday morning. Before he could enter, Vianello hurried out the front door, still pulling on his jacket. 'What is it?' Brunetti asked.

'I don't know,' the Inspector answered, grabbing him by the arm and turning him around to face the dock, where the pilot Foa stood on the deck of a police launch, unwrapping the mooring line. He raised his hand to his cap when he saw Brunetti but spoke to Vianello. 'Where to, Lorenzo?'

'Up near Palazzo Benzon,' Vianello answered.

The pilot put out a hand and helped them both on board, then turned to the wheel and pulled the boat away from the dock. At the Bacino, he pulled to the right, but by that time Brunetti and Vianello had moved down into the cabin to avoid the rain.

'What is it?' Brunetti asked, voice tight with the nervousness that radiated from the other man.

'Someone saw a body in the water.'

'Up there?'

'Yes.'

'What happened?'

'I don't know. We got the call a few minutes ago. A man on the Number One, as it was leaving Sant'Angelo. He was standing outside, and just before they got to Palazzo Volpi, he saw something in the water near the steps. He said it looked like a body.'

'And he called here?'

'No, he called 911, but the Carabinieri don't have a boat free, so they called us.'

'Did anyone else see it?'

Vianello looked out of the windows on his side; the rain was falling harder now, and a wind from the north was driving it against the windows. 'He was outside, he said.' Few people, he didn't bother to add, would choose to stand outside on a morning like this.

155

'I see,' Brunetti said. 'The Carabinieri?'

'They'll send a boat as soon as they have one free.'

Brunetti, suddenly unwilling to stay inside, got to his feet, pushed open the door, and stood on the first step, still at least partially protected from the rain. They passed Palazzo Mocenigo, then the *imbarcadero* of Sant'Angelo, and then they came abreast of the stairs running down into the water to the left of Palazzo Benzon.

It occurred to Brunetti that it might be better to stop the engine, but before he could say anything, Foa cut it and they continued to drift towards the stairs. The silence lasted only a few seconds before Foa started the engine and slipped it into reverse, slowing them, and then coming to a dead stop a few metres from the steps that led up to the pavement.

The pilot moved to the side of the boat and leaned forward. After some time, he raised his arm and indicated the surface of the water. Brunetti, followed closely by Vianello, moved out into the rain. They joined Foa at the side, looking where he pointed.

Something messy and light, swirling like seaweed, floated in the water about a metre to the left of the steps. The rain splashing on the surface of the water disguised it, whatever it was. A plastic bag? A newspaper? Then, not far from it, something else. A foot.

They saw the foot, small, and, above it, an ankle.

"Take me down to Calle Traghetto,' Brunetti told the pilot, 'and I'll come back.'

Silently, the pilot backed away from the stairs, out into the canal, then pulled in at the bottom of the stairs at the end of the next *calle*. The tide was low, and the two steps up to the pavement were covered with seaweed. Brunetti had the choice of trying to leap to the pavement, though that was slick with rain, or of holding on to Vianello's arm and stepping down on to the seaweed-covered surface of the step. He made the second choice, felt a moment's panic as his right foot slid away from him as it touched the surface, banging into the back of the stair. He lurched forward, but Vianello grabbed his arm and stopped him from falling into the water. Brunetti tried to brace himself with his free hand, but it slithered through the seaweed and hit the back of the step. He felt the rain on his back as he stepped up on to the pavement; he paused to let the shaking in his knees subside.

Brunetti heard the heavy thud as a cross-wave banged the boat against the embankment. He turned back to Vianello and helped him on to the lower step. He did not slip, and Brunetti held him steady as he climbed up beside him.

They walked down to the first crossing, turned right, then immediately right again and back towards the water. By the time they got there, the shoulders of their jackets were soaked through. Foa had the boat standing off from them, in the Canal.

Brunetti moved up beside the wall of the building and leaned forward to look into the water. The floating mass was still there, off to his right, about a metre from the bottom step. It would be within his reach if he went down to the bottom step and Vianello anchored him as he reached out.

He moved away from the wall and placed a tentative foot in the water and then moved down to the second step; the water rose to his knees. Vianello was suddenly beside him, grabbing his left wrist. Brunetti leaned far to his right, stretched out, and grabbed at the lighter shadow in the water. He heard the right side of his jacket splash into the water and felt the gelid water reach up his thighs.

Silk. It felt like silk. He latched his fingers around the strands and pulled gently. Brunetti felt no resistance, and he straightened up, pulling it effortlessly closer. As he backed up one step it floated closer, and the silk spread out and wrapped itself around his wrist. A boat loaded with boxes of fruit passed, heading towards Rialto: the man at the tiller did not bother to turn aside to look at the men at the edge of the water.

He turned to Vianello, who released him and stepped back into the water beside him. Brunetti gave a gentle tug, and it floated closer. They saw the foot, not far from the silk; then the waves of the boat reached them and the foot swung around and made its way slowly towards Vianello.

'Jesus, help me,' the Inspector muttered. He moved to the lower step, bent down, placed his fingers around the ankle and gave a gentle tug. He glanced at Brunetti, rain running down his face. 'I'll do it,' Vianello said.

Brunetti let go of the silk but remained beside his friend, ready to grab him if he slipped on the seaweed. Vianello leaned forward and put both arms under the body and lifted it out of the water. A long piece of cloth dangled down from the legs and wrapped itself around Vianello's trousers. With the body, he took a step backwards to the higher step, then another up to the pave-

159

ment. Water flowed from them.

When he was away from the water, Vianello knelt, first on one knee, then on the other, then bent forward and lowered the body to the ground in front of him. The skirt peeled itself free from his legs and slithered down on to the body of the girl. One foot was covered by a cheap pink plastic sandal; the other was bare, but Brunetti saw the lighter skin where the straps had protected it from the sun. Her cardigan was still buttoned, right up to the neck, but there was no longer any need for its warmth.

She was small, with fair hair that fanned out from her head. Brunetti looked at her face, then back to her feet, and then her hands, and finally he accepted that she was a child.

Vianello struggled to his feet like an old man. Suddenly there was a surge of noise, and then silence and only the sound of the rain hitting the water. They looked up, and there was Foa, the boat floating silently a hair's breadth from the embankment.

'Call Bocchese,' Brunetti called out to the pilot, surprised that he could speak in a normal voice. 'Get a team here. And a doctor.'

Foa waved to acknowledge that he had

heard and reached for the radio. 'Maybe he should go back and get them,' suggested Vianello. 'There's nothing he can do here.'

Even as Brunetti was telling the pilot to go back and pick up the scene of crime team, there was no thought that one of them would go back with him. When the boat was gone, they moved away from the small body and took shelter from the rain in a doorway, keeping a watch up the *calle* to stop anyone who approached. Occasionally people walked by up at the corner, going to or coming out of Campo San Beneto, perhaps in search of the eternally closed Fortuny museum. But the rain kept tourists from venturing down to the end of the *calle* to have a look at the waters of the famous Grand Canal.

After twenty minutes, Vianello started to shiver uncontrollably but refused Brunetti's suggestion that he go up to Calle della Mandola to have a coffee. Irritated by his pigheadedness, Brunetti said, 'I'm going to get one,' and left without further comment. The rain no longer made any difference; the squelching of his shoes kept him company as he walked up to the larger street and into the first bar he came to.

The barman stared at first and made some comment about the rain, but Brunetti ignored him and asked for *un caffè corretto* and one to take away in a plastic cup. The barman brought them together, and Brunetti put three sugars into each. He drank his down quickly and paid. As he was leaving, the barman told him to take the brown umbrella near the door and bring it back whenever he wanted.

Glad of the umbrella, Brunetti went back towards the water. He said nothing as he handed Vianello the coffee. The Inspector peeled off the napkin on top and drank the coffee down as if it were a dose of medicine, which in some ways it was. He started to speak, but was interrupted by the sound of a motor to their left.

A moment later they saw the police launch, Foa at the wheel, the outlines of other men visible in the cabin. Foa took the boat down to Calle Traghetto: Brunetti and Vianello waited for them, and did not step out from the doorway until the first of the technicians rounded the corner, hauling a metal case. Soon after followed the chief technician, Bocchese, and Dottor Rizzardi, the medical examiner. Behind them came two more technicians in their disposable white suits, all carrying the heavy tools of their grim trade. All of the men wore tall rubber boots.

Before Brunetti could ask how it was that he had got there so fast, the doctor explained, 'Bocchese called me at home and offered to pick me up at the Salute.' He moved past Brunetti and toward the body on the pavement. Rizzardi's steps slowed when he saw it and he said, 'I hate children.' None of them had to bother translating this: all of them hated when it was children.

It was only then that Brunetti noticed that none of the other men carried umbrellas, and he realized it had stopped raining. It had probably grown warmer, as well, but he could not sense that change through the clinging chill of his clothing. He glanced at Vianello, who had stopped trembling.

As they approached the body, Brunetti said, 'Vianello pulled her out, but she might not have gone in here.' If she had, their scrambling around on the steps would effectively have obliterated any traces of whatever might have happened before.

Bocchese, Rizzardi, and the first technician knelt around the body, and something perverse in Brunetti led his mind to the Magi and the countless paintings he had seen of three men kneeling around another child. He shook himself free of the memory and approached them.

'Ten?' Rizzardi, looking at the girl's face,

163

asked of no one in particular. Brunetti tried to remember what Chiara had looked like when she was ten, how small she had been, but the memory refused to come.

The girl's eyes were closed, but she looked anything but asleep. Where had that myth come from, Brunetti wondered, that the dead looked as if they were sleeping? The dead looked dead: there was a stillness about them that the living could not imitate. Bad painters, sentimental fiction, understandable illusion: but the dead looked like what they were.

Rizzardi picked up one of the girl's hands and felt for a pulse, an absurd formality that Brunetti found strangely touching. The doctor set the girl's hand back on the pavement and looked at his watch. He rolled back one of her eyelids, and Brunetti saw a flash of green or blue, but the doctor quickly smoothed it closed. With both hands, he opened her mouth and looked inside, then pressed on her chest with one hand, but no water came out, if indeed that was what he was expecting to happen.

Rizzardi lifted part of her sodden skirt and pulled it above one knee. The rest was trapped under her body, and he did not disturb it. He pushed the cuffs of the sweater back, but there were no marks of any sort on her wrists. He took her hand again and this time turned it over and looked at the palm. The skin was rough, torn, as though she had been dragged along some rough surface: the other palm showed the same signs. Rizzardi bent closer to examine the fingernails, then placed her hands back on the pavement.

Silently, Bocchese handed the doctor two transparent plastic bags, which he slipped over the child's hands and tied closed. 'Anyone report a child missing?' Rizzardi asked.

'Not as of yesterday, so far as I know,' Brunetti answered. He glanced at Vianello, who shook his head.

'Could be a tourist's child,' Rizzardi said. 'From the North. Hair's light enough; so are her eyes.'

The same was true enough of Paola, Brunetti thought, but he said nothing.

The doctor pushed himself to his feet, and just at that instant the sun broke through the remaining clouds and fell across them: the men standing around the body of a child on the ground. Bocchese glanced down, and when he saw that his shadow lay across the girl's face, he stepped back quickly.

'I won't know anything for sure until I do the autopsy,' Rizzardi said, and Brunetti was

165

struck by the way the doctor avoided using one of his usual expressions, such as 'open her up', or 'have a look'.

'Any idea?' Brunetti could not stop himself from asking.

The doctor shook his head. 'There's no sign of violence, except on her hands.'

Vianello made an interrogative noise.

'The scratches,' the doctor explained. 'It might help us to understand where she was before this happened.' He turned to the technician and said, 'I hope we find something for you to work on, Bocchese.'

Bocchese, not much given to talk at any time, had said nothing at all since he arrived. Hearing his name, he appeared to come out of a trance. He looked at the men around him, then asked Brunetti, 'You finished?'

'Yes.'

To his assistants, Bocchese said, 'Let's get the pictures taken.'

13

'People don't lose children,' Paola said that night, before dinner, when he had described the events of the day. 'They misplace their keys or their *telefonini,* or they lose their wallets, or have them stolen, but they don't lose their children, especially not when they're only ten.' She paused, an onion on the cutting board in front of her, and added, 'I can't make any sense of it, really. Unless it's like that scene in Luke, where Jesus goes to Jerusalem with His parents, and then they lose Him on the way back.'

Good Lord, the woman was capable of reading anything.

'When they finally did locate Him,' she said, flicking the skin aside with the blade of the knife and starting to chop, 'He was back in the Temple, preaching to the Elders.'

'And you think that's what might have happened with this little girl?' Brunetti asked.

'No,' she said and set the knife down. She turned to face him. 'I suppose I don't want to think about the alternatives.'

'That she was killed?'

Paola bent down and took a large frying pan from the cabinet. 'If you don't mind, Guido, I can't talk about this. At least not now.'

'Want me to do anything?' he asked, hoping she would say no.

'Give me a glass of wine and then go and read,' she said, which is exactly what he did.

Some months ago, Brunetti, goaded by his wife's violent denunciation of contemporary theatre and film as unmitigated garbage, had decided to reread the Greek dramatists. They, after all, had been the fathers of theatre, which perhaps made them the grandfathers of film, though this was an accusation Brunetti was reluctant to bring against them.

He had begun with *Lysistrata* — Paola had heartily approved — then the *Oresteia,* which had left him troubled that, even two thousand years ago, no one had seemed able to figure out the meaning of justice. Then *The Clouds* and its delicious sending up of Socrates, and now *The Trojan Women,* in which he knew there would be no sending up of anyone or anything.

168

They knew a thing or two, these Greeks. They knew about mercy, but more about vengeance. And they knew that Fortune was an idiot's dance, springing away, and then back, and then again away. And they knew that no one is ever always fortunate.

The book fell to his chest and he stared out the window at the growing darkness. He could not bring himself, not that night, to read of the death of Astyanax. He closed his eyes, and the greater darkness brought him the memory of the dead child, the feel of the silk threads of her hair around his wrist.

The front door opened with more noise than a door should make when opening, and Chiara banged her way into the apartment. Brunetti could never understand how a girl so delicate in appearance could be the creator of such perpetual noise. She bumped into things, dropped books, flipped pages with more noise than a motor scooter, and managed, always, to hit the surface of her plate with her knife and fork.

He heard her stop at the door and called, '*Ciao, angelo mio.*'

Her hand slapped on the wall a few times, and then the light in the corner went on. 'Ciao, *Papà*,' she said, 'You hiding from *Mamma?*' He saw her at the door, a small version of her mother, but suddenly not by much. When had she grown those last few centimetres and why had he not noticed it before?

'No, just in here reading,' he answered.

'In the dark?' she asked. 'Neat trick.'

'Well,' Brunetti explained, 'I was reading, but then I thought I'd sit here and think about what I had read.'

'Like they tell us to do in school?' she asked innocently, drawing closer. She flopped down on the sofa beside him.

'I assume that's a fake question,' he said, leaning aside to kiss her cheek.

She guffawed. 'Of course it's fake. Why else would you read, if you weren't supposed to think about it?' She settled against the back of the sofa and put her feet up on the table next to his, waving them from side to side. 'But that's what the teachers are always telling us: "think about what you read. These books are meant to serve you as examples for your lives, to enrich and improve them." ' Her voice deepened as she said this, and all trace of the Veneto cadence had dropped out as she slipped into Tuscan so pure Dante would have approved.

'Well?' he asked.

'You tell me how my mathematics book can enrich and improve my life, and I'll

170

promise to take my feet off the table and never put them there again.' She turned her left foot out and tapped at his right one a few times, reminding him of Paola's prohibition of feet on tables.

'I think your teachers might be speaking in a more general sense,' Brunetti began.

'That's what you always say when you try to defend them,' Chiara answered.

'Especially when they say something stupid?' he asked.

'Yes. Usually.'

'Do they say a lot of stupid things?' he asked.

It took her some time to answer this. 'No, I don't think so. The worst is Professoressa Manfredi, I suppose.' This was Chiara's history teacher, a woman whose remarks had been much discussed at their dinner table. 'But everyone knows she's Lega, so all she wants us to do is grow up and vote to separate from the rest of Italy and throw all the foreigners out.'

'Does anyone pay attention to what she says?'

'No, not even the kids whose parents vote for the Lega.' Chiara reflected on this and then added, 'Piero Raffardi saw her with her husband one day: they were in a store, trying to buy him a suit. And he's just this little ratty-looking man with a moustache, and every time he tried something on, he'd complain about how expensive it was. Piero was in the dressing room next to him, and when he saw who it was, well, who he was with, he decided to stay there and listen to them.' Brunetti could imagine the pleasure it would give a student to be able to eavesdrop on a teacher, especially if it were Manfredi, the black nemesis of most of Chiara's class.

She turned her head towards him and asked, 'You're not going to tell me it's impolite to eavesdrop?'

'You know it's impolite,' he said calmly, 'but, in these circumstances, I would assume it was also irresistible.'

There was a long silence, the only sounds those that came from the kitchen. 'How come you and *Mamma,*' Chiara suddenly asked, 'never tell us what's right and wrong?'

From her tone, Brunetti had no idea how serious a question this was. Finally, he answered, 'I think we do, Chiara.'

'Well, I don't,' she countered. 'The one time I asked Mamma about it, all she did was quote that stupid *Bleak House.*' With a voice that had more than a passing resemblance to Paola's, Chiara quoted, ' "knows a broom's a broom, and knows it's wicked

172

to tell a lie." ' Switching back from English, she asked, 'What's that supposed to mean?'

Had a man ever been married to a woman whose moral code was based on the British novel? he asked himself. He decided to spare his daughter this question and, instead, said, 'I think it means that you're supposed to do your job, whatever it is, and not lie.'

'Yes, but what about all that stuff about not killing your neighbour or coveting your neighbour's wife?'

He allowed himself to sink deeper into the sofa as he considered her question. After some time, he answered, 'Well, one way of looking at it is to see all those things, those ten things, as specific examples of the general rule.'

'You mean Dickens' Golden Rule?' Chiara asked with a laugh.

'You could call it that, yes, I suppose,' Brunetti admitted. 'If you do your job, you're unlikely to want to kill your neighbour, and in your case, I doubt you're going to spend much time in your life coveting your neighbour's wife.'

'Can't you ever be serious, *Papà?*' she pleaded.

'Not when I'm hungry,' Brunetti said and got to his feet.

14

The following day, Brunetti spent his first half-hour in the office reading the newspaper accounts of the discovery of the little girl's body. *Il Gazzettino* had not learned of it early enough to put it on the front page, but there had been enough time for it to reach the second section, the front page of which screamed, in red, that it was 'A Mystery'. The account gave the incorrect time of the discovery of her body, misspelled Brunetti's name, and carried a photo of steps different from the ones where she had been found. Her age was given as five, while the national papers listed it as twelve and nine. The autopsy, it was stated, would take place that day. Further, the police asked that anyone who might have information about the possible identity of a child with dark hair and eyes call them.

His phone rang and he answered with his name.

'Ah, Guido,' he heard his mother-in-law say. 'I've been meaning to call you since we got back from the Occupied Territories, but there was simply too much to do here, and then Chiara and Raffi came to lunch and I had so much fun with them that I'm afraid I forgot about calling you, though having them here should have reminded me of you, shouldn't it?'

'I thought you'd been to Palermo,' a literal-minded Brunetti said, relieved to know that the Contessa had not yet seen that day's papers. It confused him that Paola's parents could have managed another trip in the short time since they got back from Sicily.

Her laugh was musical, always brighter than her voice and very attractive. 'Oh, I'm sorry to confuse you, Guido. I should have told you. Orazio has taken to using that term to refer to Sicily and Calabria. Since both places belong to the Mafia and the government has no effective control over them, he thinks it's linguistically correct to refer to them as the Occupied Territories.' She paused for a moment, and then went on, 'And if you think about it, it's not far off the truth, is it?'

'Is this term only for domestic consumption, or does he use it in public?' Brunetti enquired, forbearing to pass judgement on the accuracy of the Count's choice of phrase and never willing to comment on his father-in-law's politics.

'Oh, I'm so seldom with him in public, I have no way of knowing about that. But you know how discreet Orazio is, so perhaps he uses it only with me. But now you know, too,' she said in a lowered tone, adding, 'Perhaps it would be wise to let Orazio decide how widespread the use of the term should be?'

Brunetti had never heard a more polite enjoinder to discretion. 'Of course,' he agreed. 'But what was it you called about?'

'That religious person,' she said.

'Leonardo Mutti?'

Yes,' she answered, then surprised him by adding, 'And the other one, Antonin Scallon.'

Brunetti thought back to his original conversation with the Contessa: he was sure he had not used Antonin's name, had referred to him only as an old friend of his brother. If he had used any name, it was Brother Leonardo's.

'Yes?' Brunetti enquired. 'And what have you heard?' He decided to leave for later the question of how the Contessa might have come to learn about his interest in

Padre Antonin.

'It seems that a friend of mine has also become attracted to Brother Leonardo's teachings,' she began, then added, 'or, as one might say, fallen under his spell.' Again, Brunetti chose not to comment.

'And it also seems,' the Countess continued, 'that this Padre Antonin learned about her . . . shall we say, about her enthusiasm for Brother Leonardo.' Before Brunetti could ask, the Countess explained, 'He's a friend of her family, this Antonin; while he was in Africa he sent them those dreadful circular letters every Christmas, and I suppose they sent him money, though I don't know that for sure. At any rate, when I asked her about Brother Leonardo, she told me how surprised she had been when Padre Antonin spoke to her about him.'

'Saying what?'

'Nothing, really,' the Countess answered. 'But from what she told me, it sounded as if he were trying to suggest she be cautious about becoming too involved with him, but being very careful not to seem as if he was doing that.'

'Will she listen to him?' Brunetti asked.

'Of course not, Guido. You should know by now that, once people reach my age, it makes no sense to try to persuade them to abandon their — well — their enthusiasms.'

He had to smile at this, thinking how charitable it was of her to limit this wilfulness to people of her age. 'Do you know if he said anything specific about Brother Leonardo?' Brunetti asked.

She laughed again. 'Nothing that exceeded the limits of clerical solidarity and good taste. Or overstepped Orazio's admonition never to speak badly of a colleague.'

In a more serious voice, she went on, 'So that you can stop worrying about how I knew you were interested in Padre Antonin, Guido, I should explain that Paola told me that he was at your mother's funeral and that he went to see you.'

'Thank you,' Brunetti said simply and then asked, 'What did your friend say about Brother Leonardo?'

The Contessa took some time to answer. 'She lost a grandson two years ago and needs whatever comfort she can find. So if what this Brother Leonardo says can lessen her grief, then I think it's all to the good.'

'Has the subject of money been raised?' Brunetti asked.

'You mean by Brother Leonardo? With my friend?'

'Yes.'

'She didn't say, and it's certainly not

anything I could ask.'

Hearing both the reproach and the warning in her voice, Brunetti said only, 'If you hear anything else . . .'

'Of course,' she said, cutting him off before he could finish the question. 'Please give my love to Paola and the children, will you?'

'Yes, of course,' he said, and then she was gone.

Just when he had thought himself free of all solicitation, Brunetti found himself reminded of Antonin and his request. Long experience had rendered Brunetti suspicious of protestations of disinterested goodwill, especially when those protestations were linked in any way to money. The only money he knew to be involved here was that given to Brother Leonardo by Patrizia's son. Brunetti went to the window and stared at the façade of San Lorenzo for some time: he found it difficult to attribute to Antonin a sincere concern for the well-being of this young man, and then came the thought that he found it difficult to attribute to Antonin a sincere concern for the well-being of anyone save himself.

The Contessa's words came back to him then, that it was difficult to persuade people her age away from their — what had she called them? — enthusiasms? He changed the word to 'prejudices', applied it to himself, and saw how apt her remark remained.

Brunetti, recalling his failure to find a Christian among his friends in the city, went downstairs to ask Signorina Elettra if she might have one among hers.

'A Christian?' she asked, surprised. She had made no reference to the newspaper accounts of the little girl's death, and Brunetti was glad enough to avoid discussion of it with her.

'Yes. That is, someone who believes and attends Mass.'

She glanced at the vase of flowers on the windowsill, perhaps to gather her thoughts, then returned her gaze to him and asked, 'May I ask what this is in aid of, sir?'

'I want to find out about a member of the clergy.' When she remained silent for some time, he added, 'Private things.'

'Ah,' she answered.

'Which means?' he asked, smiling.

She answered the smile, and then the question. 'It means that I'm not sure it's believers who should be asked about the clergy. Not, that is, if you want to hear the truth.'

'Do you have someone in mind?' Brunetti asked.

She rested her chin in her palm for a moment. Her lips disappeared, evidence of thought. She looked up and her mouth sweetened into a smile. 'I can think of two,' she said. 'One has what might be called unsympathetic opinions of the clergy.' Before he could comment, she added, 'The other has a milder view. No doubt because he has less exhaustive information.'

'May I ask who these people are?'

'One is a priest, and one used to be.'

'Which one holds which opinion?' he asked.

She sat up straight, as if trying to view this question from his perspective, and then said, 'I suppose the less interesting configuration would be for the former priest to be antagonistic, wouldn't it?'

'It's certainly more predictable,' Brunetti said.

She nodded and said, 'But that's not the way it is: it's the one who is still a priest who . . . well, who has a more adversarial stance towards his colleagues.' Absently, she pulled the cuff of her jacket forward and covered the face of her watch with it, then said, 'Yes, I think he might have more useful information.'

'What sort of information would that be?'

'He has access to the files kept by the Curia, both here and in Rome. I suppose they correspond to the personnel files we have, though we're less concerned with the private lives of our employees than they seem to be.' She clarified this by adding, 'At least from what he tells me. I've never actually seen the files.'

'But he's told you what's in them?'

'Some of it. But never using names.' Her smile became impish as she added, 'Only the titles, both of who is reported on and who is doing the reporting: Cardinal, Bishop, Monsignor, altar boy.'

It proved too much for him. 'May I ask why you're interested in them, Signorina?' Brunetti was never certain of the depth or breadth of her curiosity, nor of its purpose.

'It's like the files of the Stasi,' she surprised him by answering. 'Since the fall of the Wall, we've read about private citizens who went in and read their files and found out who had been keeping an eye on them or reporting on them. And occasionally the name of one of the people who was spying was made public, or at least was made public when people still cared about such things.'

She looked up at him as if this were sufficient, but he shook his head and she continued. 'That's why I like to learn what's in the files on the private lives of the clergy: not for what they're doing, poor devils, but for who's giving the information about them. I find that far more interesting.'

'I'm sure it must be,' Brunetti agreed, thinking of some of the things he knew to be buried in those files and who might have put the information there.

However tempting it might have been to continue this discussion, Brunetti forced himself away from it. 'I'm curious about two men,' he said. 'One of them is called Leonardo Mutti, said to be from Umbria. He is also said to be a member of the clergy, but I don't know if that's true. He lives here and directs some sort of religious organization known as the Children of Jesus Christ.'

Her lips pursed at the name, but she wrote it down.

'The second is Antonin Scallon, Venetian, who is a chaplain at the Ospedale and lives with the Dominicans in SS. Giovanni e Paolo. He was a missionary in the Congo for about twenty years.'

'Do you want to know anything specific about either one?' she asked, looking up at him.

'No,' Brunetti admitted. 'Just anything that might be interesting.'

'I see,' she responded. 'If one's a priest, then there will be a file.'

'And the other? If he's not a priest?'

'If he's running something with a name like that,' she began, tapping one incarnadined nail on her notes, 'he should be easy to find.'

'Would you be willing to ask your friend to have a look?'

'I'd be delighted,' she answered.

Questions crowded into Brunetti's mind, but he tried to flail them away. He would not ask her who this person was. He would not ask her what she might have discovered about other priests in the city. And most importantly, he would not ask her what she had given in return for this information. To stop himself, he asked, instead, 'Does he have files on all of them — priests, bishops, archbishops?'

She paused before she answered that. 'They're supposed to have a higher level of access to get a look at the prelates.'

' "Supposed to"?' he asked.

'Indeed.'

Brunetti put temptation behind him and said only, 'You'll ask him?'

'Nothing easier,' she answered, swinging around in her chair and tapping a few keys on her keyboard.

184

'What are you doing?' Brunetti asked.

'Sending him an email,' she said, not bothering to hide her surprise at his question.

'Isn't that risky?'

For a moment she didn't understand, but then he saw her get it. 'Oh, you mean for security?' she asked.

'Yes.'

'We always assume that our emails are recorded somewhere,' she said calmly, tapping a few more keys.

'So what are you asking him?'

'To meet me.'

'Just like that?'

'Of course,' she answered with a smile.

'And no one's suspicious? You send an email to a priest and ask him to meet you, and whoever is supposedly recording your messages won't be suspicious about this? About an email coming from the Questura?'

'Of course not, Commissario,' she said firmly. 'Besides, I'm using one of my private accounts.' Her growing smile told him she had not finished. 'And, you see, I have every reason to want to see him. He's my confessor.'

15

The amusement Brunetti would usually have felt at Signorina Elettra's relationship with the clergy was crushed by the lingering weight of the memory of the still unidentified child. In recent years, Brunetti had begun to see the death of the young as the theft of years, decades, generations. Each time he learned of the willed, unnecessary destruction of a young person, whether it was the result of crime or of one of the many futile wars that snuffed out their lives, he counted out the years until they would have been seventy and added up the plundered years of life. His own government had stolen centuries; other governments had stolen millennia, had stamped out the joy these kids might and should have had. Even if life had brought them misery or pain, it would still have brought them life, not the void that Brunetti saw looming after death.

He returned to his office and, to pass the

time while he waited for some word of the autopsy, read more carefully through the three newspapers he had brought with him. When he looked up from the last page of the third, all he could remember were the sixty years of life that had been stolen from the girl Vianello had pulled from the water.

Brunetti looked at the surface of his desk, folded the last newspaper and moved it aside, placing it on top of the others. With the tip of one finger, he slid some specks of dust to the edge of the desk and let them drop invisibly to the floor. Maybe she tripped and fell and, unable to swim, drowned in the canal. Even so, as Paola insisted, one did not misplace a child. This was not drawing-room comedy with an infant in a leather handbag, left unclaimed in the cloakroom of Victoria station. This was a young girl, missing, but unmissed.

The phone rang.

'I thought I'd call,' he heard Rizzardi say when he answered. 'I'll send a written report, but I thought you'd want to know.'

'Thank you,' Brunetti said, then, unable to stop himself, added, 'I can't shake loose of her.'

The pathologist limited himself to a noise of assent; there was no knowing if he felt the same way.

Brunetti grabbed a sheet of paper and pulled it towards him.

'I'd say she was ten or eleven,' the pathologist began, then paused and cleared his throat. 'The cause of death was drowning. It looks like she was in the water about eight hours.' That, Brunetti calculated, meant she had gone into the water around midnight.

'It could have been longer,' Rizzardi said. 'The water's not the same temperature as the air, and that would change the rate of rigor mortis. I sent one of my men over there to measure the temperature of the water, and perhaps when I calculate it I can get closer to the time.' A pause and then, 'You don't want to know about that sort of thing, do you, Guido?'

'No, not really.'

'Close to midnight, then,' Rizzardi said. 'Or if you prefer, you could say an hour on either side of midnight. I can't get closer than that.'

'All right,' Brunetti said, curious now about the reluctance that seeped from every word Rizzardi spoke. He knew he should ask or somehow prod the pathologist, but he was unwilling to do it: he sensed it would be better to let Rizzardi find his own way to whatever it was he did not want to say.

'There's evidence,' the pathologist began

and then paused to clear his throat again. 'There's evidence of sexual activity.'

This meant nothing to Brunetti. That is, it meant something, but he had no idea what it meant, not in a real sense. He did not know how to ask or what to ask.

'No, not rape, at least not recently. But, er, activity. I don't know what to call it. The child has had sex, though not in the near past, not any time close to when she died. Not hours, that is, probably not even days.'

Brunetti's mind leaped to the first safe place it could find. 'Could she be older?'

'Perhaps, but not by much more than a year, I'd say.'

'Ah,' Brunetti said and waited for the pathologist to continue. When he did not, Brunetti asked, 'What else?'

'The scratches on her palms. There were fragments of a reddish material in them. And under her nails. Two were broken off, one of them almost torn away. And the undersides of the toes of her left foot are badly scraped.'

'What about her knees?' Brunetti asked. He tried to remember the small body, recalled only one knee, the other under the clinging fabric of the skirt.

'One's got scratches. Same thing, a reddish, grainy material; some larger

189

fragments.'

'The other?'

'It must have been covered by her skirt. There's a place on the front of her skirt where the fabric is worn away.'

'Anything else?' Brunetti asked.

'Yes,' the pathologist said, cleared his throat, and went on. 'She had a watch, in a pocket sewn into her knickers.' Brunetti had heard of this: at the time, he had not thought to look for anything under those clinging skirts. After some time, the pathologist added, 'And there was a ring in her vagina.'

Brunetti had heard this rumour, as well, but had always chosen to dismiss it.

'It looks like a wedding ring,' the pathologist said in a neutral voice. Brunetti said nothing, and Rizzardi added, 'The watch is a pocket watch. Gold.'

A long silence stretched out as Brunetti quickly revised everything he had concluded about the girl because of her blonde hair and her light eyes. They had blinded him to the long skirt and to the fact that the skin covered by the strap of her sandal had still been fairly dark.

'Gypsy?' he asked the doctor.

'We call them Rom now, Guido,' Rizzardi answered.

Brunetti felt a flash of belligerence: no matter what we call them, no one can toss them into the water, for Christ's sake. 'Tell me about the ring and the watch,' he asked with forced calm.

'The wedding ring has initials and a date, and the watch looks antique. It's the kind that you have to open to see the face.'

'Is there anything on the inside of the cover?'

'I didn't open it. I took it out of her pocket and put it in a plastic bag with the ring. Those are the rules, Guido.'

'I know, I know. Sorry Ettore.' Brunetti allowed the anger to leak out of him and then asked, 'What do you think caused the marks on her hands?'

'That's not what I'm supposed to do. You know that.'

'What do you think caused the marks on her hands?' Brunetti repeated.

If Rizzardi had been waiting for the question, he could have answered it no more quickly. 'The evidence suggests she slid some distance, probably on a terracotta surface. The fabric is worn away down the front of the cardigan, and two buttons are missing. And, as I told you, there's the worn spot on the front of her skirt.'

'So she slid on her stomach?'

'It would seem so. As she went down the roof, she'd try to grab on to the tiles to stop herself: it's natural. That's what cut up her palms and ripped the nails.'

Again, Brunetti waited. Part of him wanted to keep Rizzardi talking about the details in which might be traced the girl's actions as she slid down a roof or from an *altana* or a terrace. He did not want to have to go back to the other things.

'And what could have happened?' Brunetti asked.

'That's another thing I'm not supposed to do, Guido,' Rizzardi protested.

'I know. But tell me.'

For some time Brunetti feared he had gone too far and that Rizzardi would hang up, but then the doctor said, 'It could be — but this is only my guess — that she was surprised wherever she was: someone came in, saw her there. She'd try to get away, but if it was a man, he'd be too big and could stop her from getting to the door, if that's how she got in. So the first thing she'd do is try a window, or the door to an *altana* or a terrace.'

As he listened, Brunetti performed a similar reconstruction of events. Any un-watched street door was fair game to the gangs of thieves who roamed the city.

Because they were minors, nothing could be done to them, and, if arrested, they were quickly returned to the care of their parents, or to the people presenting evidence that they were the parents. And then just as quickly the children were back at work.

The classic means of forced entry was the screwdriver, and who would prosecute a child found with a screwdriver in her pocket? Once inside a building, they went to the apartments which, from the outside, had been shuttered or, at night, showed no light. Nothing but *una porta blindata* could stop them entering, and once inside nothing could prevent them from taking whatever they chose, though usually they limited themselves to money and gold. Wedding rings and watches.

At the same time as one part of his mind was recalling all of this, another was drawing up a list of what had to be done: check the files to see if a child matching her description had ever been arrested; show her photo around the Questura and to the Carabinieri; have Foa check the tide charts to try to figure out where she might have gone into the water eight to ten hours before they found her. He knew it would probably be futile to find out whether anyone had reported a burglary the night of her death:

most people didn't bother, and if someone had interrupted her, then they might have seen her go into the water, and that would make it certain they would not inform the police. The way to begin, then, was to trace the ring and the watch.

Rizzardi was no longer speaking, though Brunetti had not noticed when he stopped. Suddenly annoyed with himself for avoiding what he knew he had to address, Brunetti said, 'You said there are signs of sexual activity. Could it be the . . . could it be the ring?'

'The ring didn't cause gonorrhoea,' the pathologist answered with troubling coolness. 'The lab hasn't had time to confirm the samples, but that's what it is. The results will be back in a few days, but you can be sure that's what they'll say.'

'Is there any other way she . . .' Brunetti began and let the sentence drift away.

'None. The infection is pretty well established; it's the only way she could have got it.'

'Can you tell when . . . ?' began a reluctant Brunetti.

Rizzardi cut him off. 'No.'

After some time, Brunetti asked, 'Anything else?'

'No.'

'Then thanks for calling, Ettore.'

'Let me know if . . .' began an equally reluctant Rizzardi.

'Yes. Of course,' Brunetti said and replaced the phone.

He picked it up immediately and dialled the number of the officers' room. Pucetti answered. 'Go over to Rizzardi at the hospital and ask him for a bag with a ring and a watch. Make sure you sign a receipt for it. Take them down to Bocchese and let him check them for prints and anything else he can find on them, and then bring them up to me.'

'Yes, sir,' the young officer said.

'Before you go to the hospital, go down to Bocchese and ask him to send me the photos of the head and face of the girl who drowned. And tell Dottor Rizzardi that I'd like to see any photos he took. That's all.'

'Yes, sir,' Pucetti said and was gone.

Brunetti's mind suddenly filled with a scene from *The Trojan Women*: the Greek — what was his name, Tal-something? — bringing the shattered body of little Astyanax to his grandmother. As the soldiers with the boy's body passed by the River Scamander, the soldier tells Hecuba, he had let the waters run over the child's body to clean his wounds. What was it she says to him? 'A little child like this made you afraid. The fear that comes when reason goes away.' But what to fear from this girl?

Impatience struck him, and he went downstairs to get the photos from Bocchese.

Before taking the photos back to his office, Brunetti stopped and asked Vianello to come with him, explaining to him on the way everything that Rizzardi had told him and talking about what they had to do now. Back at his desk, Brunetti opened the file of photos that the technician had given him and they saw again the face of the dead child.

There were more than twenty photos, and in all of them she lay like the princess in a fairy tale, a halo of tangled golden hair radiating out from her face. That, however, was only a first impression and quickly gone, for it was then the viewer observed the paving stones on which the princess lay and the ratty, greying cotton cardigan bunched around her neck. One photo showed the tip of a black rubber boot; another caught a single moss-covered step, a crushed cigarette packet in one corner. No prince was coming here.

'Her eyes were light, weren't they?' Vianello asked as he set down the last photo.

'I think so,' Brunetti answered.

'I suppose we should have realized; from the long skirt, if from nothing else,' Vianello said. He wrapped his arms around his chest and stood, looking at the photos on Brunetti's desk. 'There's no way of knowing, though, whether she is or she isn't,' he added.

'Isn't what?'

'A Gypsy,' Vianello said.

Voice coloured by his lingering irritation at the pathologist's words, Brunetti answered, 'Rizzardi said we were supposed to call them Rom.'

'Oh. How very correct of the doctor.'

Regretting that he had said anything, Brunetti changed the subject. 'If no one's reported a burglary,' which had been the case when Brunetti stopped in the squad room downstairs, 'then either the people haven't discovered it yet or, just as easily, they did discover the break-in and chose not to report it.'

Vianello interrupted before Brunetti could add another possibility, saying, 'No one reports a burglary any more.'

Both men had spent their professional lives working for the police and thus had long ago learned the sovereign truth of crime statistics: to the degree that the process of reporting a crime is made difficult and time-consuming, the numbers of reported crimes will diminish.

Brunetti ignored Vianello's remark and stated the next possibility: 'Or they discovered her at it, frightened her off, and saw her fall.'

Vianello turned his head quickly away and stared out of the window of Brunetti's office.

'Well?' Brunetti asked. Its unpleasantness in no way diminished its likelihood.

'There were no marks on her body?' Vianello asked.

'No. Rizzardi didn't mention any.'

Vianello considered this for a long time and then asked, 'Do you want to say it or do you want me to?'

Brunetti shrugged. He was the superior officer, so it was probably his responsibility to give voice to the last possibility. 'Or they discovered her at it and pushed her off the roof.'

Vianello nodded and remained silent. 'In either of the last cases, they'd never call us,' the Inspector finally said. 'So what do we do?'

'We see if there's any way to identify the owner of the watch and the ring, and then we go and talk to them.'

'I'll go down and ask Foa about the tides,' Vianello said and left to do that.

16

Vianello was back quickly, explaining that Foa had had no need to consult a map. If the girl had gone into the water any time around midnight and had been found in front of Palazzo Benzon before nine, then it was most likely that she had gone in somewhere along Rio de Cá Corner or Rio di San Luca or, more likely, Rio di Cá Michiel, which ran right alongside the *palazzo*. The tides had been very low the previous night, and so the body would not have travelled far in the time it was in the water. The pilot had also explained that, if no damage was visible on the body, then it was unlikely that it had floated into the heavier traffic in the centre of the canal and all but impossible that it had floated across from the San Polo side.

Vianello had no sooner finished repeating all of this than Pucetti came in, carrying more photos in a folder and a small envelope with the ring and the pocket watch. He handed them to Brunetti, saying, 'Bocchese said the only things on these are smudges that are probably from the girl. Nothing else.'

Brunetti opened the folder and was relieved to see that it contained photos only of the girl's head and face. Her hair had been brushed back, and in one photo her eyes were open: a deep emerald green. Not only years, but great beauty, had been stolen from her.

He opened the envelope and slid the ring and watch out on to the desk. Judging by the size, the ring was a man's, a broad gold band with a tiny hatching pattern around both edges. 'Hand-made, I'd say,' offered Vianello.

He held it up to the light and looked inside. 'GF — OV, 25/10/84.'

'How does it open?' Pucetti asked, nodding toward the watch, which he did not touch. A few grains of Bocchese's black dusting powder had fallen from it on to Brunetti's desk.

Brunetti picked it up and pressed the knob on the top. Nothing happened. He turned the watch over and saw a tiny flange on the edge, then prised the back open with his fingernail. In a delicate italic script was written, *'Per Giorgio, con amore, Orsola.'* The date was 25/10/94.

'Well, it lasted at least ten years,' observed Vianello.

'Let's hope they got married here,' Brunetti said, reaching for the phone. As indeed they had. Giorgio Fornari had married Orsola Vivarini on the twenty-fifth of October 1984.

Vianello took the phone book and flipped to the Fs. He quickly found a Giorgio Fornari, but the address was in Dorsoduro. Looking up, he said, 'Whatever happened, it didn't happen there, did it?' Before either of them could answer, he flipped to the back of the book and checked the Vs. 'Nothing.'

'Pucetti,' Brunetti said, turning to the young officer. 'Take the photos downstairs and see if anyone recognizes her. If not, or even if someone does, take them over to the Carabinieri and see if you can get anything from them.' Brunetti knew that photos were taken of the children who were arrested for burglary, but since regulations demanded that the photos be sent to the Ministry of the Interior, the local police were left with no visual record save memory by which to identify repeat offenders.

When the younger man was gone, Brunetti said, 'I think we should go over to Dorsoduro and see how Signor Fornari lost his watch and his wedding ring.' He glanced at his own watch and saw that, if they left now and walked along the *riva* to the *traghetto* at San Marco, they would be there before lunchtime. Before they left the Questura, however, Brunetti checked the address in *Calli, Campielli, e Canali* and located the building at the end of Fondamenta Venier.

By the time they reached Ponte del Vin, they found themselves encased in people walking in the direction of the Piazza or strolling towards them from it. On the top of the bridge, Vianello gazed at the sea of heads and shoulders in front of them. 'I can't,' he whispered. Brunetti turned and led them back towards the *imbarcadero* and the boat that would take them to the San Zaccaria stop.

Despite their change of direction, the tide continued to sweep around them: comment was superfluous. When they reached the *imbarcadero,* they found that the snake of people waiting for the boat extended all the way back to the *riva.* Without hesitation, both men walked around to the right and up to the metal chain blocking entry. Immediately they were approached by a hatchet-faced blonde dressed in jeans so tight they seemed to put her breathing, if not her life, at risk.

'This is an exit,' she said in a shrill voice, shooing her hands at them in a flutter of exasperation. 'And you'll block the people who want to get off.'

'This is a police warrant card,' Vianello said, producing it from his pocket and stepping over the chain to show it to her, 'and you're blocking the police in the performance of their duties.' She acknowledged no defeat, but whatever she said was drowned as the engine of the approaching vaporetto slipped into reverse. She wheeled around and stood, hands on hips in front of them, as though afraid they would try to slip on to the boat while the arriving passengers were still trying to get off.

They waited patiently, and when the flood from the boat ebbed, she had to move away to unhook the chain that blocked the waiting passengers. They walked on board with them.

As the boat pulled away from the landing, Brunetti nudged Vianello with his elbow and said, 'Resistance to an officer in performance of his duties. Three-year suspended sentence if it was a first offence.'

'I'd make it five,' Vianello said. 'For the jeans if for nothing else.'

'Ah,' Brunetti sighed with mock exaggeration, 'where have they gone, those good old days when we could intimidate anyone we wanted to?'

Vianello laughed out loud. 'I think having this many people around all the time makes me bad tempered.'

'Get used to it, then.'

'To what?' Vianello asked.

'Bad temper, because it's just going to get worse. Last year sixteen million, this year twenty: God alone knows what it'll be like in a year.'

Talking about this and saying the things each of them had said a hundred times, they passed the time until the vaporetto pulled up at the Zattere stop. It was not yet twelve, so they decided to see if they could find Fornari before they thought about lunch.

The day had softened, and the walk along the Zattere smothered them in light and beauty. Vianello, who appeared not to have freed himself of the weight of all those tourists, asked, 'What do we do when the Chinese start coming?'

'They already have, I think.'

'Part of the twenty million?' Seeing Brunetti's nod, Vianello added, 'Then what do we do when there are twenty million of them, plus the others?'

'I don't know,' Brunetti said, letting his

eyes feast on the façade of the Redentore on the far side of the canal, 'Ask for a transfer, I suppose.'

After considering this possibility, Vianello asked, 'Could you live anywhere else?'

By way of answer, Brunetti nodded with his chin at the church across the canal. 'No more than you, Lorenzo,' he answered.

They cut to the left before the ex-Swiss Consulate, then right, and into Calle de Mezo, and then they were there. Only there was no there there. That is, Signor Fornari and his wife, though they did indeed own the apartment on the third floor, did not live in it. Or so they were informed by the woman who owned the apartment two floors down, whose bell they rang when they saw that neither Fornari nor Vivarini was listed on the bells beside the front door.

French people lived there now, she informed them, as though Signor Fornari had rented the place to a pack of marauding Visigoths. He and his wife lived now in her mother's apartment, had been there ever since the old Signora had had to be put into the Casa di Dio six years ago. Lovely people, yes, Signora Orsola and Signor Giorgio, he selling kitchens and she running the family business: sugar. And such lovely children, Matteo and Ludovica, both of them so beautiful, and . . .'

Before she could continue, perhaps, with praise of the next generation, Brunetti asked if she by any chance had the phone number and address of Signor Fornari. This conversation took place entirely between the woman at her front window and Brunetti standing on the pavement below, and was open to anyone who passed by or who chose to open a window in any of the nearby buildings. At no time did the woman enquire who the Veneziano-speaking man was, nor did she display any reluctance in giving him both the address and phone number of Giorgio Fornari and his wife.

'San Marco,' Vianello repeated as they turned away from the closing window. Impatient, the Inspector dialled Pucetti and asked him to check where the address was. While they waited for the young officer to locate it, the two men continued to walk towards Cantinone Storico, having decided it was the best bet for lunch.

Vianello stopped walking. He pressed the phone closer to his ear, muttered something Brunetti did not hear, then thanked Pucetti and snapped the phone closed. 'It looks like the building backs on to Rio di Cá Michiel,' Vianello said.

Because they were in a hurry, they decided not to have pasta and settled for a single dish of shrimp with vegetables and coriander. They shared a bottle of Gottardi pinot noir, turned down dessert, and finished with coffee. Feeling full but still faintly unsatisfied, Brunetti and Vianello walked out to the Accademia. Crossing the bridge, they discussed things other than what they might expect at the address they were heading towards. By unspoken agreement, they ignored the rows of *vu cumprà* who lined the steps of the bridge on both sides, confining their discussion to the sorry state of the surface of the steps and the growing need for repair or replacement of many of them.

'You think they deliberately choose materials that will wear out quickly?' Vianello asked, pointing down at one of the gaps in the surface beneath them.

'Humidity and millions of feet are just as sure to do the job for them, I think,' Brunetti said, knowing as he spoke that, however true, this explanation in no way excluded the other.

Talking idly, they crossed in front of the people seated at Paolin, eating the first *ge-*

lati of springtime, turned left and wove their way back towards the canal. At the end of a narrow *calle* that led down to the Grand Canal, they rang the bell marked Fornari.

'*Sì?*' a woman's voice enquired.

'Is this the home of Giorgio Fornari?' Brunetti asked in Italian, rather than Veneziano.

'Yes, it is. What do you want?'

'This is Commissario Guido Brunetti, of the police, Signora. I'd like to speak to Signor Fornari.'

'What's wrong?' she asked with that involuntary intake of breath he had heard many times.

'Nothing, Signora. I'd like to speak to Signor Fornari.'

'He's not here.'

'May I ask who you are, Signora?'

'His wife.'

'Then perhaps I could speak to you?'

'What is this about?' she asked with mounting impatience.

'Some missing property,' he said.

After a moment's silence, she said, 'I don't understand.'

'Perhaps I could come up and explain it to you, Signora,' Brunetti suggested.

'All right,' she said. A moment later the latch on the front door snapped open.

'Take the lift,' the woman's voice came from the speaker beside them. 'Top floor.'

The lift was a tiny wooden box which held them with room to spare for a third person, a very thin third person. In mid-passage, the box gave a sudden small jerk, and Brunetti turned aside in surprise. He saw two grim-faced men looking as startled as he felt, then recognized himself and Vianello, who met his eyes in the mirror on the side wall.

The box shuddered to a stop and continued to vibrate for a few seconds, before Brunetti pushed back the swinging doors. At a doorway on the right stood a woman of medium height, medium build, with medium-length hair of an indeterminate colour somewhere between red and brown.

'I'm Orsola Vivarini,' she said without extending her hand or smiling.

Brunetti stepped from the box, followed by Vianello. 'Guido Brunetti,' he repeated, then turned to Vianello and gave his name.

'Come into the study,' she said and led them down a bright corridor at the end of which light flooded in from a tall window that looked across at the buildings and rooftops on the other side of the Grand Canal. She stopped halfway down and opened a door on the right that led into a long narrow room two walls of which were covered almost to the ceiling with bookcases. There were three windows, but the building opposite was so close that less light penetrated than from the single window in the hall.

She led them towards a pair of comfortable-looking sofas that faced one another across a low walnut table covered with the scars of decades of feet and spills. A book lay face down on the sofa the woman chose; before sitting on the other, Brunetti closed a magazine and placed it on the table. Vianello sat beside him.

She regarded them levelly, without smiling 'I'm afraid I don't understand why you've come, Commissario,' she said.

Her voice flowed in the Veneto cadence: in other circumstances, Brunetti would have slipped into Veneziano, but she was speaking in Italian, and so he did his part to retain the formality of their exchange. 'It's about two objects belonging to your husband which have been found.'

'And they thought it necessary to send a commissario to give them back?' she asked in a tone in which scepticism took the place of surprise.

'No, Signora,' Brunetti answered. 'There's a possibility that this is part of a wider investigation.' The remark, though it often served as a multi-purpose lie, this time was true.

She raised both hands from her lap and opened the palms in a gesture of confusion. 'I'm afraid I'm completely at a loss here, then.' She tried unsuccessfully to smile. 'Perhaps you'd tell me what this is all about?'

Instead of answering, Brunetti took the manila envelope from his pocket and passed it across to her. 'Could you tell me if these belong to your husband, Signora?'

She unlooped the red string which held the flap and poured the objects out into the palm of her left hand. She gasped and involuntarily sought to cover her mouth with her other hand, though all she succeeded in doing was crushing the envelope against her lip. 'Where did you get these?' she demanded, looking up at him.

'Then you recognize them?' Brunetti asked.

'Of course I recognize them,' she said sharply. 'It's my husband's wedding ring and his watch.' As if uncertain, she prised open the back and, after reading the inscription, held it towards Brunetti. 'Look. Our names are there.' She set the watch on the table and held the ring up to the light, then passed it to Brunetti. 'And our initials.' When he said nothing, she demanded, 'Where did you get these?'

'Could you tell me the last time you saw these objects, Signora?' Brunetti asked, ignoring her question.

For a moment, he thought she would object to his question, but then she said, 'I don't know. I saw the ring last week, when Giorgio came home from the doctor.'

Brunetti saw no relation between the two parts of her answer, but he said nothing.

'The dermatologist,' she explained. 'Giorgio's developed a rash on his left hand, and the dermatologist said it might be an allergy to copper.' She pointed to the ring, still in Brunetti's hand, and said, 'See how red it is. That's the copper alloy. At least that's what the doctor thinks. At any rate, he told Giorgio to try not wearing the ring for a week or so to see if the rash disappeared.'

'And has it?' Brunetti asked.

'Yes. I think so. I don't know if it's disappeared completely, but it wasn't so bad before he left.'

'Left?'

She seemed surprised at his question, almost as if he should have known her husband was away. 'Yes. He's in Russia.' Before either man could ask, she said, 'On business. His company sells ready-made kitchen units, and he's there negotiating a contract.'

'How long has he been gone, Signora?' Brunetti asked.

'A week.'

'And when do you expect him back?'

'Towards the middle of next week,' she said, then added, unable to disguise her impatience and disgust, 'Unless he has to stay on longer to bribe some other people.'

Brunetti let that pass, saying only, 'Yes, I've been told it's difficult.' Then he asked, 'Did he remove the watch at the same time, do you know?'

'I think so. The clasp on the chain broke, weeks ago, so it really wasn't safe for him to carry it, and he said he was afraid someone would steal it. Before he left, he tried to find someone to fix it, but the jeweller who made the chain is gone, and Giorgio didn't have time to look any further. I said I'd try to get it done while he was away, but I suppose I forgot about it.'

'Do you have any idea when you saw it last?' Brunetti asked.

She glanced back and forth between the faces of the two men, as if hoping to read there some explanation of their curiosity about these objects. Then she closed her eyes for a moment, opened them and said, 'No, I'm sorry, I don't. I don't even remember watching Giorgio put it on the dresser. Maybe he told me he did, but I have no conscious memory of seeing it there.'

'And the wedding ring? When did you last see that?'

Again, the quick glance to see if they'd reveal the reasons for these questions; again, the failure. 'He carried it home in his watch pocket and said he wasn't going to wear it for a while. There's no other place he'd put it, but I can't remember seeing it on the dresser.' She tried to smile, good manners rising above irritation. 'I'm afraid I have to ask you what this is all about, Commissario.'

Brunetti saw no reason not to answer her, at least in the most general of terms. 'These objects were found in the possession of a person we believe to be involved in a series of other crimes. Now that you have identified these objects as belonging to your husband, we need to find out how they came into the possession of the person who had them.'

'What person?' she demanded.

Brunetti felt Vianello shift his weight on the sofa beside him. 'That's not something I'm at liberty to tell you, Signora. It's too early in our investigation.'

'But not too early for you to come here,' she shot back. When Brunetti made no rejoinder, she asked, 'Have you arrested anyone?'

Brunetti answered neutrally, 'I'm afraid I'm not at liberty to discuss that, either, Signora.'

Her voice took on a harder edge and she asked, 'And if you do, will my husband and I be told?'

'Of course,' he answered and asked her for the address of her husband's hotel, which she gave him. A silent Vianello wrote down the name. Brunetti did not want to irritate her further and so did not ask for the phone number.

'Could you tell me who lives here with you, Signora?' Brunetti asked, quite as if he had never heard the names of her children. This was the point, Brunetti thought as he waited for her to answer, when people usually began to protest or to refuse to answer further questions.

With no hesitation, she said, 'Only my two children: they're eighteen and sixteen.'

Glancing around the room with what he thought was an appreciative look, Brunetti asked, 'Is there anyone who helps you care for the apartment, Signora?'

'Margherita,' she answered.

'And her surname?'

'Carputti,' she answered and immediately went on, 'But she's worked for us for ten, no, for thirteen years. She'd no sooner steal anything than I would.' Before Brunetti could comment, she added, 'Besides, she's from Naples: if she did decide to steal from us, she'd be much more clever about it than to waste her time taking those things.' Brunetti hoped he would remember this explanation if it ever fell to him to defend the probity of his Southern friends.

'Do your children bring friends home, Signora?'

She looked as if it had never occurred to her that children might have friends. 'Yes, I suppose they do. They come and do homework together, or whatever it is young people do.'

As a parent, Brunetti had a set of ideas regarding what young people did in one another's homes; as a policeman, he had an entirely different set.

'Indeed,' he said, getting to his feet, followed by Vianello. Signora Vivarini got quickly to her feet.

'Would you be kind enough to show us where you last saw these objects, Signora?' Brunetti asked.

'But that's our bedroom,' she protested,

and Brunetti found himself liking her for it. He flicked his eyes in Vianello's direction, and the Inspector sat back down on the sofa.

For some reason, this seemed to satisfy Signora Vivarini, and she led Brunetti back into the corridor and across to the room opposite. She left the door open and preceded him.

It had the same comfortable feeling as did the study. An old Tabriz lay at the foot of the large double bed, faded from too many years beneath west-facing windows and worn ragged at one corner. Grey linen curtains were drawn back from the windows on the far wall, beyond which Brunetti saw the windows of the building on the opposite side of the canal. Between the windows were bookcases, with books stuffed in horizontally on top of every row.

The last window on the right led to a low-walled terrace, just big enough to hold the two chairs Brunetti saw on it. 'That must be a wonderful place to sit and read in the evening,' Brunetti said, waving towards the glass door.

She smiled for the first time and her face suddenly ceased to be ordinary. 'Yes. Giorgio and I spend a lot of time there.' Then she asked, 'Are you a reader?'

'When I have time, yes, I try to be,'

Brunetti answered. It was no longer possible to ask another person how they voted, and in a Catholic country it was hardly necessary to ask about a person's religion. Questions about sexual behaviour were impolite, and food was usually discussed during meals: so perhaps the only personally revealing question left was whether a person read or not, and if so, what. Tempting as it would be to follow this reflection, Brunetti asked, 'Would you show me where these objects were, Signora?'

She pointed to a low walnut bureau with four wide drawers that looked as if they would be hard to open. As Brunetti approached, the first thing he saw was a framed wedding photograph. Even more than twenty years younger and in her wedding dress, she had still been a completely ordinary-looking woman, but the man beside her, happiness radiant in his face, was more than handsome. To the right of the photo was a porcelain tray with an image of two brightly coloured dancing peasants in the centre. 'It was my mother's,' she said, as if to justify the workmanship and colours. The tray held two separate keys, a pair of nail scissors, a few seashells, and a book of vaporetto tickets.

She stood looking at the objects on the

tray for some time. She glanced away from them and around the room, then out beyond the terrace, then back at the objects on the tray. Lightly, she placed a finger on the vaporetto tickets and slid them to one side, then turned over two of the seashells. She said, 'There was a small garnet ring here, too, and a pair of cuff links with small pieces of lapis; they're gone, as well.'

'Were they valuable?' Brunetti asked.

She shook her head. 'No. It wasn't even a real garnet: just a piece of glass. But I liked it.' She paused, then added, 'The cuff links were silver.'

Brunetti nodded. It would be impossible for him to tell what was or what was not lying, just now, on the top of the dresser in his and Paola's bedroom. The emerald ring Paola's father had given her when she finished university was often left there, as was her IWC watch, but Brunetti had no idea when he had last seen them.

'Is anything else missing?' he asked.

'I don't think so,' she said, running her eyes across the surface of the bureau.

Brunetti walked over to the door to the terrace and looked at the house opposite. To see the canal, he would have to lean out from the terrace. Instead, he thanked her and went out into the corridor. When she joined him, he asked, 'Signora, could you tell me where you were on Wednesday night?'

'Wednesday,' she repeated, but not as a question.

'Yes.'

'At the opera, with my son and my sister and her husband, then at dinner with them.'

'May I ask where?'

'At their home. They had invited me and my husband, but he was away on this trip, so Matteo took his place.' She added, making it sound as if she thought it best to ask pardon for it, 'My son likes the opera.' Brunetti nodded, knowing her story could be easily checked.

As if reading his mind, she said in a voice grown louder, 'Her husband's name is Arturo Benini. They live in Castello.'

Again she anticipated his next question and said, 'We were there until at least one.' Sounding as if she might soon run out of patience, she added, 'My daughter was asleep when I got in, so I'm afraid there's no one you can check with about when we got back.' Brunetti heard the difficulty with which she controlled the anger that was seeping into her voice.

'Thank you, Signora,' he said and started back towards the room where Vianello waited. But suddenly the door at the end of the corridor opened and Botticelli's Venus walked into the apartment.

17

Married for more than twenty years to a woman he thought beautiful, with a daughter who was quickly becoming just that, Brunetti was accustomed to the sight of female beauty. He lived in a country that bombarded his eyes with lovely women: on posters, on the street, standing behind the counters in bars; even one of the new officers at the station in Cannaregio had caused his heart to stop the first time he saw her. Officer Dorigo, however, had turned out to be both a complainer and a troublemaker, so Brunetti's appreciation of her had turned into something that resembled window shopping: he was perfectly happy to observe her, just so long as he did not have to speak to or listen to her.

Nevertheless, he was still not prepared for the sight of the young girl who came in the door, turned to close it, and walked towards them smiling, saying, '*Ciao, Mamma,* I'm home.'

She kissed her mother, put out her hand to Brunetti in what he thought a charming imitation of adult sophistication, and said, 'Good afternoon. I'm Ludovica Fornari.'

Closer to, Brunetti saw that the resemblance to Botticelli's painting was superficial. The long blonde hair was the same, surely, but the face was more rectangular, the eyes, a translucent blue, more broadly spaced. He took her hand and gave his name but not his rank.

She smiled again, and he saw that her left incisor was faintly chipped. He wondered why it had not been fixed: certainly a family with a house like this could afford it. Brunetti found himself feeling protective of this girl and wondered if something could be said to her mother. Good sense intervened here, and he turned to Signora Vivarini and said, 'I won't keep you, Signora. Thank you for your time. I'll just get Ispettore Vianello.'

The girl made a noise and put her hand to her mouth, then started to cough. When Brunetti turned to look, the girl was bent over with her hands braced on her knees while her mother patted her repeatedly on the back. Uncertain how to help, he watched as the girl brought the coughing under control. She nodded, said something to her mother, who took her hand away, and then the girl stood upright.

'Sorry,' she whispered to Brunetti, smiling, tears in her eyes and on her cheeks. 'Something stuck,' she said, pointing at her throat. Saying that launched her into another fit of coughing. After a time, she held up one hand and smiled. She took a few quick, shallow breaths, then said to her mother, her voice hoarse, 'It's all right now, *Mamma.*'

Relieved, Brunetti crossed the corridor and opened the door to the other room. Vianello sat on the sofa, reading the magazine they had found there. The Inspector got to his feet, placed the magazine on the table, and joined Brunetti at the door. Emerging into the corridor, Vianello saw the girl, who smiled in his direction but did not extend her hand. The two men left the apartment, ignored the lift that still stood there with one door open, and took the stairs.

As soon as they were outside, Vianello asked, 'The daughter?'

'Yes.'

'Pretty girl.'

Instead of answering, Brunetti walked

down to the edge of the canal, where he turned back and studied the façade of the building they had just left.

Vianello asked, looking in the same general direction, 'What are you looking for?'

'The roof, to see what sort of angle it has,' Brunetti answered, shielding his eyes from the sun with an upraised hand. They were too close, so they saw only the façade and the underside of the gutters; there was no way they could back up to improve the perspective.

'Their bedroom is at the back,' Brunetti said, thrusting his hand away from his face and gesturing towards the building. 'There were two other doors on that side of the corridor.'

'And?' Vianello enquired.

'And nothing, I'm afraid,' Brunetti answered and started back down the *calle*. As Vianello drew abreast of him, Brunetti said, 'She told me she was at the opera with her son and then they went to dinner with her sister and her brother-in-law. So we check that first.'

'And then?'

'If it's true, then we try to find out something about the girl.'

After a moment's hesitation, Vianello asked hesitantly, 'The Gypsy?'

226

'Yes, of course,' Brunetti answered, slowing for a moment and giving him a curious look.

Vianello met his glance, looked away, and when he looked back, asked, 'Did Rizzardi really say that? About gonorrhoea?'

'Yes.'

They came out into Campo Santo Stefano and by mutual consent started towards the Accademia Bridge and the boat that would take them back to the Questura.

As they passed behind the statue, Vianello said, 'Why do I keep thinking it's worse because of her age?'

They walked in front of the church and turned towards the bridge. 'Because it is worse,' Brunetti said.

Pucetti came in to report soon after the other men returned to the Questura. By then, Brunetti had located Signora Fornari's brother-in-law, who confirmed her story, even adding that he had walked her and her son to the 1.07 vaporetto.

Pucetti had done as told and had shown the photos of the dead girl to his colleagues downstairs; he had left copies of the photos at the Carabinieri station at San Zaccaria, asking that they be circulated to see if anyone recognized her. As he spoke, he placed the folder with the remaining photos on his superior's desk.

When the younger man had stopped talking, Brunetti asked, 'But no one recognized her?'

'No one here, not yet. I put two of the photos on the notice-board,' Pucetti said. 'One of the Carabinieri over at San Zaccaria said he thought she'd been brought in there about a month ago, but he wasn't sure. He said he'd check the records and talk to the men who filed the report.'

'Let's hope he does it,' remarked Vianello, who had greater experience of the Carabinieri and their ways.

'I think he will,' protested Pucetti. 'The fact that it's a child seemed to bother him. Seemed to bother everyone I spoke to, in fact.'

Glances passed between the three men.

'You going to speak to her son?' Vianello asked, reminding Brunetti that the boy had still to be questioned to corroborate his mother's story.

'She wouldn't risk that,' Brunetti said, not certain why he knew this but no less certain about it for that.

'Commissario,' Pucetti began in a tentative voice, 'may I ask something?' At his superior's nod, the young officer continued,

'You sound, at least from what I've heard you say, like you think this Vivarini woman is guilty of something, or trying to hide something.'

Brunetti resisted the urge to pat Pucetti on the shoulder, nor did he smile. 'Signora Vivarini said she didn't notice that anything was missing. A wedding ring, a pocket watch, a pair of cuff links, and another ring.'

Pucetti listened attentively, filing away what Brunetti said.

'She was surprised when the police showed up, I think genuinely.' Pucetti nodded, adding this to his information. 'And as anyone would be expected to be,' Brunetti added, and Pucetti nodded again.

Brunetti toyed with the idea of asking Pucetti to comment on this, to tell them what he thought, but he resisted the temptation and continued. 'At no time during our conversation — and Vianello and I were in her house for at least half an hour — did she think to ask about the child who was pulled out of the water near her home.'

'Does that mean you suspect her of that?' Pucetti asked, unable to stop his astonished emphasis of the last word.

'No,' Brunetti said. But she didn't ask about the child, even when I told her we found the objects in the possession of someone we were investigating. That's why I'm suspicious.'

The first expression Brunetti saw flash across Pucetti's face was akin to dislike, and he was surprised at how much it offended him to see it there. But the younger man shook his head, glanced at his feet for some time, then came up with a smiling face. 'She should have, shouldn't she?'

Brunetti glanced across at Vianello and was relieved to see that he was smiling, too. The Inspector said to Pucetti, 'Little kid drowns in front of your house, and then the police show up, asking about things that have gone missing. Seems to me that, if the cops are there for half an hour, you'd have enough time to begin to wonder if maybe there's some sort of connection between the two things. After all, it's not as if people drown here every day, is it?'

'But what connection are you looking for?' Pucetti asked.

Brunetti raised his eyebrows, tilting his chin to one side to suggest endless possibilities. 'It could be nothing but coincidence. We've got the advantage that we know the girl had the ring and the watch, so we know that she was in the house. Signora Vivarini doesn't necessarily have to know the girl was there, so she might not see the connection, but it's still strange that she didn't ask about her.'

'That's all?' Pucetti asked.

'For the moment, yes,' Brunetti answered.

18

Later in the same day on which Pucetti had distributed the photos of the Gypsy girl, Brunetti found himself at his desk, the file with the remaining photos placed consciously to one side, as if that would help him to put them to the back of his mind. Almost with relief, he heard someone knock on his door and called, *'Avanti.'*

Signorina Elettra entered, saying, 'Do you have a moment, Commissario?'

'Of course, of course,' he said, gesturing to a chair.

She closed the door and crossed the room, and sat down, crossing her legs. She carried no papers, but her posture suggested she planned to be there for some time.

'Yes, Signorina?' Brunetti said with an easy smile.

'I've done what you asked, Dottore, and been busy finding out about that priest.

'Which one?' he asked.

'Ah, there's only one: Padre Antonin,' she answered, then, before he could enquire, she added, 'The other one, Leonardo Mutti, is a member of no religious order, at least not one that has the sanction of the Vatican.'

'May I ask how you discovered this?'

'It was easy enough to get his date and place of birth: he's resident here, so all I had to do was check the files at the Comune.' A minimal gesture of her right hand indicated the surpassing ease of this. 'And then all my friend had to do was run his name and date of birth through their files.' She paused here to add, 'The record-keeping at the Vatican is a marvel: they keep track of everything.'

Brunetti nodded.

'There's no sign of anyone called Leonardo Mutti either as a member of the regular clergy or in any recognized order of monks or priests.'

'Recognized?'

'My friend tells me they've got files on all of the acknowledged orders — that is, the ones they control — as well as on some of the fringe groups — those Lefèvre lunatics and people like that — but Mutti's name doesn't appear as a member of any of them, either.'

'Were you able to check those records

yourself?' Brunetti asked, more from politeness than from any clear understanding of what this might entail.

'Ah, no,' she said, hand raised to wave off the very thought. 'They're too good for me. I told you, they're a marvel: it's almost impossible to get into their system. Only with the proper authorization.'

'I see,' he said, as though he did. 'And Antonin? What did your friend find out about him?'

'That he was removed from his parish in Africa four years ago and sent to some small town in Abruzzo, but then it looks like some strings got pulled for him, and he ended up here, chaplain in the hospital.'

'What sort of strings?'

'I don't know, and he couldn't find out. But Antonin was in what you might call internal exile for a year or so before he was transferred here.' When Brunetti remained silent, she said, 'Usually, when they're sent back like that — under a cloud, as it were — they stay where they've been sent for far longer, often for the rest of their careers.'

'Why was he removed?' Brunetti asked.

'He was accused of running a scam,' she said, then added, 'I should have told you that to begin with, I suppose.'

'What sort of scam?'

'The usual thing they do in Africa and in lots of the missions in the Third World: letters back home, telling how great the need for help is, how little they have, and how poor the people are.' To Brunetti it sounded so very much like the letters Antonin had sent to Sergio.

'But Padre Antonin's mission moved into the modern age,' she said with something like admiration in her voice. 'He set up a website with photos of his jungle parish and his happy congregation filing into church for Mass. And the new school that had been built with donors' money.' She tilted her chin and asked, 'When you were a boy, Signore, did you get to ransom babies?'

'Ransom?'

'With the little cardboard collection box that you put your pocket money in, and the money went to ransom a pagan baby and save him for Jesus?'

'I think they had them at school, but my father wouldn't let me give them anything,' Brunetti said.

'We had them, too,' she said, failing to say whether she had or had not contributed to the salvation of pagan souls for Jesus. There was something she wasn't telling him; he had no idea what it was, but he had no doubt that it would soon be revealed. 'Padre

Antonin used the same tactic on his website,' she explained. 'By sending money to a bank account, you could pay for the education of a child for one year.'

Brunetti, who had a number of Indian orphans in his fiscal care, found himself growing uncomfortable.

'He spoke of education and vocational training, not about religion, at least on the website,' she explained. Then, before he could ask, she said, 'I suppose he assumed that people who consulted a website would be more interested in education than in religion.'

'Perhaps,' Brunetti said, then asked, 'And?'

'And then the whole thing blew up when someone looking at the website noticed that the photos of Antonin's happy congregation were also used on the site of a school run by some bishop in Kenya. Not only that, but the pious stories of hope and faith were the same, as well.' She smiled. 'I suppose they thought there would be no ecclesiastical crosschecking, if I might call it that.' Then, her cynicism slipping through, she asked, 'Besides, all Black people look alike, don't they?'

Ignoring this last, Brunetti enquired, 'What happened?'

'The person who noticed it was a journalist working on an article about these missionary groups.'

'A journalist with or without sympathy?' Brunetti asked.

'Luckily for Antonin, with.'

'And so?'

'And so he reported it to someone at the Vatican, who had a quiet word with Antonin's bishop, and Padre Antonin found himself suddenly transferred to Abruzzo.'

'And the money?'

'Ah, here it becomes interesting,' she said. 'It turns out that Antonin had nothing to do with the money: it all went to an account his bishop had set up in his own name, along with a percentage of the money raised by the bishop in Kenya who was using Antonin's photos. Antonin never had any idea how much money they raised: he didn't care so long as they had enough to run the school and feed the children.' She smiled at the simplicity of the man.

'He served as a kind of front man, I suppose you could say,' she went on. 'He was European, had contacts in Italy, knew people here who could design a website, and he knew how to appeal to people's generosity.' She smiled again, a cooler smile. 'If it hadn't been for the journalist, he'd probably still be there, saving souls for Jesus.'

Indignant, as much for Antonin as because of what his initial response to the story revealed about his own prejudices, Brunetti said, 'Didn't he protest? He was innocent.'

'Poverty. Chastity. Obedience.' She paused after each word. 'It seems Antonin takes them all seriously. So he obeyed the command of Rome and came back, did his job in Abruzzo. But then it seems someone found out what had really happened — the journalist probably told someone — and Antonin was sent here.'

'Has he told anyone the truth?' Brunetti asked.

She shrugged. 'He does his job, takes care of the people in the hospital, buries the dead.'

'And tries to stop people from being caught up in similar scams?' Brunetti ventured.

'So it would seem,' she said reluctantly, preferring, regardless of the evidence, to keep her suspicions of the clergy intact. She leaned forward and began to get to her feet. 'Do you want me to continue looking into Leonardo Mutti?'

Though Brunetti's best instincts warned him not to waste more time on this, he now felt he owed Antonin a favour. 'Yes, please. Antonin kept insisting that he was from Umbria, so perhaps you could see if you can find anything there.'

'Yes, Commissario,' she said, finally getting to her feet. 'Vianello told me about the little girl. Terrible.'

Did she mean the death, or the disease, or the fact that she probably died while robbing an apartment, or that no one had come to claim her? Rather than answer this, Brunetti said, 'I can't get rid of the sight of her.'

'Vianello said the same, sir,' she said. 'Perhaps it will be better when it's settled.'

'Yes. Perhaps,' Brunetti replied. When he said no more, she left his office and went back to her own.

Three days later, a phone call from the Carabinieri sub-station at San Zaccaria was transferred to him. 'You the one looking for the Gypsy?' a man's voice asked.

'Yes.'

'They told me to call you.'

'And you are?'

'Maresciallo Steiner,' the man answered, and at the name Brunetti realized that the accent lurking in the man's voice was German.

'Thank you for calling, Maresciallo,' Brunetti said, opting for politeness, though he had a feeling it might not cut much ice.

'Padrini showed me the photo your guy left, said you wanted to know about her.'

'Yes, that's correct.'

'My boys brought her in here a couple of times. Usual stuff: call a female officer, wait for her to get here, then search the kid. Search the other ones that got brought in with her, too. That happened twice. Then get in touch with their parents.' A pause followed, then Steiner added, 'Or the people who say they're the parents. Then wait for the parents to come, or if they don't show up, take the kids out to the camp and hand them over. That's the procedure. No comments, no charges, and not even a little tap on the back of the wrist to remind them not to do it again.' Steiner's words suggested sarcasm, but his tone expressed only tired resignation.

'Could you tell me exactly who recognized her?' Brunetti asked.

'As I told you, two of my men. Pretty girl: didn't look like one of them. So they remembered her.'

'Could I come down there and talk to them?' Brunetti asked.

'Why? You guys going to handle the case?'

Immediately on his guard to avoid whatever turf war the Maresciallo might be
imagining, Brunetti said amicably, 'I'm not
sure there's much of a case to handle,
Maresciallo. What I'd like to do is get a
name and, if possible, an address from your
records, then get a positive identification
from her parents . . .' Brunetti paused here,
then added in a tone of complicit camaraderie, '. . . or the people claiming to be her
parents.'

All Brunetti heard was a muffled grunt
from Steiner, perhaps of agreement, perhaps
of appreciation. He went on. 'As soon as we
have that, we can consign her body to them
and close the case.'

'How'd she die?' the Carabiniere asked.

'Drowned. Just as it said in the papers,'
Brunetti answered, then added, 'for once.'
This time Brunetti heard a short grunt of
agreement. 'No signs of violence: I figure
she fell into the canal. Probably didn't know
how to swim,' he said, without a thought of
adding, 'poor thing.'

'Yeah, it's not like they spend a lot of time
at the beach, is it?' Steiner asked, and
Brunetti mumbled something that might
sound like agreement.

'You still want to bother coming down
here?' Steiner asked. 'I can give you all the

information on the phone.'

'No, it'll look better on my report if I can say I came down and talked to you about it,' Brunetti said, as if confiding in an old friend. 'Any chance I could talk to your men, too?'

'Wait a minute and I'll see who's here,' Steiner said and set the phone down. After a long time, he picked it up. 'No, both of them have gone off duty. Sorry.'

'Could I get the information from you, then, Maresciallo?'

'I'll be here.'

Brunetti thanked him, said he'd be there in ten minutes, and replaced the phone.

Because he was in a hurry, he didn't stop to tell anyone where he was going. It might be better, in any case, to visit Steiner alone, if only to make it appear to him that the police had no great interest in the death of the child and were merely trying to clear their records. Brunetti had no particular reason to want to keep information from the Carabinieri: his urge towards secrecy was entirely atavistic.

On his walk to the Carabinieri station, Brunetti's imagination conjured up a picture of Steiner as a kind of Tyrolean *Ubermensch:* tall, blond, blue-eyed, firm of chin and purpose. The man into whose office he was shown, however, was so short and dark that he must often be mistaken for a Sardinian or a Sicilian. He had black hair so dense and wiry Brunetti thought he would have the devil's own time finding anyone able to cut it for him. Strangely enough, his eyes were clear grey and looked out of place on his dark-skinned face.

'Steiner,' he said as Brunetti entered. The two men shook hands, and Brunetti, after turning down the ritual offer of a coffee, asked the Maresciallo to tell him whatever he could about the girl or her family.

'I've got the file here,' the Maresciallo said, picking up a manila folder and putting on a pair of thick-lensed glasses. He waved the file in the air. 'They're busy people.' Setting it down on his desk, he added, 'Everything's here: our reports, more from the squad in Dolo, also from the social services.'

Steiner opened the file; he picked up the first few pages and began to read: 'Ariana Rocich, daughter of Bogdan Rocich and Ghena Michailovich.' Steiner glanced at Brunetti over the top of his glasses, and when he noticed that he was taking notes, said, 'The file is yours. I had copies made of everything.'

'Thank you, Maresciallo,' Brunetti said and replaced the notebook in his pocket.

Steiner returned his attention to the papers and went on, as though there had been no interruption, 'Or at least those are the names on their papers. Doesn't mean much.'

'Fake?' Brunetti asked.

'Who knows?' Steiner asked in return and let the pages flutter to his desk. 'Most of the ones we have here come from ex-Yugoslavia: they've come in with UN refugee status, or their documents are from countries that don't exist any more.' With a finger that was surprisingly long and delicate, he pushed the folder forward on his desk, saying, 'Some of them already have Italian passports: been here so long. This bunch, though, came from Kosovo. Or said they did. No way of knowing. Probably doesn't make any difference, anyway. Once they're here, there's no getting rid of them, is there?'

Brunetti muttered something, then asked, 'You said that your men brought other children in with her.' Steiner nodded. 'Same parents? What's their name? Rocich?'

Steiner leafed quickly through the papers and placed some to the side, face down. Finally he pulled one out and read through it, then said, 'There are three of them. That is, this girl Ariana, and two others.' He looked up and said, 'You know we can't

244

keep records for children, but I asked around: that's what's in here.' At Brunetti's nod, Steiner went on. 'My boys told me they've caught her twice, both times during a burglary.' Brunetti knew that no one under the age of fourteen could be arrested by the police, only taken into protective custody until they could be returned to their parents or the adult in whose care they were. No records could be kept, but memory was not yet illegal.

'The other two kids,' the Maresciallo continued, 'belong to the same family — at least the same surname is on their papers — though with them you never know who the real father is.'

'Do they live in the same place?' Brunetti asked.

'You don't mean in a house, do you, Commissario?' Steiner asked.

'Of course not. I mean camp. Do they all live in the same one?'

'It would seem so,' Steiner said. 'Outside of Dolo. It's been there about fifteen years, ever since things fell apart in Yugoslavia.'

'How many people are there?'

'You mean in that camp or altogether?'

'Both, I suppose.'

'It's impossible to say, really,' Steiner answered, removing his glasses and tossing them down on the open file. 'In the camp, there can be from fifty to a hundred, sometimes more if they have a party or a meeting: a wedding or some sort of celebration. The best we can do is count the caravans or the cars and then multiply by four.' Steiner smiled and ran one hand through his hair: Brunetti thought he could hear the noise it made. 'No one knows why we use that number,' Steiner confessed, 'but we do.'

'And in total? In Italy, I mean.'

This time Steiner ran both hands through his hair, and Brunetti really did hear the noise. 'That's anyone's guess. The government says forty thousand, so it could be forty thousand. But it could just as easily be a hundred thousand. No one knows.'

'No one counts?' Brunetti asked.

Steiner looked across at him. 'I thought you were going to ask if no one cares,' he said.

'That, too, I suppose,' Brunetti answered, no longer feeling so distant from the man.

'Certainly no one counts,' Steiner said. 'That is, they count the people in the camps, if you can call what we do counting. And then they count the camps all over the country. But the numbers change every day. They move around a lot, so some never get counted and some get counted more than once. Sometimes they move when it begins to be dangerous for them to stay in one camp.' Steiner gave him a long look and then added, 'And if you'd like me to say something I shouldn't say, I'll add that the people who see them — or who want them to be seen — as a danger to society tend to count more of them than people who don't.'

'Why is that?' Brunetti asked, though he had a pretty good idea.

'The neighbours get tired of having their cars stolen or their houses broken into or having their children beaten up in school by the kids from the camps. That is, the ones who go to school. So groups, or you could call them gangs, start to form outside the camps, and if the number of nomads in the country is a high one, then these groups feel justified in wanting to get rid of them. And they begin to make life uncomfortable for them.'

Seeing that Brunetti was following his explanation, he decided not to describe how life was made uncomfortable and went on, 'So one morning there are fewer campers and fewer Mercedes. And for a while no one breaks into houses in the area and their kids go to school and behave better while they're there.' Steiner gave Brunetti a long look and then asked, 'You want me to speak frankly?'

'It's what I most want.'

'Another thing that makes them move is if we start coming around too often with their kids, bringing them back after we've found them in houses or coming out of houses or walking around with screwdrivers stuck in their socks or in the waistbands of their skirts. After we've brought them back five or six times, they move.'

'And then what happens?'

'They go somewhere else and begin to break into houses there.'

'Just like that?' Brunetti asked.

Steiner shrugged. 'They pack up and move and continue living as they always have. It's not as if they've got rent or mortgages to pay or jobs to go to, like the rest of us.'

'It sounds like you have very little sympathy for them,' Brunetti risked saying.

Steiner gave a shrug. 'No, it's not that, Commissario, but I've been arresting them and taking their children home for years, so I don't have any illusions about them.'

'And you think people do?' Brunetti asked.

'Some do. About equality and respect for culture and different traditions.' Much as he listened for it, Brunetti could detect no hint of sarcasm or irony.

'There's also guilt about what happened

to them during the war,' the Carabiniere continued, adding, 'Understandably so. As a consequence, they get treated differently.'

'Which means what?'

'Which means if you or I refused to send our children to school and, instead, sent them out to rob houses, we wouldn't keep those children very long.'

'And that's not the case for them?'

'I hardly think you have to ask me that, Commissario,' Steiner said, more than a bit of asperity in his tone. He ran his right hand through his hair again then changed the subject by asking, 'Now that you know who she is, what do you plan to do?'

'Her parents have to be informed.'

Steiner nodded.

After giving the Maresciallo some time to comment, an opportunity the other man ignored, Brunetti said, 'I found the body, so I suppose I should be the one to tell them.'

Steiner studied Brunetti for a moment, then said, 'Yes.'

'Is there someone from the social services who knows them?' Brunetti asked.

'There's a number of them.'

'I'd prefer it to be a woman,' Brunetti said. 'To tell the mother.'

Brunetti thought he saw Steiner grimace, but then the Maresciallo got to his feet. He picked up the file, came around the desk, and held it out to Brunetti. 'Some of the reports of the social workers are in here.' Brunetti looked at the folder but made no move to take it.

Steiner gave a smile and a small shake of the folder. 'I need a cigarette, but I have to go outside to smoke it,' he said. 'Read this while I'm gone, and when I come back, tell me what you'd like to do, all right?'

Brunetti reached up and took the file. Steiner left the office, closing the door quietly behind him.

19

What was that book Paola always talked about whenever she taught Dickens? *London Something and the London Something?* Brunetti had been shocked the first time she read to him from it, shocked not only by the information the book contained, but by the apparent gusto with which she read it to him. When he had balked at the accounts of scores of people living in windowless rooms, of young children hunting for re-sellable garbage in a faeces-filled river, she had called him 'lily-livered', whatever that meant. When he had refused to believe the accounts of precocious sexuality presented by the author or had blanched at the list of occupations pursued by children, Paola had accused him of wilful blindness.

His thoughts fled to those passages as he read the reports of the social workers who had visited the Rom camp outside Dolo where the Rocich family lived. The family's home was a 1979 *roulotte* for which no registration papers existed. Nor, apparently, did it have a source of heat.

As Steiner had suggested, to call it the family's home was to impose the conventions of one society upon members of another. The car which was parked nearest to the *roulotte* was registered to Bogdan Rocich, possessor of a UN refugee document. The woman sharing the *roulotte* with him, also the possessor of a UN document, was Ghena Michailovich. Three children, Ariana, Dusan, and Xenia, were entered on the passport of the woman, whose name appeared on their birth certificates, as did that of Bogdan Rocich.

Bogdan Rocich, also known to the authorities by a long list of aliases, had a long criminal record, stretching back sixteen years, when he presumably entered the country. The crimes he had been arrested for included: robbery, assault, the sale of drugs, possession of a weapon, rape, and public drunkenness. He had been sentenced only for possession of a weapon: the witnesses of his other crimes, most of whom had been his victims, had in every case retracted their accusation before the case came to trial. One witness had disappeared.

The woman, Ghena Michailovich, born in

what was now Bosnia, had also been arrested many times, though her crimes consisted of nothing more serious than shoplifting and pickpocketing. She had been convicted twice, and both times had been consigned to house arrest because she was the mother of three children. She, too, enjoyed the use of a list of aliases.

Brunetti read through all of the arrest reports of the parents, then turned to the documents concerning the children. All three were known to the social services. Because they had been born in Italy, there was no uncertainty about their age. The oldest, Xenia, was thirteen; the boy, Dusan, twelve. The dead girl, Ariana, had been eleven.

When he read the age of the dead child, Brunetti lowered the papers to the desk and turned his head to gaze out the window and into the courtyard at the centre of the Carabinieri station. A pine tree stood at the far corner, some sort of fruit tree a few metres in front of it, so Brunetti saw the sweet green of the still unfolded leaves outlined against the darker green of the needles. Below them, the new grass was almost electrically bright, and against the low stone wall of the inner courtyard he saw the thin shoots of what would become tulips poking up from the earth. Suddenly a bird swooped in from the left and disappeared into the upper branches of the pine tree, emerging a few seconds later to fly off. He sat for a few minutes, watching the bird return again and again. Building a house.

He looked back at the papers. The three children were enrolled at two schools in Dolo, though all of them were so frequently absent as to render the word 'enrolled' notional.

The documents from the schools gave no indication of their scholastic achievements and were confined to listing the days on which the children did not appear in class and the days on which they did not present themselves for their year-end exams. Dusan had twice been sent home for being involved in fights, though the report contained no explanation of the cause of those fights. Xenia had once attacked a boy in her class and had broken his nose, but nothing had come of that, either. No special mention was made of Ariana.

The door opened behind him and Steiner returned. He carried two small white plastic cups. 'There's only one sugar,' he said, as he set the coffee down in front of Brunetti.

'Thank you,' Brunetti said, as he closed the folder and set it on the desk in front of him. The coffee was bitter: he didn't mind.

Steiner walked around his desk and sat down again. He finished his coffee, crushed the cup and tossed it into the wastepaper basket. 'You willing to talk about what you've found?' he asked Brunetti. As if to emphasize the question, he leaned forward and placed his extended palm on the folder.

'The girl had a ring and a watch,' Brunetti said, reluctant to explain where Rizzardi had found the ring. 'They belong to a man called Giorgio Fornari, who lives in San Marco, near where the girl's body was found. I spoke to the wife — went to see her — and she seemed surprised when I produced them. When she showed me where they had been left, she realized another ring and a pair of cuff links were missing. I think she was genuinely surprised the things had been stolen.'

'Was there anything else worth stealing in the house?'

'Nothing Gypsies steal,' Brunetti said. 'Rom, I mean,' he quickly added.

'That's just for the reports,' Steiner said. 'You can call them Gypsies here.'

Brunetti nodded.

'Who else lives in the house?' Steiner asked.

'Her husband was away, in Russia on

some sort of business trip, and should be back soon. There's a son, eighteen, who was at the opera with his mother that night.' Steiner raised his eyebrows at this, but Brunetti ignored him. 'And there's a daughter, sixteen. She came in while we were there.'

'Anyone else?'

'A cleaning woman, but she doesn't live with them.'

Steiner leaned back in his chair, and in a gesture Brunetti found familiar, he pulled a side drawer open with one foot and crossed both of them on top of it. He folded his arms, rested his head against the back of his chair. He stared out the window and studied the trees. Perhaps he even watched the bird.

Finally Steiner said, 'Either someone came in and surprised her or not. Either she fell or someone helped her to fall.' He studied the trees and the bird a bit longer. 'We can't be certain about either of those things, at least not now. But we can be sure of one thing.'

'That she wasn't alone?' Brunetti offered.

'Exactly.'

'The other two have been arrested with her a few times,' Brunetti added.

This time, Steiner brought both hands to his head and scratched at it vigorously, as though it were a friendly dog. When he finished, he returned his attention to the tree for some time, then glanced over at Brunetti and said, 'I think this is where we have to stop and consider things.'

'Like the fact that they're minors?' Brunetti suggested. At Steiner's nod, he added, 'and the fact that jurisdiction becomes an issue.'

Again, the Carabiniere nodded, then surprised Brunetti by asking. 'Is your boss Patta?'

'Yes.'

'Humm. I've worked for men like him. I suppose you're used to putting things to him in — well — in inventive ways?'

Brunetti nodded.

'You think you can convince him to let you run with this? It's not that anything much is likely to come of it, but I don't like it that it's a kid.'

'Of the possibilities you gave, is there one you believe?' Brunetti asked and was reminded of his own dogged questioning of the pathologist.

Before Steiner answered, he consulted the trees and the bird again, and then said, 'As I said before, either she fell or she was pushed. And the other kids must have been there, so they know which one it was.'

'They would have said something,' Brunetti suggested, though he didn't believe it and offered it only to see how the other man would react.

Steiner let out a huff of disbelief. 'These aren't children who talk to the police, Commissario.' After a moment's reflection, he added, 'I don't know if they're even children who talk to their parents.'

Brunetti spoke before he thought. 'You can't set out as three and go home as two and no one notices it or asks about it.'

Steiner took his time before he answered, 'It's probably something that happens to them all the time. If you think about it. They see the police and scatter; someone comes in while they're in a house, and they run; someone sees them prising open a door and screams at them, and they run in different directions to make it harder to catch them. I'm sure they know the best way to escape from any situation.'

'The girl didn't,' Brunetti said.

'No,' Steiner agreed in a soft voice. 'She didn't, did she?'

After a moment, Brunetti said, 'It's strange that they never notified us that the girl was missing.'

'Not really,' Steiner said. 'If you think about it, that is.'

Silence fell between them, but it was the silence of empathy and common purpose. Finally Brunetti said, 'I've got to go and tell the mother.'

'Yes,' Steiner said, 'you do.' After a pause, he asked, 'How do you want to do it?'

'I'd like to take my assistant with me. Vianello.'

'Good man,' Steiner surprised Brunetti by saying.

Choosing not to comment, Brunetti said, 'I'd like one of you to come with me. And I'd like to arrive in one of your cars.' Steiner nodded, as if to suggest that nothing would be easier. 'And,' Brunetti continued, 'I think it would be best to take someone from the social services with us.' As he spoke, he realized he was now including the Maresciallo in his plans.

Steiner agreed. 'I'll tell my superior.'

'And I'll think of a way to tell mine.'

Steiner pushed himself to his feet and walked towards the door. 'It will take me about twenty minutes to get this organized: a boat and a car and someone from the social services. I'll come and get you in one of our boats: say half an hour.'

Brunetti extended his hand, thanked the Maresciallo, and left, heading back to the Questura.

20

There was no sign of Vianello. Brunetti stopped at the officers' squad room, but the Inspector was not there, nor did anyone know where he might have gone. Brunetti went down to Signorina Elettra's office on the odd chance that the Inspector might be there, or, less likely, in with Patta.

'You seen Vianello?' he asked without greeting as he went in.

She looked up from the papers on her desk and, after a pause that went on a bit too long, said, 'I think he's waiting for you in your office, sir.' Her head bent back over the papers.

'Thank you,' Brunetti said. She did not reply.

It was only when he was on the steps that he registered the abruptness of his tone and the coolness with which she had answered him, but he had no time for such niceties. Brunetti found Vianello in his office, standing at the window, gazing across the canal. Before Brunetti could speak, the Inspector said, 'Steiner called me, said the boat was just arriving there, and he'd be here in a few minutes.'

Brunetti grunted in acknowledgement, went over to his desk, and picked up the phone. When Patta answered with his name, Brunetti said, 'Vice-Questore, it's Brunetti. It seems the Carabinieri have located the parents of the girl who drowned last week. Yes, sir, the Gypsy,' Brunetti answered, wondering if there were perhaps other girls who had drowned in the last week that Patta had failed to tell him about.

'The Carabinieri want someone from the Questura to go along while they inform them,' he said, doing his best to fill his voice with irritation and impatience. He listened for a moment, then answered, 'Near Dolo, sir. No, they didn't tell me exactly where. But I thought you, as the ranking person here, would be the most suitable person to accompany them.'

In response to his superior's question, Brunetti said, 'With the boat ride and the wait for the car at Piazzale Roma — they told me there's been some sort of mix-up and it won't be there until three — I'd say it wouldn't take much more than two hours, sir, maybe a bit more, depending on the car.' Brunetti listened for some time and then said, 'Of course I understand, sir. But there's no other way to inform them. There are no phones out there, and the Carabinieri don't have a *telefonino* number to contact.'

Brunetti glanced across at Vianello and held the phone away from his ear as Patta presented his reluctance to the listening air. Suddenly Vianello leaned forward and pointed towards the entrance to the canal and the approaching boat. Brunetti nodded and pulled the phone back to his ear.

'I understand that, Vice-Questore, but I'm not sure it's convenient . . . Of course I understand the importance of maintaining good relations with the Carabinieri, but surely they'd prefer that an officer of higher . . .'

Brunetti caught Vianello's eye and made a rolling motion with his outstretched finger, suggesting that this conversation might go on for some time. It did, until Vianello started towards the door, when Brunetti interrupted to say, 'If you insist, sir. I'll give you a full report when I get back.'

He replaced the phone, grabbed the envelope with the photos of the dead child, and hurried after Vianello, who was already halfway down the stairs.

Outside, Vianello jumped on to the waiting launch and shook hands with Steiner, then held out a hand to steady Brunetti as he jumped aboard. Vianello addressed the Maresciallo as 'Walter', and left it to Brunetti to decide which form of address to use with the other man. He opted to follow in the wake of Vianello's friendship and used the more familiar *tu,* giving his first name, after which Steiner touched him on the upper arm and told Brunetti to call him Walter.

Still standing on deck, Brunetti explained that Patta had asked him to take the news to the child's parents, thinking it best to provide no explanation of how this had come to pass. Steiner's face remained impassive; he permitted himself to say only, 'The most successful superiors understand how important it is to know how to delegate.'

'Indeed,' Brunetti replied, and the familiarity begun by the use of *tu* grew even stronger.

The men moved down into the cabin as the boat made its slow way up towards Piazzale Roma, where a woman from the social services would meet them. Brunetti used the time to tell Steiner about finding the body and the complete results of the autopsy.

Steiner nodded and said, 'I've heard that they hide things that way, though we've never encountered it.' He shook his head a few times, as if attempting to expand his understanding of the limits of human behaviour, then said, 'The kid's eleven years old, and she's hiding jewellery in her vagina.' He was silent for a while, then muttered, *'Dio buono.'*

The boat passed under the Rialto, but none of the men in the cabin noticed. 'The woman who'll meet us, Cristina Pitteri, has worked with the Gypsies for about ten years,' Steiner said in a voice so neutral it forced Vianello and Brunetti to exchange a quick glance.

'What's she do?' Vianello asked.

'She's a psychiatric social worker by training,' Steiner explained. 'Used to work at Palazzo Boldù. But she asked for a transfer: she ended up in the office that deals with the different nomad groups.'

'There's others?' Vianello asked.

'Yes. The Sinti. Not as criminal as the Gypsies, but they come from the same places and live much the same way.'

'What does she do?' Brunetti asked.

Steiner considered this until the boat was passing under the Ponte degli Scalzi and then in front of the train station. 'She's in charge of something called "inter-ethnic liaison",' he answered, using the foreign words.

'Which means?' asked Vianello.

Steiner's face softened into a grin, but only momentarily, and then he said, 'As far as I can see, I think it means she tries to make them make sense to us and us to them.'

'Is that possible?' Vianello asked.

Steiner got to his feet and pushed open the door that led to the steps. He turned and said over his shoulder, 'Better ask her', and went up on deck.

The pilot brought the boat to a halt in one of the taxi docks to the right of the *imbarcadero* of the 82. The three men stepped on to the dock; Brunetti and Vianello followed Steiner up to the road, where a dark Carabinieri estate car waited, motor running. A robust woman with short dark hair who looked to be in her late thirties stood on the pavement next to the car, smoking a cigarette. She wore a skirt and sweater under a box-cut jacket, and dark brown walking shoes that had the glow of expensive leather. She had a round face in which the features all seemed to have been squeezed too close together. Her eyes were close set, and her upper lip much thicker than the lower, giving the impression that, in a kind of continental shift, her features were slowly migrating towards her nose.

Steiner approached her and extended his hand. She paused long enough for everyone to register that she had done so, then gave her hand to the Maresciallo.

'Dottoressa,' he said with neutral deference, 'this is Dottor Brunetti and Ispettore Vianello, his assistant. They're the ones who found the girl.'

She flicked the cigarette aside and briefly studied Brunetti's face, and then Vianello's, before she extended her hand to Brunetti. Her grip was as fleeting as it was limp; they exchanged titles as a form of greeting. She nodded at Vianello, turned, and got into the back seat of the car. A silent Steiner got into the front seat beside the driver, leaving the other two, in the absence of any motion on the part of Dottoressa Pitteri to slide across the seat, to walk around the back of the car to the door on the other side. Brunetti opened it a few centimetres then waited for a break in the traffic before climbing in. Taking his place on the uncomfortable middle of the seat, he was careful to angle his knees and thighs to the left to keep from touching those of the woman beside him. Vianello clambered in and slammed the door, pressing himself close against it.

The driver, a uniformed officer, said something softly to Steiner, who answered '*Sì,*' after which the car pulled away from the kerb. 'Dottoressa Pitteri has worked with the Rom for some time now, Commissario,' Steiner said. 'She knows the girl's parents, and so I'm sure her presence will be a great help to us when we tell them.'

'And to the girl's family, as well, I should hope,' Dottoressa Pitteri interrupted, speaking with muffled indignation. 'I think that's rather more important.'

'I hardly thought it needed saying, Dottoressa,' Steiner said blandly. As he spoke, his eyes remained on the road before them, as though he considered it his duty to keep the driver constantly warned of approaching danger.

They started across the causeway, and Brunetti's eyes were pulled to the left and to the smokestacks and holding tanks of Marghera. The newspapers had told him that morning that cars with even-numbered licence plates were permitted on the street today; the odd-numbered ones could drive tomorrow. There had been no substantial rain for a month: it had done nothing but sprinkle, and so only God knew what was swirling around in the air they breathed. 'Microdust', it was called, and Brunetti could never read the name without conjuring up tiny particles of chemicals, all those poisons Marghera had been hurling up into the atmosphere for three generations, digging their way ever deeper into his lungs and into his tissues.

Vianello, whose ecological sympathies used to be, but were no longer, a source of fun at the Questura, looked in the same direction. 'Try to close it,' Vianello said with no introduction, nodding towards the representative smokestacks of the industrial area, 'and they're out in protest the next day. "Save our jobs." ' The Inspector gestured to the left, then let his hand fall to his lap in what Brunetti thought a melodramatic gesture of frustration and despair.

No one in the car spoke for a while, but then Dottoressa Pitteri asked, 'Would you rather they starved, Ispettore? And their children?' Her voice held a combination of irony and condescension and she spoke with great clarity, as if she feared a man as simple-minded as a police inspector might not be able to understand a more complex question.

'No, Dottoressa,' Vianello said, 'I'd like them to stop pumping *Cloruro vinile mono-*

mero into the air our children breathe.'

'Certainly they've stopped that in the last years,' she said.

'So they say,' Vianello replied, then added, 'If you choose to believe them.'

In the ensuing silence, the noise of a passing truck sounded uncommonly loud.

Brunetti had followed the play of emotion on the woman's face in the rearview mirror, and he saw her purse her lips as she turned away from the offending smokestacks.

Though Brunetti was curious to learn whatever the woman could tell him about the Gypsies, the obvious antipathy between her and Steiner made him reluctant to raise the subject while the other man was present. 'Have you been out there before, Maresciallo?' he asked, using the formal *Lei* to address the other man.

'Twice.'

'For these same people, the Rocich?'

'Once. The other time it was to bring back a woman who tried to pick a tourist's pocket on the vaporetto.' Steiner's voice was a study in neutrality.

'What did you do?'

'I put her in the car and brought her back out here.' For a moment, Brunetti thought Steiner had stopped, but after a pause the Maresciallo resumed. 'It was the usual story: she said she was pregnant. We were short-staffed that day, and I didn't want to waste time on it: take her to the hospital to verify the pregnancy, take witness statements from the man and from the two witnesses who saw what happened, then call the social services . . .' He let his voice trail off for a moment. 'So I decided to take her to the place where she said she was living and let the matter drop.'

'And so you never bothered to get witness statements about what really happened?' Dottoressa Pitteri suddenly asked. 'You just assumed she was guilty?'

'It wasn't necessary to get them.'

'But I'm asking you why, Maresciallo. Because you simply assumed that, if she was a Rom, she had to be guilty of anything she was accused of doing? Especially by a tourist?' She pronounced the last word with heavy emphasis, dragging out each syllable.

'No, not for that,' Steiner said, eyes still forward.

'Then why?' she demanded. 'Why was it so convenient simply to assume she was guilty?'

'Because one of the witnesses put her hand on the woman's arm as she was taking the man's wallet out of his pocket and because both witnesses were nuns.' Steiner gave that information enough time to settle and then added, 'I assumed they wouldn't lie.'

She paused, but only for a moment, before she asked, 'And you honestly think this woman would have risked doing something like that in front of two nuns?'

'They weren't wearing habits,' Steiner said.

Brunetti had kept himself from looking at her while all of this was going on, but now the urge to do so proved irresistible. She glared at the back of Steiner's head with such intensity that, had his hat and hair begun to smoulder and then burst into flames, Brunetti would not have been at all surprised.

They all lapsed into silence. Occasionally, the dispatcher's voice spoke from the radio, but it was too low for anyone in the back seat to understand, and neither Steiner nor the driver seemed concerned with anything that was said. The driver took the ramp leading to the road to the airport. It had been some time since Brunetti had been to the airport in anything except a boat or taxi, so he was surprised at the sudden appearance of roundabouts in place of crossroads. He drove so infrequently, and so badly, that he had no way of telling whether they were an improvement or not, and he did not want to break the silence by asking.

They passed the airport on the right and soon pulled up at traffic lights. All at once, from the driver's side, a long-skirted woman holding something that might have been a baby or might have been a swaddled football approached the window. With one hand she pressed the side of her kerchief over her nose and mouth as if to protect herself from the fumes of the idling motors. She held the other out in a pleading gesture, hand cupped.

The five people in the car looked stonily ahead. Seeing the two men in uniform in the front seat, she swerved away from the car and went to the one behind it. The light changed and they moved off.

The silence in the car grew more leaden as time passed. From the autostrada they saw fields and trees, occasionally a single house or small group of farmhouses. Some trees were in blossom. Brunetti turned his attention from side to side, and he found that, regardless of the tension in the car, he could still enjoy the rare sight of vast swaths of burgeoning nature. They should go somewhere green this summer, spend their holidays amidst fields and forests: no beaches, no sand or rocks, no matter how much the children complained. Long walks, mountain air, streams, happy clouds beyond the glistening glaciers. Alto Adige, perhaps. Didn't Pucetti have an uncle who ran some sort of *agriturismo* near Bolzano?

He felt the car slowing. He looked up as they sailed through the exit of the autostrada, came to the end of the exit ramp, turned right, and found themselves on a highway that passed between low buildings on both sides: factories, used cars, petrol stations, a bar, a parking lot, another. At the second traffic light they turned right and drove by rows of single houses set back on both sides of the road, each in its patch of land. The houses disappeared, replaced by green fields.

More traffic lights, more houses, but now they were surrounded by wire fences. He saw dogs in many of the gardens, large dogs. They drove another kilometre and then the driver signalled, slowed, and turned to the right.

Brunetti saw that they had stopped in front of a metal gate. The driver sounded the horn once, twice, and when nothing happened, he got out of the car, leaving the door open, walked to the gate and opened it himself. Once he had driven through the gate, at a word from Steiner he stopped the car and went back and closed it.

Ahead of them Brunetti saw a ragged half-moon of cars and behind them a row of trailers parked any which way. Some were metal, some wooden, some quite modern and sleek. One had a short metal chimney in the middle of the peaked roof that made Brunetti think of the drawings in children's books. Objects piled up against the sides of the trailers spilled out into the spaces between them: plastic boxes, cardboard cartons, collapsible tables, metal barbecues, countless shredded and tattered plastic bags. Beyond them, a few footpaths appeared to have been beaten down into the field of high grass and nettles behind the camp, though none appeared to extend far before petering out. Brunetti saw the odd piece of rusted metal jutting up amidst the weeds: a refrigerator, an old-fashioned washing machine with a hand wringer, at least two metal bedsprings, and an abandoned car.

The cars in front of the trailers were in far better shape, most of them apparently new, or at least they seemed that way to Brunetti, who was no judge of these things.

If such a disorderly arrangement of cars could be said to have a centre, the driver pulled the car into it, then turned off the engine. Brunetti heard the soft ticks and pings as it cooled, then the sound of Steiner's door being pushed back and yanking at the springs. Then birdsong, coming perhaps from the trees on the other side of the wire fence that surrounded the camp.

As he watched, first one, then another, then two more of the doors of the campers were pushed open and men stepped out and started down the steps. The men did not speak, and they seemed to have no communication with one another, but they came and stood in an uneven row in front of the car.

Vianello and then the driver pushed open their doors and got out of the police car. When Brunetti looked back at the men standing in front of them, three more had joined them. And the birdsong had stopped.

21

The men stood there, and slowly the sound of birdsong returned. The air was soft, as the gentle rays of the afternoon sun embraced them all. Beyond the fence Brunetti saw the field rolling up and away from them, gently green, to a stand of chestnut trees: surely, some of the birdsong came from there. How sweet life is, Brunetti thought.

He lowered his eyes from the trees and considered the men, now nine of them, who stood facing them. He was struck by the fact that all of them wore hats, dirty fedoras that might once have been different colours but now looked a dull, dusty brown. None of them was close shaven. With many Italian men of all ages, this look was considered a fashion statement — Brunetti had never been quite sure what the statement was, but he knew it was meant to be one. These men, however, looked as if they could not be bothered to shave or somehow considered it a sign of weakness. Some of the beards were patchy, some were longer than others; none of them looked particularly clean.

All of the men were dark-skinned and dark-eyed, and all of them wore woollen trousers, sweaters, and dark jackets. Some had shirts underneath. Their shoes were thick-soled and scuffed.

Steiner and his driver were in Carabiniere uniform, so the men of the camp kept their eyes on them, though an occasional curious glance was cast towards Brunetti and Vianello. A dull thud from his right made Brunetti flinch. He looked at Steiner and noticed that the Maresciallo, as he turned toward the noise, had put his hand on the butt of his revolver.

When Brunetti followed Steiner's eyes, he saw Dottoressa Pitteri standing at the side of the car, her hand still on the handle of the door she had slammed, a small smile on her lips. 'I didn't mean to startle you, Maresciallo,' she said, her smile turning acid. 'Do please forgive me.'

Steiner returned his attention to the men in front of them. His hand fell to his side, but his instinctive reaction had not passed unobserved. Two of then, indeed, could not stop themselves from smiling, though not at Steiner.

Dottoressa Pitteri moved away from the car and approached the men. They gave no hint of recognition, let alone pleasure, as she walked over. She stopped and said something Brunetti could not hear. When none of the men responded, she spoke a bit louder. Though this time Brunetti could hear her words, he could not understand what she said. She stood with her feet apart, and from the back he saw how thick her calves were. Her feet seemed anchored to the ground.

As he watched, one of the men, who was standing to the right, spoke to her. She turned to him and said a few words; the man responded in a louder voice, loud enough for the police to hear, 'Speak Italian. It's easier to understand you.' Though he was not the oldest man in the group, he spoke with the air of command. His accent was marked, but they could hear that he spoke Italian with ease.

Brunetti had the impression that the woman had sunk both feet more deeply into the ground-up earth in front of the caravans. Her hands hung by her sides — she had left her bag in the car — and he saw that she had drawn her fingers up into fists.

'I'd like to speak to Bogdan Rocich,' Brunetti heard her say.

Beyond her, the man's face remained impassive, but Brunetti noticed that two of the others exchanged a glance, and a third glanced aside at the man who had spoken.

'He's not here,' the man answered.

'His car is here,' she said, and the man's eyes moved to a sun-faded blue Mercedes with a large dent in the right fender. 'He's not here,' he repeated.

'His car is here,' she said, as though the man had not spoken.

'He went with a friend,' one of the other men volunteered, and was about to say more but was cut off by a fierce glance from the leader. The man in charge took a sudden step towards the woman, then another, and Brunetti was impressed to see that she did not move back, did not flinch: if anything, she dug her feet more deeply into the earth.

The man stood less than an arm's length from her and, though he was not tall, seemed to loom above her. 'What do you want with him?' he demanded.

'To talk to him,' she answered calmly, and as Brunetti watched, her fists opened and her fingers stretched towards the ground.

'You can talk to me,' the man said. 'I am

his brother.'

'Signor Tanovic,' she said, 'you are not his brother, and you are not his cousin.' Her voice was calm, relaxed, as if the two of them had met in the park for a chat. 'I have come to speak to Signor Rocich.'

'I told you he is not here.' His face could have been carved, so impassive did it remain all during this conversation.

'Perhaps he's come back,' she suggested, offering him a way out. 'And no one told you.'

Brunetti, keeping his face as motionless as the man's, watched him consider the possibility being offered to him. The man looked at Dottoressa Pitteri, then ran his eyes across the faces of the men in front of him, two in uniform and the others no doubt bearing the unmistakable scent of police.

'Danis,' he said, turning away from them and speaking to the man at the far left of the line. All Brunetti understood was the name 'Bogdan.'

The man peeled away silently and walked off towards the caravan behind the blue Mercedes. One of the men lit a cigarette, and when the man addressed as Tanovic said nothing, two others did as well. No one spoke.

Danis walked up the steps to the caravan and raised his hand, but before he could knock on the door it was pulled open and a man dressed like the others came out; they exchanged a few words, and he followed the other man down the steps. He left the door open, and a flash of something light behind it caused Brunetti to keep his eyes on the door while everyone else watched the man approach Tanovic and Dottoressa Pitteri.

The interior of the camper was dark, but Brunetti thought he saw one side of a human figure, or the shadow of a human form, at the door. Yes, there was movement, some sort of swinging motion of the lower, lighter part of the figure.

He was conscious of the man as he came closer to them all, then of his stopping, not by Dottoressa Pitteri but by the man who had summoned him and who had taken a half-step back. Brunetti listened, but the men spoke to one another in a language utterly foreign to him. He risked a glance and saw that the attention of everyone in the circle around the two men was riveted on the conversation.

Brunetti glanced back at the door, and as he did, fingers emerged and wrapped themselves around it, pulling it open a bit more, and then just above the hand a woman's face appeared. He could not see her clearly, but he could see enough to observe that she was an old woman, perhaps the mother of the man who had emerged from the caravan, perhaps Ariana's grandmother.

She leaned forward, following the man with her eyes, and Brunetti saw the motion again as her skirt swung forward beneath her.

When the men seemed to have stopped talking, Dottoressa Pitteri said, 'Good afternoon, Signor Rocich,' and Brunetti switched his attention to the man who had come out of the caravan.

He was shorter than the other men, and he was thicker-set. His hair was as black and dense as Steiner's, though longer, straight and slicked back from his forehead with pomade or grease. He had enormous black eyebrows under which his dark eyes disappeared: it was difficult to tell what colour they were. He looked more prosperous than the others: his beard was trimmed, his shoes were cleaner, as was the collar of the shirt he wore under his sweater.

He looked across at Dottoressa Pitteri, and his glance was so neutral that it was impossible to tell if he knew her; indeed, there was no telling if he had ever seen her before. 'What you want?' he finally asked.

'It's about your daughter,' she answered. 'Ariana.'

'What happen Ariana?' he asked. When he spoke, he did not take his eyes from hers.

'I'm afraid I have to tell you that your daughter has died in an accident, Signor Rocich.'

His eyes turned slowly towards the caravan, and as the others followed his look the woman's form retreated inside, though everyone could still see her four fingers on the outside of the door.

'She die?' he asked. At the woman's nod, he asked, 'How? In car traffic?'

'No. She drowned.'

It was obvious from his expression that he did not understand the word. Dottoressa Pitteri repeated it a bit louder, then one of the other men said something, and the understanding came into his face. He looked at his shoes, then at her, then at the men who stood behind him, first to one side and then to the other. No one said anything for a long time.

Finally Dottoressa Pitteri said, 'I'd like to tell your wife,' and turned to take a step towards the caravan.

The man's hand shot out like a snake, and he grabbed her upper arm, stopping her on the spot. 'I no like,' he said in a tight voice, though he spoke no more loudly. 'I tell,' he said, and took his hand from her arm. Brunetti could see that the cloth of her sleeve still bore the imprint of his hand.

'She mine,' he said decisively to Dottoressa Pitteri, as if to put an end to any possibility of discussion, and turned towards the caravan. His wife or his daughter, Brunetti found himself wondering, to which of them was he staking a claim? Probably both, from the sound of him.

The man continued walking towards the caravan, but then he turned and came back. He stopped in front of Dottoressa Pitteri and said in an openly belligerent voice, 'How I know? How I sure she Ariana?'

The woman turned to Steiner and said, 'I think this question is for you, Maresciallo.' Brunetti saw the looks that passed among the line-up of men at the sound of her voice, saw how their attention turned to the man in uniform to whom a woman spoke in this manner.

Brunetti stepped forward, pulling the photos from his pocket. He handed the envelope to the man, saying nothing. The man opened it and pulled them out, looked at all three, once, and then again. He slid them back into the envelope and turned back towards the caravan. He went up the steps.

Dottoressa Pitteri returned to the car. Speaking to the policemen, she said, 'I think our work here is finished.' She did not bother to wait for agreement or dissent from them but climbed into the back seat, slamming the door after her.

The leader of the men turned away from them silently and went inside his caravan. The others dissolved.

Keeping his voice low, though there was no longer anyone to hear him, Brunetti walked up beside Steiner and said, 'Well?'

Before the Carabiniere could answer, a high-pitched keening broke from the still open door of the Rocich caravan. Brunetti's eyes swung towards it and then were diverted by a sudden motion from beyond it, at the top of the hill. The sound had startled the birds into flight, and a cloud of them circled the clump of chestnuts like a restless, dark halo. The sound went on, rising, falling, but never growing softer. His eyes on the branches of the trees, Brunetti thought of Dante and of the way he had broken off a branch, only to hear the agonized cry of the suicide to whose pain he had added, 'Is there no pity left in any soul?'

By silent agreement, the men turned back

towards the car. Steiner and the driver got into the front seat, and Brunetti was just ducking his head to climb into the back seat when the door of the caravan slapped open with a slam like a pistol shot.

The woman who had been hiding inside and listening leaped through the door, appeared to fly down the steps, and stopped at the bottom as if blinded by the sudden light. One hand held the crushed envelope and the other the three photos, cupped delicately in her palm as if she feared damaging them in some way.

Brunetti had seen moles dug up, and they had been as startled by the light as she. At no time in all of this did her wailing cease. Suddenly she hurled the envelope to the ground and fell to her knees. She threw her head back and began to howl. With her free hand, she began to rake at her cheek. Brunetti, who was closest to her, saw the red trails appear, as though they were being slashed on with a row of red crayons.

Without thinking, he ran to her and grabbed her hand, holding it out to the side. He saw her start to swing at him with the other hand, but then she remembered the photos and stopped, though she reeled back and spat at him, again and again, spattering his shirt and the front of his trousers with her spittle.

'You kill my baby!' she shrieked. 'You kill my baby. In water, you kill her. My baby.' Her face was distorted by rage, and Brunetti saw that she was not an old woman, only a young one who had been aged by life. Both cheeks had caved in to fill the places of her missing teeth; two of the remaining front ones were chipped. Her hair was dry and pulled roughly under a kerchief, and her dark skin was oily and coarse.

Suddenly Dottoressa Pitteri was beside him, leaning over the woman. She said some words to her again and again, always the same phrase. She put her hand beside Brunetti's on the kneeling woman's arm, then gestured to him to let her go.

Brunetti obeyed, and as soon as his hand was removed, the woman seem to grow calmer. Her shrieks stopped and she bent forward, one arm wrapped around her stomach, the other holding the photos safely to the side. Her moans continued, and she muttered something Brunetti had no way of understanding. Dottoressa Pitteri took a handkerchief from the pocket of her jacket and pressed it against the woman's cheek, holding it there, saying nothing. There was no change in the woman's sobs, and she continued to mutter the same words. Dottoressa Pitteri turned the handkerchief to a fresh side, and Brunetti saw the streaks of blood.

Strong hands gripped Brunetti's upper arms, and he was thrust aside with force. He turned, crouching into a defensive stance, but it was the girl's father. Brunetti stood upright and watched as he approached the two women. When he reached them, he put his hands on Dottoressa Pitteri's arms. As Brunetti watched, he actually lifted her from the ground and stepped aside to set her down a metre from his wife.

He went back to the keening woman and said something to her. She ignored him or didn't hear him and continued moaning, like an animal in pain. The man reached down and grabbed her by the upper arm. She was so thin that he had no trouble in pulling her to her feet.

She gave no sign that she saw him or knew what was happening to her. He swung her around until she was facing the caravan and used his other hand to give her a strong push in the middle of her back. She staggered forward and, almost losing her balance, instinctively put both hands out to steady herself. As Brunetti watched, the three photographs fluttered to the ground. The man, either seeing them or not seeing them, followed the woman. His foot came down on the face of one of the photos, sinking it into the dirt and mud. The other two fell face down.

As they watched, the woman stumbled up the steps and into the caravan. The man followed and slammed the door. Again, at the sound, the birds fled the branches of the trees and fluttered helplessly, filling the air with a higher-pitched version of the woman's cries.

Brunetti stooped and picked up the photos. The one the man had stepped on was beyond saving, crushed under the weight of the foot that had pressed mud into every crease. He slipped it into the pocket of his jacket. He walked over to the caravan and placed the other two on the top step, then went back to the car.

They drove back to Venice in silence.

22

As Brunetti had warned Patta, more than two hours had passed by the time he and Vianello finally returned to the Questura. When they got to the first floor, Brunetti suggested Vianello go back to the duty room, saying he would see to informing the Vice-Questore about the events of the afternoon.

Signorina Elettra looked up when he came in, and he watched recent events play across her face. He saw her remember his brusque question, her own umbrage at that, but then he saw her register the general state of his being, though he had no clear idea of how she registered it or what there was to register.

'What's wrong, Dottore?' she asked with real concern, all memory of their previous meeting cancelled.

'We went out to tell the girl's parents,' he explained, then told her, as briefly as he could, what had happened.

'Ah, the poor woman,' she said, when he had finished. 'How terrible, to have a child disappear and then to be told this.'

'That's what's so strange,' Brunetti said. In the car, the tense silence had kept him distracted during the ride back, and it was only now that he could begin to consider the response of the girl's parents.

'What?'

'The girl's been gone almost a week, and none of them — not the mother, not the father — reported it to us.' He thought back to their time at the nomad camp and said, 'And when we got there, the man in charge — at least that's what I think he is — he didn't want to let us see them or talk to them.'

When she remained silent, Brunetti asked, 'Can you imagine if a child went missing here? It would be all over the papers, on every television station.' Still she did not answer, and so Brunetti asked, 'Well? Isn't that true?'

'I'm not sure they can be expected to respond the way we would, sir.'

'What do you mean?'

He watched her strive for words, and finally she said, 'I think their attitude towards the law is more tentative than ours.'

'Tentative?' he asked with a sharpness of tone that surprised even him. Deliberately softening his voice, he asked, 'What do you mean?'

Finally, she set her pen down and pushed herself back from her desk. She looked different, somehow, when she did that, and he wondered if she had lost weight or got her hair cut or had done one of those other things women do. 'It's not as if their first thought, when something goes wrong, is to call the police, is it, sir?' When he said nothing, she added, 'Which is certainly understandable, given the way people in their community are treated.'

'No one out there — except the mother — showed much concern that the girl was dead,' Brunetti allowed himself to be goaded into saying.

'And you think they'd do that in front of four policemen, sir?' she asked mildly.

He would stand no more of this. 'Why do you look different, Signorina?' he asked.

She was unable to disguise how much his question surprised her. 'You noticed?' she asked.

'Of course,' he answered, still puzzled.

She got gracefully to her feet. She extended her arms to the side, curved them upwards, then leaned towards him as she swept her right arm in his direction. 'I've started taking lessons,' she said, leaving him none the wiser. Yoga? Karate? Ballet?

His confusion must have been evident, for she laughed, then bent her knees, turning to face him sideways, her right hand cupped around an invisible something that she jabbed in his direction.

'Fencing?' he asked.

If so graceful a motion could be thought of as a lunge, she lunged forward and took two tiny steps in his direction, only to come up against the side of her desk.

The door to Patta's office opened suddenly, and the Vice-Questore emerged, a folder in his right hand, eyes on a single sheet he held in his left, the perfect image of a busy commander of men. By the time he glanced up, Signorina Elettra's rapier had disappeared, and she was just turning to him. 'Ah, Vice-Questore, I was coming in to tell you that Commissario Brunetti was here to report to you.'

'Ah, yes,' Patta said, giving Brunetti a speculative glance, as if he could free himself from the weight of the cares of office for just long enough to speak to him. 'All right, Brunetti,' he finally said. 'Come in and tell me.'

Patta put the folder of papers on Signorina

Elettra's desk, keeping the single sheet in his hand. He left the door of his office open after he went in, an invitation to Brunetti to follow.

Brunetti attempted to intuit how much time Patta would allow him. Usually, if the Vice-Questore went back to his desk, it meant he wanted to be comfortable, and that meant he was willing to listen for more than a moment or two. If, however, he stood by the window, it meant he was in a hurry and whoever spoke to him had best be quick about it.

In this case, Patta walked over and placed the paper on his desk, then glanced at Brunetti and turned it upside down. He turned and leaned back against the desk, hands braced on either side of him. This left Brunetti in a kind of procedural limbo: he certainly could not sit down in the presence of his standing superior, and the thought that Patta might well launch himself to some other place in the room made him uncertain where to stand.

He took a few steps towards Patta, who today wore a slate grey suit so sleek of line as to render him both taller and more slender. Brunetti's eyes were drawn to a small gold pin — was it some sort of cross? — on Patta's lapel. Refusing to allow himself to be distracted, Brunetti said, 'I went out there, as you asked me to, Vice-Questore.'

Patta nodded, a hint that his role today was as the silent, watchful guardian of public security.

'A maresciallo of the Carabinieri came along, as well as a woman from social services who works with the Rom.'

Patta nodded again, either to acknowledge that he was following Brunetti's account or in tribute to the political correctness of Brunetti's choice of noun.

'At first, the man who seems to be the leader didn't want to let us talk to the parents, but when we made it clear that we were going to stay until we did, he called the father and I told him about the child.' Silence from Patta. 'He asked how we could be sure of her identity, and I gave him the photos. He showed them to the mother. She was' — Brunetti had no idea how to describe the woman's agony to Patta — 'she was distraught.' Brunetti could think of nothing more to say. Those were the facts.

'I'm sorry,' Patta surprised him by saying.

'For what, sir?' Brunetti asked, wondering if perhaps some opportunity of publicity had presented itself in the afternoon and Patta now regretted not having gone out to the camp.

'For the woman's pain,' Patta said soberly. 'No one should lose a child.' With a sudden lightening of tone, he asked, 'And the other woman?'

'You mean the woman from the social services, sir?'

'No. The one whose house you went to. About the jewellery.'

'The child must have been in their home,' he answered. Seeing Patta start to speak, he added, 'How else can the ring and the watch be explained?' As soon as he said that, Brunetti realized he was sounding too involved, too interested, so he tempered his voice and said, 'Well, that is, it's difficult to think of some other way she might have got them.'

'But that doesn't mean much, does it?' Patta asked. 'I mean, that's no reason to believe that anything happened to her while she was in there, that she did anything but trip and fall. Why, people are falling off roofs all the time.'

Brunetti had heard of one case in the last ten years, but he knew better than to argue. Perhaps roofs were more dangerous in Patta's home town of Palermo. Most things were.

'They usually work in groups, sir,' Brunetti observed.

'I know, I know,' Patta answered, waving a hand in Brunetti's direction as though he were a particularly annoying fly. 'But that doesn't mean anything, either.'

As if he were indeed a fly, Brunetti's antennae began to pick up another strange buzz in this room, some other emanation coming at him from Patta, either from his eyes or his tone or the way the fingers of his right hand occasionally moved towards that sheet of paper, then suddenly skittered back to his side.

Brunetti made his face display the play of thought. 'I suppose you're right, sir,' he finally said, careful to speak with acquiescent disappointment. 'But it might be useful to be able to talk to them.'

'To whom?'

'The other children.'

'Out of the question,' Patta said in an unrestrainedly loud voice. Then, as if sharing Brunetti's surprise at the volume with which he had spoken, the Vice-Questore continued more softly, 'That is, it's too complicated: you'd need an order from a judge from the minors' court, and you'd need someone from the social services to go along with you and be there while you talked to them, and you'd need a translator.' Patta spoke as though the matter had been settled, but then, after a careful pause, he added, 'Besides, you'd never be sure you'd got the right children in the first place.' He shook his head in contemplation of the impossibility of Brunetti's ever being able to achieve all of this.

'I see what you mean, sir,' Brunetti said with a resigned shrug, lowering his voice and closing his heart to the temptations of irony or sarcasm. For he did indeed see what Patta meant: the prosperous middle class was involved here, so Patta had decided it would be best to avoid any examination of what might have happened on that roof.

And Brunetti, like a snail that brushes something rough with one of its feelers, opted to retreat into his shell. 'I hadn't considered all of that, sir,' he admitted grudgingly. He waited to see if Patta would drive another nail into the coffin of possibility, and when he did not, Brunetti did it for him and said, 'And there's no chance that we could ever get these kids to testify, anyway, is there?'

'No, none,' Patta agreed. He shoved himself away from his desk and walked behind it to his chair. 'See if there's anything that can be done for the mother,' Patta said, and Brunetti rejoiced greatly in the request, for to learn what might be done for her, he would surely have to go and talk to her, would he not?

'I'll leave you to your work, sir,' Brunetti said.

Patta was already too busy to reply, and Brunetti left him there to get on with it.

Signorina Elettra looked up as he emerged from Patta's office. 'The Vice-Questore,' Brunetti said, having been careful to leave the door to the office open behind him, 'thinks there's no point in pursuing this.'

Glancing at the open door, she fed him his next line, 'And do you agree with him, Commissario?'

'Yes, I think I do. The poor girl fell from the roof and drowned.' He suddenly remembered that no disposition had been made for the girl's body. Now that Patta had effectively closed the investigation, she should be returned to her family, though in a case of accidental death, Brunetti had no idea whose responsibility that would be.

'Would you call Dottor Rizzardi and see when the body can be released?' he asked. For a moment, Brunetti considered accompanying the girl's body, but he was not prepared to do that. 'There's a woman at the social services, Dottoressa Pitteri — I can't remember her first name. She's been working with the Rom for some time, so she might have an idea of what . . . well, of what they might want to do.'

'With the girl, do you mean?' Signorina Elettra asked.

'Yes.'

'All right,' she said, then, 'I'll call her, Commissario, and let you know what happens.'

'Thank you,' he said and left her office.

23

As he climbed the steps to his office, Brunetti was suddenly overcome with a desire to turn around and leave the Questura and, as he had sometimes done as a schoolboy, take the vaporetto out to the Lido and go for a walk on the beach. Who would know? Worse, who would care? Patta was probably congratulating himself at his easy success in having protected the middle class from any embarrassing investigation, while Signorina Elettra was busy with the sombre task of finding a way to send the dead child back to her family.

He went up to his office and immediately dialled down to Signorina Elettra's office. When she answered, he said, 'When Patta came out of his office, he had a sheet of paper in his hand. Have you any idea what it was?'

'No, sir,' came her answer, as laconic as it could be.

'Do you think you might have a look?'

'One moment, and I'll ask Lieutenant Scarpa,' she said, then he heard her asking, voice a bit fainter as she held the receiver away from her mouth, 'Lieutenant, do you know what's wrong with the photocopying machine on the third floor?' There was a long silence, and then he heard her add, voice even louder, as if she were now talking to someone at a greater distance, 'It seems there's a paper jam, Lieutenant. Would you mind having a look?'

There was a brief silence, into which Brunetti said, 'You shouldn't bait him, you know.'

'I don't eat chocolates,' she answered sharply. 'Baiting the Lieutenant provides the same pleasure, but there's no risk of getting fat.' It did not seem to Brunetti that Signorina Elettra ran much of a risk of that, and it was hardly his place to question anyone else's pleasures, but to go out of her way repeatedly to antagonize Patta's assistant seemed riskier behaviour than eating a chocolate truffle or two.

'I wash my hands of you,' he said, laughing as he did so. 'Though I must say I admire your courage.'

'He's a paper tiger, sir; they all are.'

'All who?'

'Men like him, who make a habit of being tough and silent and looming over your desk. They always want to make you think they're getting ready to tear you into little pieces and use tiny slivers of your bones to pick your flesh out of their teeth.' He wondered if this would be her assessment of the men at the Gypsy camp, but before he had even finished formulating the thought, she added, 'Don't worry about him, Commissario.'

'I think it would be wiser not to antagonize him.'

A hard edge came into her voice and she said, 'If it ever came to a choice, the Vice-Questore would cut him loose in a moment.'

'Why?' Brunetti asked, honestly puzzled. Lieutenant Scarpa had been the faithful henchman of the Questore for more than a decade: a fellow Sicilian, a man who appeared to enjoy feasting on the scraps that fell from the table of power, he had always seemed, to Brunetti, utterly ruthless in his desire to aid Patta in his career.

'Because the Vice-Questore knows he can trust him,' she answered, confusing Brunetti utterly.

'I don't understand,' he confessed.

'He knows he can trust Scarpa, so he knows it would be safe to get rid of him, so long as he saw to it that he went to some better job. But he's not sure he can trust me, so he'd be afraid, ever, to try to get rid of me.' He hardly recognized her voice, so absent was its usual bantering tone.

But then she went on in her usual pleasant voice, 'And to answer your question, the only person who went into his office today, aside from you, was Lieutenant Scarpa. He was in with him for an hour this morning.'

'Ah,' Brunetti allowed himself to say, thanked her, and replaced the phone. He pulled a sheet of paper towards him and began to make a list of names. First the owner of the ring and watch. He knew Fornari's name was familiar: he stared at the far wall and tried to summon the memory. His wife had said he was in Russia, but the name of the country was no aid. What was it he sold? Kitchen appliances? No, ready-made units, and he was trying to export them there. Yes, that was it, right on the edge of memory: export, licences, Guardia di Finanza, factories. Something about money or some foreign company, but no, it wouldn't come, so Brunetti decided to leave it.

He wrote the wife's name, the daughter's, the son's, even the cleaning woman's. They were the only people likely to have been in the apartment the night the girl died. He added the words, 'Zingara', 'Rom', 'Sinti', 'Nomadi', to the bottom of the list, and then he pushed his chair back and resumed his contemplation of the far wall, and the likeness of the dead girl slipped into his memory.

The woman looked old enough to be the child's grandmother, yet that seamed, hollow-cheeked face was the face of the mother of an eleven-year-old child. All three children were younger than fourteen, and so could not be arrested. He had seen no children when he was there; stranger still, there had been no sign of children, no bikes or toys or dolls left lying about in the midst of all that litter. Italian children would be at school during the day; the absence of the Gypsy children, however, suggested that they were at work, or what passed as work for them.

Surely, the Fornari children should have been at school at that time of day. If the girl was sixteen, then she would be finishing middle school; the son might well have already started university. He picked up the phone and redialled Signorina Elettra's number. When she answered, he said, 'I've got another favour to ask. Do you have access to the files of the schools in the city?'

'Ah, the Department of Public Instruction,' she said. 'Child's play.'

'Good. The Fornaris' daughter is called Ludovica — she's sixteen. She's got a brother who's eighteen, Matteo. I'd like you to see if there is anything worth knowing about them.'

He thought she might remark that this was a rather vague category, but all she did was ask, 'What are the parents' full names?'

'Giorgio Fornari and Orsola Vivarini.'

'Oh my, oh my,' she said when she heard the second name.

'Do you know her?' Brunetti asked.

'No, I don't. But I'd certainly like to meet the woman who got stuck with a name like Orsola but still named her daughter Ludovica.'

'My mother had a friend named Italia,' he said. 'And lots of Benitos, a Vittoria, even an Addis Ababa.'

'Different times,' she said. 'Or a different idea, to give a child a name that's really more a boast than a name.'

'Yes,' he said, thinking of the people with names like Tiffany and Denis and Sharon he'd arrested. 'My wife once said that if an American soap opera had a main character named Pig Shit, we'd have to prepare ourselves for an entire generation of them.'

'I think the Brazilians are more popular, sir,' she said.

'Excuse me?'

'The soap operas.'

'Of course,' he said and found he had nothing further to say.

'I'll see what I can find out about them,' she said. 'And I'll call this Dottoressa Pitteri.'

'Thank you, Signorina,' he said.

Brunetti knew he could run some sort of computer check on the name Giorgio Fornari, but the part of his memory in which the name was lodged was the same part where gossip and rumour found their home; so he knew that what he was looking for was the sort of information that was not to be found in newspapers or magazines or government reports. He tried to reconstruct the situation in which he had first heard Fornari's name. Something to do with money, and something to do with the Guardia di Finanza, for it was when reading a reference to the tax police in the paper some days ago that Fornari's name had sounded in the back of his memory.

A former classmate of his was now a captain in the Guardia di Finanza, and Brunetti still recalled with delight the afternoon — it must be three years ago —

they had spent together in the *laguna*. The patrol boat, with what looked like action film turbines on both sides, had astonished Brunetti, accustomed as he was to the boats of the police and Carabinieri. He had spent the afternoon redefining the term, 'high speed', as the pilot took them through the Canale di San Nicolò and then straight ahead, as if he would not stop until they saw the islands off the coast of Croatia. Brunetti's friend had justified the trip as what he called 'liaison with other forces of order', but in the end, with the full complicity of the pilot, it had turned into a school-boy outing — complete with hoots of glee and much back-slapping — and would not have stopped had the radio not received a call, asking their location.

Ignoring the call, the pilot had swooped the boat around and shot back towards the city, passing fishing boats as though they were tiny islands and then deliberately slamming and bumping across the wake of one of the cruise ships that was heading towards the city.

Struck by memory, Brunetti spoke the words aloud, 'The cruise ships.' Still looking at the wall, he allowed the story to trickle back into his memory. Giorgio Fornari was also a friend of Brunetti's captain friend and had once called to tell him about something he had heard from the owner of a shop on Via XXII Marzo who found himself caught in the middle of yet another inventive method of growing rich off the city.

It seemed, according to what Fornari had been told, that the passengers of these cruise ships were routinely warned that Venice was a city where it was not safe to shop or eat. Since most of the passengers were Americans, who knew themselves to be safe only when at home in front of their own television sets, they believed this and were relieved when the boat provided them with a list of 'safe' shops and restaurants where they were sure not to be cheated. Not only were the places guaranteed not to cheat them — and here the Captain had not been able to keep himself from laughing as he told Brunetti — but these same establishments would provide a 10 per cent discount to ship's passengers: all they had to do was provide their passenger identification and ask.

With mounting glee, the Captain had gone on to explain that, always eager to cause more joy, the staff of the ships offered some sort of lottery to the passengers returning to the ships: if they submitted the receipts of their purchases or for their lunch, the number of chances they got in the lottery would be calculated in relation to how much they had spent.

'Everyone happy, everyone content with their discounts,' Brunetti remembered the Captain saying with a wolfish smile. And the next day members of the ship's crew made the rounds of the 'safe' shops and restaurants and collected *their* 10 per cent, a small enough consideration for the businesses to see that their names appeared on the safe list. If the shops tried to understate what the passengers had spent, why, did they not have the receipts that proved a higher total sum? Safe, indeed.

And Giorgio Fornari had asked the Captain if there were any way this could be stopped. The Captain, in the spirit of true friendship, had warned Fornari to keep his mouth shut and had told him to warn the owners of the shop to do the same. Brunetti recalled what the Captain had said, 'I think he was offended because he thought it was wrong. Imagine that.'

Brunetti knew this incident could hardly be used as a portrait of Fornari, but perhaps it could serve as a snapshot. Caught in a particular situation, he had reacted as an honest man. His friend had told him about

Fornari's indignation that the city could be used like this by people — the owners of the ships being foreigners — who were neither Venetians nor Italians. It was then that the Captain had had to remind Fornari that a scam such as this could not continue, perhaps could not even be organized, without the tacit consent, perhaps even the involvement, of 'certain interests' in the city.

But by then they were pulling up to the dock at the end of the Giudecca, the boys' outing at an end, and the story of Giorgio Fornari's indignation at dishonesty had been filed in Brunetti's memory.

'Imagine that,' he said aloud.

Brunetti was distracted from further contemplation of this marvel by a call from Signorina Elettra, who began by saying, 'I've found a number of things about that Mutti person.'

Her pronunciation of the name was as good as a shriek. 'Found what?' he enquired.

'As I told you, sir, he's never been a member of any religious order.'

'Yes, I remember,' Brunetti said, then added, for her tone demanded he do so, 'But?'

'But Padre Antonin was right when he mentioned Umbria. Mutti was there for two

311

years, in Assisi. He wore a Franciscan habit then.'

In response to her careful phrasing, Brunetti asked, 'What was he doing?'

'Running a sort of wellness retreat centre.'

'Wellness retreat centre?' Brunetti repeated, feeling himself taking yet another step forward into the time in which he was living.

'A place where wealthy people could go for a weekend of . . . well, of purification.'

'Physical?' he asked, thinking of Abano, where she had so recently been, though not forgetting the mention of the Franciscan habit.

'And spiritual.'

'Ah,' Brunetti allowed himself to say, then, 'And?'

'And both the health authorities and the Guardia di Finanza were obliged to step in and close it down.'

'And Mutti?' Brunetti enquired, omitting the clerical title.

'He knew nothing about the finances of the place, of course. He was there as a spiritual consultant.'

'And the financial records?'

'There were none.'

'What happened?'

'He was convicted of fraud, given a fine,

and released.'

'And?'

'And apparently he transferred himself to Venice.'

'Indeed,' Brunetti said and then, deciding, 'I'd like you to call the Guardia di Finanza. Ask for Capitano Zeccardi. Tell him everything you've just told me and say that he might want to take a closer look at whatever Mutti's up to.'

'Is that all, Commissario?'

'Yes,' Brunetti said, and then, remembering, contradicted himself and said, 'No. Tell the Captain this is to thank him for the ride he gave me in the *laguna*. He'll understand.'

During dinner he was perhaps less talkative than usual, though none of the others seemed to heed it, so involved were they in a discussion of the street war that seemed to be in process in Napoli.

'Two of them got shot today,' Raffi said, reaching for the bowl of *ruote* with *melanzane* and *ricotta*. 'It's like the Wild West down there. You walk out of your house, going down to the corner for a litre of milk, and *Zacchetè!* — someone blows your head off.'

In the voice she used to cool the enthusiasm of youth, Paola said, 'I suspect, if it's

313

Napoli, they are more likely to be going down to the corner for a litre of cocaine.' Without a break, she asked, 'Chiara, would you like more pasta?'

'They aren't all like that, are they?' Chiara enquired of her father, nodding in response to her mother's request.

'No,' Brunetti said, slipping into his role as source of police authority. 'Your mother is exaggerating again.'

Chiara said, 'Our teachers say that the Mafia is being fought by the police and the government.' To Brunetti, this sounded like something that had been memorized.

'And how long has that fight been going on?' her mother asked her in a deceptively reasonable voice. 'Ask them that, the next time one of them is stupid enough to say such a thing,' Paola concluded, once again doing her best to foster her children's faith in their teachers, to make no mention of the government.

Brunetti started to protest, but she cut him off, saying, 'Can you name a war that's been going on for sixty years? In Europe? We've had it ever since the real war ended and the Americans brought the Mafia back to help fight the menace —' and here her voice took on the tones of soft and liquid faith, as it tended to do when she mouthed any of the pieties that disgusted her — 'of international Communism. So, instead of having the risk that the Communists might have entered the government after the war, we've got the Mafia, and we'll have them around our necks for ever.'

As a member of the forces of order, it was here Brunetti's duty to oppose her in this belief and maintain that, under the serious leadership of the current government, the police and the other organs of state were making great strides in their fight against the Mafia. Instead, he asked what was for dessert.

24

A day passed, during which Brunetti was kept busy compiling a report on patterns of crime in the Veneto: Patta would use this information for a speech he was to deliver at a conference to be held in Rome in two months. Rather than foist the research on to Signorina Elettra or the men in his department, Brunetti decided to do it himself and thus spent hours each day reading police files from all over the Veneto as well as checking figures available from other provinces and countries.

As he searched the current statistics, he was assailed by those four words: Zingari, Rom, Sinti, Nomadi, for the majority of the people arrested for certain crimes belonged to them. Robbery, theft, breaking and entering: time and time again, those arrested were nomads of one sort or another. Even without records of the arrest of children for these crimes, a reader did not have to be particularly skilled in the arcana of police files to be able to interpret the repeated explanation given for the use of police vehicles for trips on the mainland: 'return child to guardian', 'return unaccompanied minors to parents'.

Brunetti read of one case of a young man who had been arrested numerous times but who had repeatedly claimed to be only thirteen and thus too young to be arrested. In the absence of written proof of his identity, the presiding magistrate ordered a complete body X-ray to be taken of him so as to determine his age by the condition of his bones.

The nomads had, all these centuries, managed to keep themselves almost completely separated from the societies in whose midst they lived. Horse-traders and trainers, tinkers, gem-setters by trade, most of their jobs had been rendered obsolete in the modern age. But they continued to live off what they called the *gadje* — considering theft not much different from trade. During the last war, this alienation had cost them dear, for they had gone to their death in frightening numbers.

As he continued to compile statistics from other regions, the pattern became more common: break-ins, pickpocketing, burglary: all over the country, members of the nomad groups were arrested in disproportionate numbers and with disproportionate frequency. But there were some cases — especially a particularly vile one in Rome — of organized prostitution, the children rented out, it would appear, by members of the clans to the men interested in their services. Brunetti thought of the autopsy report.

Though he forced himself back to the examination of general crime statistics, that particular case continued to nag at him, and the girl's face, both in death and in the photos he had placed on the steps of the caravan, would return to him at odd times and more than once in his dreams. Pushing those memories aside, he forced himself back to the business of tabulating comparisons among the numbers of crimes, but when he found himself at a loss for the Venetian equivalent of automobile theft, he stopped and gave up for the moment.

'See if there's anything that can be done for the mother,' Patta had enjoined him. Brunetti had no idea what could be done for the mother of an eleven-year-old girl who had drowned, and he suspected that the Vice-Questore would also be at a loss. But Patta had given the command, and

Brunetti would obey it.

This time the car that took him there belonged to the Squadra Mobile, and the driver, when Brunetti told him where he wanted to go, recognized the name of the camp. 'Be easier if we just ran a normal service like a bus, Commissario,' he said. He was a man in his forties and had slipped into the dialect he heard Brunetti speak. He was tall and fair-skinned, with an open, relaxed manner.

'Why's that?' Brunetti asked.

'Because we go out there so often. Or maybe it's more like a taxi service for their kids.'

'Like that, eh?' Brunetti asked, noticing that the trees were in stronger bloom today: the green was darker, more sure of itself. 'Sounds bad.'

'Not my place to say whether it's bad or good, sir,' the driver said. 'But after you do it for a while, it's got to look pretty strange.'

'Why?'

'It's like there's a different law for them than there is for the rest of us.' He risked a side glance at Brunetti, and sensing that the Commissario was both listening and interested, the driver went on. 'I've got two kids at home: six and nine. Can you imagine what would happen if I refused to send them to school and if they got brought home for stealing? Six times? Ten times?'

'What would be different?' Brunetti asked although he had a pretty fair idea.

'Well, for one thing, I'd pound both of them into next week,' the driver said with a smile, making it clear that 'pound' would translate into strong words and no television for a month. 'And I'd lose my job. That's for sure. Or it would be so hard for me to keep it that I'd quit.' That, Brunetti suspected, was a bit of an exaggeration, but he was reminded of similar cases, when the children of policemen had been arrested, and their fathers' careers had been damaged seriously.

'How else?'

'Well, if they kept away for a long time, I suppose the social services could step in and take the kids away, maybe send them to foster homes. I don't know.'

'You think that would be right?' Brunetti asked.

The driver changed lanes smoothly and didn't speak for some time, eyes careful on the road. 'Well, speaking for myself, sir, for my own family, I think it would be too much. Really I do. I'd find a way to stop them.' He thought about this, then said,

'Well, maybe these people wouldn't like to have their kids taken away, either, now that I think about it.' Another long silence, and then the driver said, 'I guess we don't all have to love our kids in the same way, eh?'

'No, I suppose not,' Brunetti agreed.

'And the kids, what do they know about anything?'

'I'm not sure I follow you,' Brunetti said.

'What they get is normal, isn't it? I mean, to them it is. All kids know about a family is what they see around them. That's what's normal. For them, I mean.' He let Brunetti consider this and then added, 'When I take them back, it's obvious the kids love their families.'

'And the parents?'

'Oh, they love the kids; at least the mothers do. That's obvious, too.'

'Even though it's the police who's bringing them back?' Brunetti asked.

The driver let out a surprised laugh. 'Oh, that doesn't matter to them, sir. They're happy, and the kids are, too.' He stole a glance at Brunetti in the mirror and said, 'I guess family's always family, eh, sir?'

'I suppose so,' Brunetti agreed. 'Still, if the police brought your kids home . . .'

'That wouldn't happen to begin with, sir. My kids are in school, and if they weren't there, we'd know about it.' Then, suddenly changing the subject, the driver said, 'I never got much of an education, sir. So here I am, driving a police car for a living.'

'Don't you like it?' Brunetti asked, not certain how one subject had led to the other.

'No, sir, it's not that I don't like it. Times like this, when I get to talk to someone, well, someone who talks to me like I was a person or something, I like it. But what sort of life is this for a man? Driving other people around, and knowing those other people are always going to be more important than I am? I'm a police officer, yes, and I get the uniform and a gun, but all I'm ever going to do is drive this car. Until I retire.'

'Is that why you think it's important your children go to school?' Brunetti asked.

'Exactly. They get an education, they can do something with their lives.' He put on the indicator and started up the exit ramp of the autostrada. He glanced briefly at Brunetti and said, 'I mean, that's all that matters, isn't it, that our kids have a better life than we did?'

'Let's hope, eh?' Brunetti asked.

'Yes, sir,' the officer answered.

He drove through the exit from the autostrada, stopped at a red light and looked both ways, then turned to the left. Because of the oncoming traffic or perhaps because he had said all he had to say, the driver grew silent, and Brunetti shifted his attention to the passing scenery. It was difficult for him to understand how drivers found their way back to a place. So much could change: trees and flowers blossomed or died, fields were ploughed or harvested, parked cars changed their places. And if a driver lost his way, it was difficult to pull over and stop, even worse to try to go back in the direction from which he had come. And there was the perpetual irritation of traffic, cars buzzing at them like insects from every side.

They made another turn. Brunetti looked around and recognized nothing. The houses disappeared and the world turned green.

After some time the car pulled up at the gates to the camp. The driver got out and opened them, came back and drove inside, then got out again and closed them. If they were so easy to open, what purpose did the gates serve?

Two men sat on the steps of one of the caravans; three others stood around the open bonnet of a car, bent over and peering inside. None of them acknowledged the arrival of the police car, though Brunetti saw from the sudden stillness that passed over their bodies like a wave that they were aware of it.

Brunetti got out of the car, motioning to the uniformed driver to remain inside. He walked towards the three men at the car. *'Buon giorno, signori,'* he said.

One after the other, they glanced at him, then back into the viscera of the car. One of them said something Brunetti could not understand, pointing to a plastic bottle with a hose running through a red cap on the top. He reached forward and prodded it so hard that the liquid inside it could be seen to ripple, then the other two remarked on what he had done.

The three men stood upright and, as if they had practised the manoeuvre, pushed themselves away from the car at the same instant and headed back towards the caravans. After a time, Brunetti approached the two men sitting on the steps. They glanced at him as he approached.

'Buon giorno, signori,' he said.

'No italiano,' one of them said, smiling at his friend.

Brunetti walked back to the police car. The driver rolled down the window and looked at Brunetti, who asked, 'You know a lot about cars?'

'Yes, sir, I do.'

'Anything wrong with any of the cars you see here? I mean legally wrong.' Brunetti added, pointing with his chin to the circle of cars in front of them.

The driver opened the door and got out. He took two steps nearer the cars and ran his eyes carefully over them. 'Two of them have broken tail lights,' he turned to tell Brunetti. 'And three of them are driving on tyres that are almost bald.' He looked at Brunetti, then asked, 'You want more?'

'Yes.'

The driver walked over to the line of cars and, one by one, made a careful circuit of them, glancing into the back seats to check for seat belts, looking for broken headlights and the absence of green insurance cards.

He walked back to Brunetti and said, 'Three of them can't be driven legally. One has tyres that might as well not be there, and two of them have insurance cards that expired more than three years ago.'

'That enough to get them towed away?' Brunetti asked.

'I'm not sure, sir. I've never worked in traffic.' He glanced back at the cars, then added, 'But it might be.'

'We'll see,' Brunetti said. 'Who's got jurisdiction here?'

'The province of Treviso.'

'Good,' Brunetti answered.

Brunetti had often reflected on the meaning of the phrase 'net worth', especially as it was used in an attempt to calculate the wealth of a person. It usually included their investments, homes, bank accounts, possessions: only those things which could be seen, touched, counted. Never considered, as far as he could tell, were such intangibles as the good or ill will which followed a person through life, the love he gave or the love which was felt for him, nor, important in this instance, the favours he was owed.

Brunetti, whose net financial worth could easily be quantified, had vast other resources upon which he could draw, in this case a university classmate who was now Vice-Questore of Treviso and upon whose order, thirty minutes later, three police tow trucks, one after the other, pulled up to the gates to the nomad camp.

Brunetti's driver opened the gates, and the trucks drove in. From the first one, a uniformed police officer climbed down and, ignoring Brunetti and the driver, walked over to the first of the three cars Brunetti had reported. Using a handheld computer, he typed in the licence plate, waited for the response to come up on the screen, then typed in some more information. After a moment, the computer spat out a small sheet of white paper, which the officer tucked under the windscreen wiper of the car. He followed the same process with two other cars, and when he was finished, waved his hand to the drivers of the three trucks.

With a precision Brunetti could but admire, they drove their trucks closer to the rear of the cars, turned, backed up to them, and got out. In a motion as practised as that of the three nomads pushing themselves away from the hood of the car, they attached their tow hooks to the backs of the cars and returned to the cabs. The fourth officer saluted Brunetti, climbed back into the cab of the first truck, and slammed his door. The engines of the three trucks whined to a new pitch. Slowly, the rear ends of the cars rose into the air. Then the trucks lined up in a row and drove through the gate, each towing a car. Outside, they stopped, and the same officer got out and came back to close the gates. The trucks drove off. The entire operation had lasted less than five minutes.

Brunetti's driver returned to their car, but Brunetti remained standing in front of it. After a few minutes, the man who had acted as leader the last time Brunetti visited the camp opened the door to his caravan and came down the steps. Brunetti took a few steps forward. Tanovic walked over and stopped about a metre from him.

'Why you do that?' he asked angrily, jerking his head aside to indicate the places where the cars had stood.

'I don't want you people to run any risks,' Brunetti said. Then, before the man could speak, he added, 'It's dangerous to break some laws.'

'What laws we break?' the man asked, pumping indignation into his voice.

'Having insurance when you drive a car,' Brunetti explained. 'And headlights, and seat belts. You didn't do the things the police want you to do.'

'No need take cars,' the man said, making the jerking motion again.

'You're here, aren't you?' Brunetti asked. 'Talking to me.'

The man's eyes widened at this, as if he preferred to play the game of power without ever talking about the moves that were being made. 'I come other time,' he said. 'I busy now.'

'I don't have time to waste,' Brunetti said in a very unpleasant voice. 'You waste my time. I waste your time.'

The man did not want to enter into a discussion of this. 'What you want?'

'I'd like to speak to Signor and Signora Rocich.'

The man stared at Brunetti as though he still expected him to answer his question.

Brunetti waited for him to speak. He had seen the blue Mercedes with the damaged fender when they drove in. He waited a bit longer then sighed and turned away. He walked over to the police car, bent to the window and said, loud enough for the other man to hear, 'You think you could call them in Treviso again?'

'Wait, wait,' he heard Tanovic say from behind him. 'He just come.'

Brunetti straightened up. The other man walked over to the caravan from which Rocich had emerged the last time and stamped his foot on the bottom step: once, twice, three times. Then he backed off two steps. Brunetti joined him. The man pulled a *telefonino* from the pocket of his leather jacket and punched in a number. Brunetti heard a phone ring twice, then it was answered with a single, shouted word. The man answered with two and broke the connection. He turned to Brunetti and gave a wolfish smile, as if to offer this as his next move in whatever game they were playing.

The door to the Rocich caravan opened and the same short man emerged. He came down the steps and paused at the bottom. Brunetti felt, as if it were heat radiating from a furnace, rage emanating from the man. Nothing, however, showed on his face, as impassive as the last time.

He walked the two steps to them and asked something of the other man, who answered him quickly. Rocich began to object, or so it sounded to Brunetti, but he was cut off. As their dialogue continued, Brunetti, who gave every appearance of paying no attention at all, and who could in fact follow only the way the men moved and the rising and falling tones of their voices, felt the rage in Rocich grow.

Brunetti folded his arms and spread a look of infinite boredom across his face. He turned away from the men and let his eye roam up the hill, then, chin still raised, he took a quick glance at the caravan, where again he detected signs of motion, this time behind both of the windows, now only a few metres away. He turned his head to the other side and looked out at the road that passed the camp, pursed his lips impatiently, then looked quickly back at the caravan, where he could now distinguish what looked like two heads at the windows.

Tanovic broke away and walked back to his caravan. He walked up the stairs and

330

went inside, closing the door softly. That left Brunetti and Rocich.

'Signor Rocich, I'm sorry about the death of your daughter.'

The man spat on the ground, but he turned his head away before he did it.

'Signor Rocich, I'm the one who found her body. I took her out of the canal,' Brunetti said, almost as if he hoped this would establish some sort of a bond with the man, though well he knew the impossibility of that.

'What you want, money?' Rocich asked.

'No. I'd like to know what your daughter was doing in Venice that night.'

The man shrugged.

'Did you know she was there?'

He repeated the shrug.

'Signor Rocich, was your daughter alone?'

The difference in their heights was such that the man had to bend his head back to meet Brunetti's eyes. When he did, it was only by force of will that Brunetti prevented himself from taking a step backward and out of the radiant circle of this man's almost incandescent anger. Brunetti had encountered rage as a response to a loved one's death many times before, but this was different, for the rage was directed at Brunetti himself and not at the fate that had cost the child her life.

He had told the man in charge that he wanted to speak to Signor and Signora Rocich both, but he realized now that any attempt on his part to speak to the woman, anything in fact that called attention to her or suggested any interest in her, would probably be paid for in ways Brunetti did not want to think about.

The man spat on the ground again, then looked down as if he wanted to see how close he had managed to come to Brunetti's shoe. While Rocich's gaze was lowered, Brunetti looked boldly across at the caravan, where half of a woman's face was now visible behind the door.

Brunetti raised his voice and asked, 'Do you have a doctor here?'

Obviously the question confused Rocich, who said, 'What?'

'A doctor? Do you have a doctor?'

'Why you ask?'

Brunetti put on an air of irritated patience. 'Because I want to know. I want to know if you have a doctor, if you have a family doctor.' Again, the word 'family' slipped into his conversation and into his mind. Before Rocich could refuse, Brunetti said. 'There are records, Signor Rocich. I don't want to have to waste more time looking for them.'

'Calfi, he doctor for all,' Rocich answered, waving a hand backwards over the entire camp.

Brunetti went to the unnecessary trouble of pulling out his notebook and writing down the doctor's name.

Rocich couldn't let it go. 'Why you want?'

'Your daughter was sick when she died,' he said. True enough. 'And the police doctor wants to see the blood records of the people here.'

He wondered how much of this Rocich understood. Apparently enough for him to ask, 'Why?'

'Because when the doctor checks all the blood types he will see who she got the disease from,' Brunetti lied.

Rocich's response was involuntary. His eyes widened, and his head whipped around towards the door of the caravan, but by the time he looked, no one was standing at the door or at the window and the caravan gave every evidence of being empty. When Rocich looked back at Brunetti, the nomad's expression was blank. 'I no understand,' he said.

'It doesn't matter,' Brunetti said, 'whether you do or you don't. But we want to check.'

Rocich turned away from him then and went back up the stairs of the caravan. He went inside and closed the door. Brunetti had the driver take him back to Piazzale Roma.

25

'You think he believed you?' Paola asked Brunetti that evening as they sat in the living room, the children in their rooms and the house quiet with the late-night stillness that encourages people to abandon the day and go to bed.

'I don't know what he believed,' Brunetti said, taking another sip of the plum liqueur that one of his paid informants had given him for Christmas the year before. The man, who owned three fishing boats in Chioggia, had proven a very useful source of information on the traffic in contraband cigarettes coming in from Montenegro, and so Brunetti and his colleagues in the Guardia di Finanza never expressed any curiosity about the source of the seemingly endless supply of distilled liqueurs — all in unmarked bottles — with which he brightened the holiday season of numerous members of the forces of order.

'Tell me again exactly what you said to him,' Paola asked but then interrupted herself, holding up her glass: 'You think he makes this himself?'

'I've no idea,' Brunetti admitted. 'But it's certainly better than anything I've ever bought that had a tax stamp on it.'

'Pity, then,' Paola said.

'Pity what?'

'That he doesn't make it legally.'

'So he could make more of it?' Brunetti asked, really not understanding.

'Something like that, I suppose,' Paola said. 'Or that we could buy it openly and eliminate your sense that you owe him a favour every time he gives it to you.'

'He's been paid enough,' Brunetti said, giving no explanation of what that might mean. 'Besides, you know how hard it is to open a business, especially one where he'd have to get the licences to produce alcohol. No, he's better doing it the way he does.'

'Protected by the police?' she asked, using the vocal equivalent of a poke with a stick.

'And the Guardia di Finanza,' Brunetti added complacently. 'Don't forget them.'

She emptied her glass, set it on the table, and said, this time employing the voice she used when she had been bested, 'All right. But going back to this Gypsy, tell me again exactly what you said to him.'

Brunetti cradled the small glass between his hands. 'That she had a disease when she died. Which is true enough,' he added, realizing that it was only with Paola that he could feel comfortable talking about this. 'And that a doctor would be able to tell who she got the disease from by looking at blood types.' Brunetti had spoken impulsively, hoping that Rocich would somehow have heard enough garbled talk about disease transmission to have some vague inkling that it was possible to trace the source of a disease in this manner. And that he knew what sort of disease the girl had or was likely to have had.

'But how could anyone believe something like that?' Paola asked, making no attempt to disguise her scepticism.

Brunetti could only shrug. 'There's no telling what people will believe.'

Paola considered this for some time, then said, 'You're probably right. God knows what's percolating in the heads of most people.' She gave a weary shake of her own. 'I've got students who think you can't get pregnant the first time you have sex.'

'And I've arrested people who think you can get AIDS from hairbrushes,' Brunetti added.

'So what will you do?'

'No one's claimed the body,' Brunetti said, not by way of answer to her question; more just to say it and see what she thought. 'Or at least no one had yesterday, when I spoke to Rizzardi.'

'What's her family waiting for?'

'God knows,' Brunetti answered. Her family.

'What will happen?'

Brunetti had no answer. The idea that a parent could know that their child was lying dead, no matter where, and not rush to the body was one he found impossible to comprehend. This was the basis of Hecuba's final lament, he knew: 'I, homeless, childless, and the one to lay you in your grave, you so young and miserably dead.' He had read that just last night and had been forced to put the book aside, the play unfinished.

He would have to call Rizzardi's office again to see if the child's body had been taken away. He knew the urge to do it immediately was futile: no one would be at the morgue at this hour, and it was hardly a matter about which he could disturb the pathologist at home.

'Guido?' Paola asked. 'Are you all right?'

'Yes, yes,' he said, dragging his spirit back to their conversation. 'I was thinking about the girl.' He still lacked the courage to tell Paola he had been dreaming about the child, as well.

'What will happen?'

'If?'

'If no one claims her.'

'I don't know,' he admitted. It had happened in the past, when bodies found in the water had not been identified: then it became the responsibility of the city to see to burying them, a mass said over their nameless corpse in the hope that they were Catholic and perhaps in the added hope that this would make some difference.

In this case, however, where the dead person had been identified and yet remained unclaimed, Brunetti had no idea how to proceed: indeed, he had no idea if a correct procedure existed. Even this heartless state had not been able to imagine people who would not claim their dead. He had no idea of the child's religion. He knew that Muslims buried their dead quickly, and Christians would certainly have done it by now, yet still she rested unburied in her drawer in the hospital's morgue.

Brunetti set his glass on the table and stood. 'Shall we go to bed?' he asked, suddenly feeling very tired.

'I think we'd better,' Paola agreed. She

raised a hand, inviting him to take it and help her to her feet. She had never done this before, and he was unable to disguise his surprise. Seeing this, she said, 'You are my shield and buckler, Guido.' Usually, she said such things as jokes, but tonight she sounded serious.

'Against what?' he asked as he drew her towards him.

'Against my sense that it's all a dreadful mess and there's no hope for any of us,' she said calmly and led him to their bed.

The first thing he did when he got to the Questura the next morning was call Rizzardi and ask about the body of the girl.

'She's still here,' the pathologist answered. 'I had a call from some woman in the social services, saying that it was not their responsibility, and we had to take care of it.'

'What does that mean?'

'We informed the Treviso police. They said they'd send someone to the camp to speak to the parents.'

'But do you know if they did?' Brunetti asked.

Rizzardi answered, 'All I'm sure of is that we — the hospital administration, that is — sent the parents a letter, telling them that the child's body was here and that they could come and get her.' The doctor paused for a moment, then added, 'The letter gave the name of the company that takes care of it.'

'Of what?'

'Moving the dead.'

'Oh.'

'First to Piazzale Roma by boat, then in a hearse to wherever they have to go on the mainland.'

Brunetti had nothing to say to this.

Finally Rizzardi said, 'But no one's come in here to get her.'

Brunetti stared at the wall of his office and tried to understand what he had just been told. Into his silence, Rizzardi said, 'It's never happened before, not that I know of. I've spoken to Giacomini — he's the only magistrate I could think of who might know about something like this — and he said he'd look into it and see what the procedure is.'

'When did you talk to him?' Brunetti asked.

'Yesterday afternoon.'

'And?'

'And he's a busy man, Guido.' As he heard the mounting impatience in Rizzardi's voice, the fear came to Brunetti that the doctor, who spent his days surrounded by the silent dead, would say that the girl was not going anywhere or that he would somehow speak lightly of the situation. He could not abide the thought of that possibility, not in a man of whom he thought so highly, so he said, 'Let me know when you hear, Ettore, all right?' and, without waiting for an answer, replaced the phone.

He sat quietly for some time, looking first at the papers on his desk, reading the words and reading them again, waiting for them to make some sort of sense. But they remained letters and words on paper and nothing more. The wall offered no more than the papers. He knew Giacomini, a serious man: surely he would find the proper way to proceed.

Brunetti remembered having written down the name of the doctor: Calfi. Rocich had seemed too surprised to have had time to lie. He called down to the officers' room and asked for Pucetti. When the younger man answered, Brunetti said, 'I'd like you to find me the address and phone number of a doctor named Calfi. Somewhere out by the nomad camp. I don't know his first name.'

'Yes, sir,' Pucetti said and hung up.

Brunetti waited. He should have thought of the doctor long before this, as soon as

Rizzardi had told him the results of the autopsy. A doctor would have treated them all: the girl, the mother, the other children, perhaps even Rocich himself. How else would the man have known the doctor's name?

After only a few minutes, Pucetti called back with the doctor's first name, Edoardo; his address, in Scorzè; and the phone number of his surgery.

Brunetti dialled the number and, after seven rings, got a recorded voice asking him to describe his problem and leave his name and number, and the doctor would call him back. 'Describe my problem,' Brunetti said while he waited for the machine to click to recording mode. 'Dottor Calfi, this is Commissario Brunetti from Venezia. I'd like to ask you some questions about patients of yours. I'd be very grateful if you would call me here at the Questura.' Brunetti gave his direct number and hung up.

Which of the family were his patients? Did he know that the girl was infected with gonorrhoea? Did her parents know? Had he any idea how she might have contracted the disease? As Brunetti ran through the list of questions he wanted to ask, his thoughts turned to the doctor who had cared for his family when he and his brother were children. As he recalled him, his mother slipped back into his memory, for she had always stayed with him those few times he had been sick as a child. She had always brought him mugs of hot water, lemon and honey, telling him it was nature's best way to fight a cold, or flu, or just about anything that went wrong with him. To this day, it was the remedy he insisted on using with his own children.

His reflections were interrupted by a call from Signorina Elettra, who, with thinly veiled contempt for the ease with which the Department of Public Instruction allowed its files to be 'accessed', told Brunetti that both of the Fornari children were excellent students, the son already accepted at the Bocconi Business School in Milano. He thanked her for the information, got up, and went down to the officers' room in search of Vianello, who had chosen to accompany one of his informants the day before when she spoke to a magistrate and had thus been unable to accompany Brunetti to the nomad camp.

When Brunetti turned into the final flight of steps, he saw Vianello at the bottom. 'You coming up?' Brunetti asked.

'Yes,' the Inspector answered, starting up the steps towards him. 'I'd like to know what happened when you went out there.'

As they walked slowly back to Brunetti's office, he told Vianello about his visit to the camp, concluding with his phone call to the doctor. Vianello listened closely and, when he was finished, complimented Brunetti for having thought to call the tow trucks.

Brunetti was flattered that Vianello saw the humour, as well as the ingenuity, of this.

'And you think she heard you?' Vianello asked.

'She must have,' Brunetti answered. 'She was standing just behind the door: we were less than two metres from her.'

'If she understands Italian.'

'One of the children was there, too,' Brunetti explained. 'They're more likely to speak it.'

Vianello grunted in acknowledgement and followed Brunetti into the office. As he took his seat, the Inspector said tiredly, 'There are times when I find myself wishing we had more tow trucks.'

'To do what?' Brunetti asked.

'Move them somewhere else.'

Brunetti stopped himself from staring, but he did say, 'I've known you to say kinder things, Lorenzo.' At Vianello's shrug, he added, 'I've never heard you say you don't like them.'

'I don't.' Vianello shot back, voice entirely level.

Surprised to hear not so much the statement as the heat with which Vianello gave it, Brunetti didn't bother to disguise his reaction.

Vianello stretched his legs out in front of him and appeared to study his shoes for a moment, then looked at Brunetti and said, 'All right: what I said is an exaggeration. It's not that I particularly dislike them more that I don't particularly like them.'

'It still sounds strange to hear you say it,' Brunetti insisted.

'And if I said I didn't like white wine? Or spinach? Would that sound strange?' Vianello asked, his voice moving up a notch. 'And would your voice have that same air of disappointment that I'm not thinking the proper thoughts or feeling the proper sentiments?' Brunetti declined to answer, and Vianello went on. 'So long as I say that I don't like a thing, an object, or even a movie or a book, it's perfectly all right to say it. But as soon as I say I don't like Gypsies, or Finns or people from Nova Scotia, for God's sake, all hell breaks loose.'

Vianello glanced at Brunetti, giving him the opportunity to say something if he chose; when he still remained silent, the

Inspector went on. 'I told you, I don't feel any active dislike towards them; I simply feel no active sympathy.'

'There are wiser ways to express your lack of feeling,' Brunetti suggested.

His words might have been ironic, but the tone was not, as Vianello clearly heard. 'You're right,' the Inspector answered, 'that's what I should say: it's the acceptable way to talk. But I think I'm tired, tired to death, of always having to be careful to express the right sympathies, of always having to make sheep's eyes and say pious things whenever I'm confronted with one of life's victims.' Vianello considered this and then added, 'It's almost as if we were living in one of those Eastern European countries, years ago, where you had one way to speak publicly and a different way to speak honestly.'

'I'm not sure I follow.'

Vianello looked up and met Brunetti's eyes. 'I think you do.' When Brunetti looked away, the Inspector continued, 'You've listened to enough people, the way they say all those things about how we can't have bad feelings and have to accept minorities and respect their rights and be tolerant. But as soon as they've finished saying it, if they trust you, they say what they're really thinking.'

'Which is?' Brunetti enquired mildly.

'That they're fed up with watching this country turn into a place where they don't feel safe and where they lock their doors when they run next door to a neighbour's to borrow a cup of sugar, and whenever the prisons are full the government says some noble words about giving people another chance to insert themselves into society and tosses the doors open to let the killers out.' Vianello stopped as suddenly as he had started.

After what seemed like a long time had passed, Brunetti asked, 'Will you say the same things tomorrow?'

Vianello shrugged and finally looked across at him and said, 'Probably not.' He smiled and gave a different kind of shrug. 'It's hard, never to say these things. I think I'd feel less guilty about thinking them if I could admit to them once in a while.'

Brunetti nodded.

Vianello gave himself a shake, much in the manner of a large dog getting to its feet. Then, his voice steady with friendship, he asked, 'What do you think's going to happen?' He sounded entirely normal, and Brunetti had the strange sensation that he had just watched Vianello's spirit slip back into his body.

'I have no idea,' Brunetti said. 'Rocich is a ticking bomb. The only way he knows how to deal with anything is by hitting at it. The boss or the leader, or whatever he is, is too powerful for him to try going up against. That leaves the woman and the children.' He hesitated an instant, but then decided that he would say what he was thinking, 'and he'd be violent even if he weren't a Gypsy.'

'I agree,' Vianello said.

'I don't want to call attention to the woman. Can't call her in here for questioning, can't go back there and try to talk to her.'

'And so?'

'And so I wait for this doctor to call me. And after he does or I get tired of waiting for him to call, I go back and talk to the Fornaris again and have another look at their apartment.'

26

Brunetti did not have long to wait for Dottor Calfi to return his call: the phone rang only minutes after Vianello had gone back down to the squad room. Brunetti lifted the phone and gave his name.

'Commissario, this is Edoardo Calfi. You asked me to call.' The voice was a light tenor, the accent Lombard: perhaps Milano.

'Thank you for calling, Dottore. As I told you in my message, I'd like to ask you some questions about patients of yours.'

'What patients are those?'

'Members of a family known as Rocich,' Brunetti said. 'They are nomads living in the camp near Dolo.'

'I know who they are,' the doctor said sharply, and Brunetti began to think the call was going to be a failure. This impression grew stronger when Calfi added, 'And they are not "known as" Rocich, Commissario: it is their name.'

'Good,' Brunetti said, working to keep his voice calm and pleasant. 'Could you tell me which of the family members are patients of yours?'

'Before I do, I'd like to know why you're asking this question, Commissario.'

'I'm asking you, Dottore,' Brunetti said, 'in order to save time.'

'I'm afraid I don't understand.'

'With a judge's order, I could perhaps get the information from the central records in that district, but since these are questions I'd like to address to their doctor personally, I'm trying to save time by establishing that they are your patients.'

'They are.'

'Thank you, Dottore. Could you tell me which members of the family you've treated?'

'All of them.'

'And that would be?'

'The father and mother, and the three children,' the doctor answered, and Brunetti fought down the impulse to say he made it sound just like the three little bears.

'It's about the younger daughter I'd like to ask information, Dottore.'

'Yes?' The doctor's voice was cautious.

'I'd like to know if you've ever treated her

for a venereal disease,' Brunetti said, as if she were still alive.

That was quickly put paid to by the doctor, who said, 'I *do* read the newspapers, Commissario, so I know Ariana is dead. Why do you want to know if I treated her' — he asked, placing great emphasis on the past tense '— for this sort of disease?'

'Because signs of gonorrhoeal infection were found during the autopsy,' Brunetti said in a neutral voice.

'Yes, I knew about the disease,' the doctor said. 'She was under treatment for the problem.' Brunetti forbore to ask whether, as a doctor, he had thought it proper to report this 'problem' to someone at the social services.

'Could you tell me how long she had been under treatment?'

'I don't see how this is relevant,' the doctor said.

Brunetti doubted that but answered only, 'It might help us in our investigation of her death, Dottore.'

'Some months,' Calfi acquiesced by saying.

'Thank you,' Brunetti said, deciding not to ask for clarification but to settle for what he could get.

'I'd like to say something if I may,' the

doctor began.

'Of course, Dottore.'

'This family has been in my care for almost a year. And during that time I've come to take a great interest in them and in the troubles they meet with here.' At this point, Brunetti could pretty well predict what he was going to hear. Dottor Calfi was a crusader, and he knew he could do nothing more with crusaders than listen to them, agree with them entirely, and then try to get out of them what he wanted.

'I'm sure many doctors come to feel a strong concern for their patients,' Brunetti said in a voice he washed clean of any sentiments save warmth and admiration.

'Life's not easy for them,' Calfi said. 'It's never been easy for them.'

Brunetti made a noise of assent.

For the next few minutes, Calfi catalogued the misfortunes of the Rocich family, at least the version he had been given of those misfortunes. All of them had, at one time or another, been the victims of brutality. Even the wife had been beaten by the police in Mestre, one eye blackened and her neck badly bruised on both sides. The children had suffered persecution in school and were afraid to return. Rocich himself was unable to find work.

When the doctor stopped speaking, Brunetti asked, voice warm with concern and fellow feeling, 'How did the child contract the disease, Dottore?'

'She was raped,' Calfi said indignantly, almost as if Brunetti had tried to deny this or had perhaps been involved in some way in the deed. 'Her father told me that she was walking back to the camp late one afternoon and was offered a ride by a man in a big car. At least that's what she told him.'

'I see,' said a very concerned Brunetti.

'The man pulled off the road on the way to the camp and raped her,' Calfi said, voice rising with anger.

'Did they report it to the police?' asked an equally angry Brunetti.

'Who'd believe them?' Calfi asked in a tone now of indignant disgust.

Not many, thought Brunetti, but what he said was, 'Yes, you're probably right, Dottore.' Using the same tone, Brunetti asked, 'Did they bring her to you?'

'Not until some months later,' the doctor explained, then before Brunetti could ask about this, added, 'She was ashamed about what had happened, so she wouldn't let them bring her to me until there were symptoms they couldn't ignore.'

'I see, I see,' Brunetti said, then allowed himself to mutter an audible, 'Terrible.'

'I'm glad you see it that way,' the doctor said, and Brunetti had to admit that he did indeed think the whole thing was terrible but not, perhaps, in the same way the doctor did.

'Did anything similar ever happen to any of the other children?' he asked.

'What do you mean, "similar"?' the doctor asked in a sharp voice.

Brunetti shied away from the idea of sexually transmitted disease and said, 'Violence from the people in the area.' He decided to risk it and added, 'or from the police?'

He could almost feel Calfi calming down when he heard this.

'Occasionally, but the police seem to prefer exercising their violence against women,' Calfi said, quite as if he had forgotten he was talking to a policeman.

Brunetti decided to get out while the going was good and so expressed his thanks to the doctor for his help and for the information he had given.

With a mutual exchange of courtesies, the men hung up. 'Their violence against women,' Brunetti repeated, the phone in his hand. He replaced the receiver.

■ ■ ■ ■

That left him the Fornaris. It would be advisable, he knew, to let Patta decide on the wisdom of going to speak to them again, or perhaps it would be better to leave that decision to the examining magistrate, but Brunetti chose to see his visit not as an investigative one so much as an attempt better to clarify the likelihood that the child had died in a fall from their roof. Signor Fornari should have returned from Russia by now: Brunetti wondered if he shared his wife's lack of curiosity about the Gypsy girl, found dead so close to their home.

Brunetti walked along the Riva degli Schiavoni, filtering through the people walking in his direction or coming towards him, and as he walked, he had the sensation of being observed. He paused occasionally to study the wares on offer in the ever-increasing number of waterside stalls: football-team flags, *gondolieri* boaters, thick velvet court jester hats, ashtrays — one from Capri — and the omnipresent plastic gondolas. He stood in front of each horror in turn, his attention radiating out to both sides. He replaced the gondola on the counter and swung around, studying the people behind him, but he saw no sudden motion. He thought for a moment of taking a vaporetto: this would force anyone who was following him to abandon the pursuit. But curiosity overcame him and he continued to walk, even slowing his pace to allow whoever it was, if anyone, to keep up with him.

He continued across the Piazza and down Via XXII Marzo, then turned right and past Antico Martini and in front of the Fenice. The sensation of being watched kept pace with him, though the one time he stopped and turned to study the façade of the theatre he saw no one he had seen behind him before. He walked in front of the Ateneo and down towards the Fornari house.

He rang, gave his name, and was told to come up. When Brunetti reached the top floor, Orsola Vivarini stood at the open door, and as he drew closer he thought for a moment that she had sent an older version of herself to speak to him.

'Good morning, Signora,' he said. 'I've come back to ask you a few more things. If you don't mind, that is.'

'Of course not,' she said, voice too loud.

Brunetti's easy smile gave no indication that he had noticed the change in her appearance. He followed her into the apartment. The flowers that had stood on a table to the right of the door were still there, but the water had evaporated, and Brunetti could smell the first faint scent of rot.

'Is your husband back from his trip?' he asked, following her into the room where they had spoken the last time.

'Yes. He got home yesterday,' she said and, turning to him, asked, 'Can I offer you anything, Commissario?'

'No, Signora, you're too kind. I just had a coffee. But thank you for asking.' She waved him to a chair. He crossed the room to it, but when she remained standing, Brunetti did as well.

'Please sit down, Commissario,' she said. 'I'll call my husband.'

He gave a low half-bow and rested one hand on the back of the chair. And thought again of his mother and her rule that a man did not sit when a woman was standing.

She turned away and left the room. Brunetti went to the far wall to look at a painting. Primo Potenza, he thought, one of that crop of fine painters who had flourished in the city in the fifties. Where had all the painters gone? he wondered. All he seemed to see in the galleries were video installations and political statements expressed in papier mâché. Two large groupings of what must be family photos flanked the painting; Brunetti studied them. The star of the photos was the daughter. There she was with far shorter hair, on a horse, on water skis, then standing in front of a Christmas tree next to her mother. Years passed and summer returned in the next photo. Her hair had grown to the length it was now, and she stood on a dock, her arm around a tall, gangly boy, both of them wearing bathing suits and enormous smiles. The boy had thick hair almost as blond as hers, though with a decidedly reddish cast. In the fashion of the day, he had tattoos of what looked like South Sea Island tribal patterns encircling biceps and calves. He looked vaguely familiar to Brunetti, who assumed it was her brother and what he saw was a family resemblance. The girl was absent from the next two: in one, a photo taken from the back, Signora Vivarini stood in front of an enormous abstract painting that Brunetti did not recognize, her back to the camera, her arm draped over the shoulder of what might have been the same boy. In the last photo, she faced the camera with a full smile, her hand in that of a man with kind eyes and a soft mouth.

'*Buon giorno.*' Brunetti straightened up, backed away from the photos, and turned towards the voice. Dressed in a suit and tie both of which looked as though they were being worn for the first time, the man — the same one in the photo — managed to look faintly rumpled. As he approached, Brunetti studied him and realized the cause lay in his eyes, darkly circled underneath, and in his chin, on the underside of which he saw a small patch of white bristles the man had overlooked while shaving. His hair, too, though it was well cut and clean, managed to look tired, as if all it had the strength to do was hang limply across his head.

The man smiled and extended his hand: the grip was firmer than the smile. They exchanged names.

Fornari led Brunetti over to the same chair, and this time Brunetti lowered himself into it. 'My wife tells me,' he said when he was sitting opposite Brunetti, 'that you'd like to speak to me about this robbery.' His eyes were the same clear blue as his daughter's, and Brunetti saw in his face the source of her beauty. The straight, thin nose was the same, as were the perfect teeth and dark lips. The angles of her jaw were softer, but their strength came from his.

'Yes,' Brunetti said. 'Your wife has identified the objects.'

The man nodded.

'We're curious about the circumstances of the theft,' Brunetti said. 'And about any information you or your wife might be able to give us.'

Fornari gave a small smile that remained on his lips without reaching his eyes. 'I'm afraid I can't tell you anything about it, Commissario.' Before Brunetti could question him, Fornari said, 'I know only what my wife has told me, that someone managed to get into the apartment and take those things.' He smiled again, this time a bit more warmly. 'You've returned what was of greatest value to us,' he said with a gracious nod in Brunetti's direction. 'The other things, the ones still missing, they really don't matter.' In response to Brunetti's reaction, he clarified this by adding, 'They have no sentimental value, that is. And not much material value, either.' He smiled again and added, 'I say that to try to explain our response to the robbery. Or lack of response.'

It seemed to Brunetti, as he listened to Fornari and watched the man exercise control over his features, that he was working very hard to make it appear that he had little interest in the crime. Brunetti had no idea how he himself would respond to the theft, however temporary, of his wedding ring: he doubted that he would accept it with lofty philosophical tranquillity, as Fornari seemed to do. The cost of the man's attempt to remain calm was increasingly evident to Brunetti in the rhythmic motion of his right forefinger on the velvet fabric of the arm of his chair. Back and forth, back and forth, and then a sudden rectangle, and then quickly back and forth again.

'I can certainly understand that,' Brunetti said easily. 'Unless something really important is taken, most people — well,' he said with a nervous smile to suggest that he really ought not to be telling this sort of thing to a civilian — 'they won't even bother to report a break-in.' He shrugged at this evidence of human behaviour as if to demonstrate sympathy with it.

'I think you're right, Commissario,' Fornari said, as if the idea were a new one to him. 'In our case, we never even noticed the things were missing, so I can't say what we would have done had we realized a robbery had taken place.'

'I see,' Brunetti said and smiled. Then he said, 'Your wife told me that your daughter was here that night.' Fornari's finger stopped moving, and Brunetti watched it join the others in a tight grip on the arm of the chair.

After a long pause, he said, 'Yes, that's what Orsola told me. She said she checked on her before she went to bed.' Fornari smiled tightly at Brunetti and asked, 'Do you have children, Commissario?'

'Yes. Two teenagers. A boy and a girl.'

'Then you know how hard it is to break the habit of checking on them at night, I suppose.' Fornari's tactic, however obvious, was clever, one Brunetti had often employed: find common ground with your subject and use it to lead the conversation where you want it to go. More importantly, use it to lead a conversation away from where you do not want it to go.

While Fornari continued speaking, Brunetti considered the possibility that Fornari's daughter knew something her father did not want Brunetti to know. He nodded towards Fornari, not really listening, though he thought he heard the man begin a sentence with, 'Once, when Matteo was a child . . .'

Suddenly Brunetti was overcome by the temptation to do something he would despise himself for doing, something, in fact, that he had promised himself he would never do and then, after those times when he had done it, had promised himself he would never do again. Informers were everywhere: the police had them inside the Mafia; the Mafia had them even at the highest level of the *magistratura;* the military was full of them, as no doubt was industry. But no one had so far bothered to penetrate the world of teenagers and bring from it reliable information. He foresaw no danger to his own children in asking them to supply information about Fornari's, but the essence of danger was that it was unforeseen, wasn't it?

When he tuned back in, Fornari was coming to the end of a story about one of his children: Brunetti did not know which one. Brunetti smiled, then got to his feet and extended his hand to Fornari. 'I suppose they're all much the same,' he said. 'They just don't pay attention to the same things we do.' He hoped it was an appropriate response to whatever story Fornari had been telling, and from the man's reaction it appeared that it was.

They shook hands, Brunetti thanked him for taking the time to speak to him, asked him to extend the same thanks to his wife, and left the apartment. On the way downstairs, he wondered which of his children he was willing to turn into a spy and how he would deal with Paola when she found out.

27

When he reached the *calle,* Brunetti turned to the right and, more from habit than conscious thought, started back the way he had come. He was halfway down Calle degli Avvocati when he changed his mind and decided to take the vaporetto back to the Questura. He turned abruptly, and when he did he noticed a sudden motion on the left about ten metres away as something slipped back around the corner of Calle Pesaro. Reminded of the sensation that he had been followed from the Questura, Brunetti decided to abandon caution and took off at a fast run towards the corner.

When he wheeled around it, he saw motion ahead as someone, perhaps a woman, ran down the other side of the bridge and to the right into Calle dell'Albero. Brunetti followed over the bridge, down the *riva* and left at the end. He paused only long enough to look down the *calle* at the right, which he knew to be a dead end.

And heard retreating footsteps. He followed them: the walls of the buildings on either side grew closer together as the *calle* narrowed, and then ahead of him he saw the tall metal doors of a *palazzo*. For a moment, he wondered if he had been imagining it all, but then he heard a sound on the left. He moved forward slowly, and as he walked he unbuttoned his jacket to put his pistol within reach.

He saw it then, in a doorway on the left, and at first it looked to him like a discarded overcoat or a garbage bag over which someone had tossed an old sweater. He approached, and the object moved, backed up somehow to get closer to the door, then slid silently to the right and pressed up against the wall.

Brunetti was still not sure what sort of creature he had cornered. He bent down to take a closer look, and it erupted in his direction, crashing against his legs. Instinctively, Brunetti grabbed at it, but it was like holding an eel or some sort of wild animal. It thrashed, and then two skinny legs began to kick at him.

Knowing then at least what manner of being he was dealing with, Brunetti lifted it from the ground and turned it so that the feet were facing away from him and would perhaps do less damage. Then he wrapped his arms around the upper part and pulled it to his chest, muttering the sort of things he had said to their dogs when he was a boy.

'It's all right. It's all right. I'm not going to hurt you.' It kicked a few more times. Brunetti heard gasps, but gradually they subsided and the kicking stopped. It hung limp in his arms. 'I'm going to put you down now,' Brunetti said. 'Be careful where you put your feet, and don't fall.' The creature remained limp and unresponsive.

'Do you understand?'

Something under the hood of a dirty sports jacket nodded, and Brunetti lowered it to the ground. He felt the feet touch the ground one after the other, and, his hands still on the arms, he felt the entire body grow tense and prepare to flee. Effortlessly, he picked the child up again and said, 'Don't try to run away again. I'm much faster than you are.'

The tension relaxed and Brunetti lowered the child once more. The top of the hood came a few centimetres above Brunetti's belt. 'I'm going to let go and move away from you.' He did just that and then spoke to the back of the jacket. 'When you want, you can talk to me.'

There was no response. 'Is that why you were following me?' he asked. 'Do you want to talk to me?'

He saw a motion of the head, but it could have meant anything. 'All right. Then let's talk.'

A small, dirty hand came out of the sleeve of the jacket and motioned Brunetti to move farther away. Because the *calle* was a dead end and he was blocking the exit, he did this, moving back a full two paces. 'All right, I'm far enough away from you now. So we can talk.'

Brunetti leaned back against the wall of a building and folded his arms. He looked at the wall opposite him, though his attention was entirely on the child.

After what could have been a minute but might have been more, the child turned around. In the shadow created by the hood, Brunetti could make out eyes and mouth but not much more. He put his hands in his pockets and took another step away from the child, leaving an opening in front of him large enough for the child to try to bolt through. He watched as the child considered doing this and then discarded the idea.

The child slipped the same hand that had done the waving into the front pocket of the jacket. When it came out, the child took one step towards Brunetti and opened the fingers. In the palm Brunetti saw some small objects. He took a slow step closer, then leaned forward to see better. There was a ring and a cuff link.

Brunetti crouched down and extended his hand towards the child, who took one small step towards him. Brunetti saw that it was a boy, looking no older than eight, though he knew that the dead girl's brother was twelve. The boy let the jewellery drop into Brunetti's outstretched palm.

He pulled the objects closer and looked at them. The silver of the cuff link surrounded a small rectangle of lapis lazuli. Even Brunetti could see that the red stone in the ring was only a piece of glass. He glanced at the child, who was looking at him. 'Who sent you?' Brunetti asked.

'*Mamma,*' the child answered in a very light voice.

Brunetti nodded. 'You're a good boy,' he said. 'And very brave.' He didn't know how much of this the boy would understand, but when he saw the answering smile, he knew. 'And very clever,' Brunetti added, tapping the side of his own head, and the smile grew larger.

'What happened?' Brunetti asked. When

the child did not answer, Brunetti asked, 'That night, what happened?'

'The tiger man,' the boy said.

Brunetti cocked his head to one side to show his confusion. 'What tiger man?' he asked.

'In the house,' the child said, waving his hand in the general direction of the houses to Brunetti's left, where stood Palazzo Benzon and the home of Giorgio Fornari.

Brunetti raised his palms in the universal sign of confusion. 'I don't know a tiger man,' he said. 'What did he do?'

'He saw us. He came in. No clothes. Tiger man.' To show what he meant, the boy stuck his fingers in his hair and ruffled it out above his head, then made cutting motions, first with one hand, then with the other, at the top of his arms. 'Tiger. Bad tiger. Loud noise. Tiger noise.'

'Did the tiger man give you these?' Brunetti asked, holding the jewellery out towards the boy.

The boy's face grew cloudy with confusion. 'No, no,' he said with a violent shake of his head. 'We take. Tiger man see.' His eyes contracted as though he were trying to remember something, or trying not to remember something. Then he said, 'Ariana. He took Ariana.' To show Brunetti what he meant, he stuck his arms out in front of him and pretended to pick something up. 'Like you do me,' he said, making it clear and raising his hands with the emptiness suspended between them. He froze.

Brunetti waited.

'Door. Ariana out door,' he said, pushing his arms away from him violently and letting his hands fly open. Brunetti saw that the boy was crying.

His knees had begun to ache, but he remained crouched down, afraid of the effect on the child if he suddenly got to his feet. He let the boy cry for some time, and when he seemed calmer, Brunetti asked, 'Who was with you?'

'Xenia,' he said, raising one of his outthrust hands to the level of his shoulder.

'Did she see the tiger man?'

The boy nodded.

'Did she see what he did?'

He nodded again.

'Does your mother know about this?' Brunetti asked.

He nodded.

'Will she talk to me?'

The boy stared at Brunetti for some time and then shook his head.

'Because of your father?'

The boy shrugged.

'Why are you in the city?' Brunetti asked.

'Work,' the boy said, and Brunetti was left speechless at the use of the word.

'Will you tell your mother that you talked to me?'

'Yes. She want.'

'Does she want anything else?' Brunetti asked.

'Tiger man. Tiger man die,' the boy said fiercely, and Brunetti realized it was not only the boy's mother who wanted him dead. 'Like Ariana,' the boy said with adult savagery.

Brunetti had had enough. He spread his fingers on the ground in front of him and pushed off, rising slowly to his feet. He heard his right knee creak. As he had feared, the boy took two steps backwards and raised an involuntary arm across his face.

Brunetti backed farther away. 'I won't hurt you.' The boy let his arm fall to his side.

'You can go now, if you like,' he said. The boy at first seemed not to understand, so Brunetti turned and walked to the end of the *calle,* where it formed a T junction with Calle dell'Albero. Brunetti called back to the boy. 'I'm going back to the Questura. Tell your mother I would like to talk to her.'

The boy had materialized around the

corner behind him. He shook his head at Brunetti's request, but he said nothing.

Pressing his back against the wall of the building opposite Brunetti, the boy squeezed past him. He turned left into the *calle,* heading towards the bridge they had both run down.

He paused at the bottom but did not look back at Brunetti. As the boy put his foot on the first step, Brunetti called after him. 'You're a good boy.' The boy ran up the bridge and disappeared down the other side.

28

' "Tiger man"?' Vianello repeated after Brunetti told him about his meeting with the Fornaris and the child. 'He didn't give you any better idea of what he was talking about?'

'No. Nothing. Someone who looked like a tiger to him — came in while they were inside the place and picked the little girl up and threw her out the door.' Brunetti paused, ran a hand through his hair, and added, 'At least that's what it sounded like.'

'And for this the boy wants to *kill* him?'

'There was a door to the terrace in the parents' bedroom,' Brunetti reminded him. 'She could have fallen off and slid down the roof from there.'

'You might be right about that,' Vianello conceded, 'but I don't remember seeing a tiger skin.'

'Don't be literal-minded, Lorenzo. He's a child. Who knows what he means by a tiger man? It could be someone in striped pyjamas; it could be someone who yelled at them in a deep voice.'

Vianello considered this, then added, 'We don't even know if the kid's using the right word, do we?' When Brunetti said nothing, Vianello said, 'You told me he barely spoke Italian. You think he'd know the word?'

Brunetti thought the boy's understanding of Italian was more than adequate, though what Vianello said might be true. Then he remembered the way the boy had fluffed out his hair like the head of a beast and had made those motions to suggest a tiger's stripes. But the world of a child's imagination did not have to correspond to an adult's.

'Poor devil,' Vianello said.

'You mean the kid?' Brunetti asked.

'Of course I mean the kid,' Vianello said quickly. 'How old is he? Twelve? He ought to be in school, not coming to the city to go *to work* by breaking into houses.' Brunetti restrained himself from commenting on the inconsistency of Vianello's opinions and waited for him to continue.

'He's a kid,' the Inspector repeated indignantly. 'He's not doing these things because it's his idea to do them.' He threw up his hands in disgust and made an angry noise in his throat.

'It sounds as if you do have a certain sympathy for at least one of them,' Brunetti observed, but he smiled after he said it, and Vianello did not take offence.

'Well, you know how it is: it's always easy to have sympathy in a particular case. It's when we look at things in general that we lump them all together and say those things. Stupid things.' Presumably, Vianello meant the things he had said earlier, which would make this an apology or something close to one.

'It's just that I get crazy, not being able to do anything,' Vianello went on, and Brunetti remained silent. 'I was talking to Pucetti before I came up. They had a call from that grocery store over by the Miracoli. Seems they had a drug addict in there this morning, waving a metal rod and threatening to break the place up if they didn't give him money.'

This was a story Brunetti had heard many times, and he feared he already knew the outcome. 'They gave him twenty euros,' Vianello went on, 'and all he did was go to the bar next door and buy a bottle of wine and then sit on the bench in front of the store and start to drink it. That's when the owner called us.' Vianello stretched his legs out and stared at his feet. He too had heard this same story many times.

'So Pucetti went over. He tried to get Alvise to go with him.' Vianello, gave a deep sigh, and shook his head. 'But he was too busy. So he took Fede and Moretti, and when they got there the guy was still sitting on the bench, like he'd just been passing by and decided to rest a while. The owner identified him, Pucetti wrote out a formal *denuncia,* and they brought the guy back here. And after two hours we let him go.'

Vianello appeared to have finished, but then he said, 'It's just like the Mutti guy. He's disappeared. Your friend Zeccardi called earlier.'

'What did he say?'

'Mutti was living in Dorsoduro. So the guys from the Finanza paid him a visit, asked to see the financial records of his organization, and he told them to come and see him in the group's office the next day.'

'And?' Brunetti asked, though, given the context into which Vianello had placed the subject, he was fairly certain what the story would be.

'They did. And he was gone. The address he gave for the office was a bar, where they'd never heard of him, and when they went back to where he was living, he'd cleared out the place. No one knew where he'd gone.'

'Raptured?' Brunetti asked, using the English word.

'What?' Vianello asked.

'Nothing, nothing,' Brunetti said. 'Bad joke.'

The prisons were overflowing, Brunetti knew, and the government had had too much flak over the last amnesty to be willing to declare another one so soon, so bulletins from the Ministry discouraged the police from arresting anyone except the most violent criminals. The resulting feeling of impotence, both on the part of the police and on the part of the public, was a cause of simmering anger to both, but there was no way of changing anything.

'All right,' Brunetti said, pushing himself to his feet. 'This isn't going to help us or get us anywhere, sitting here and moaning.'

'What do you suggest?'

'That we go and get a coffee and see about finding a way to get someone to watch the Fornari place.' When he saw Vianello's expression, Brunetti explained, 'I'm curious to see if anyone goes to see them.'

'Anyone like who?' asked Vianello, intrigued.

'That's what I'd like to find out. Because

that might tell me why they went.'

Over coffee, the two men discussed the problem of staffing and logistics but came up with no way to keep the Fornari house under surveillance. Anyone seen lurking in a dead end *calle* such as that one would soon call attention to himself. They discussed and dismissed every possibility until Vianello was finally forced to ask, 'Who do you think it is that will go calling?'

'The girl's father.'

The answer appeared to surprise the Inspector. 'You think he cares?'

'No, but I think he might see it as an opportunity to get some money out of them.'

'You're assuming he knows what happened to the girl, aren't you?' Vianello asked. 'And that the Fornaris do, too.'

Before he answered, Brunetti recalled his initial visit, when Fornari's wife had seemed curious to find the police in her house, but hardly worried; and his second, when both she and her husband had given signs of great distress. They must have learned something in the ensuing time: Brunetti wanted to know what it was and who had been the bearer of that information.

A silence fell between the men as each considered the possibilities of action open to them. After some time, Brunetti said, making it sound the sort of natural everyday thing a father would do, 'I can ask my kids.'

'Ask them what?' Vianello said, unable to disguise his astonishment.

'If they know either of their children. And what they might have heard about them.' Vianello's look was so long and serious that it made Brunetti uncomfortable.

'They're of an age,' Brunetti said, then added, 'well, close to it.'

'Thank God mine are still too young,' Vianello said with suspicious blandness.

'For what?' Brunetti asked, though he knew what was coming.

'To work for us,' the Inspector said.

Brunetti resisted the impulse to defend himself. He looked at his watch and saw that it was almost three. 'I'm going home,' he said, getting to his feet.

Vianello too had apparently said as much as he chose to say.

'If anyone wants me, tell them I had to go out, all right?' he asked Vianello.

'Of course.'

Even the Chief Augur would not have been able to find a hidden message in Vianello's voice, though Brunetti knew there was one. Brunetti walked around his desk, and patted Vianello on the shoulder.

Then he left the Questura and went home.

He broached the subject at dinner, between the risotto with spinach and the pork with mushrooms. Chiara — who appeared to have abandoned vegetarianism — looked somehow different that evening, said that she didn't know Ludovica Fornari but knew of her.

'Of?' Brunetti asked, placing another piece of pork on his plate.

'Even I've heard about her,' Raffi offered, then returned his attention to the bowl of carrots with ginger.

'What have you heard?' Brunetti enquired mildly.

Paola shot him a glance as sharp as it was suspicious and interrupted to ask, 'Chiara, is that my Passion Flower you're wearing?' Brunetti had no idea to what the name referred. Because Chiara was wearing a white cotton sweater, it was not likely to be an article of clothing: that left lipstick or whatever else might be applied to a face. Or perfume, though he had not been aware of any, and Paola usually never wore scent.

'Yes,' Chiara said with a certain hesitation.

'I thought so,' Paola said with a wide smile. 'It looks very good on you.' She tilted her head to one side and studied her daughter's face. 'Probably better on you than it does on me, so maybe you'd better keep it.'

'You don't mind, do you, *Mamma?*' Chiara asked.

'No, no, not at all.' Looking brightly around the table, Paola said, 'There's only fruit for dessert, but I think tonight might be a good time to open the *gelato* season. Anyone willing to go over to Giacomo dell'Orio to get it?'

Raffi speared the remaining wheels of carrot and put them into his mouth, set his fork down, and raised his hand. 'I'll go.'

'But what about flavours?' Paola, who had never in her life shown any interest at all in the flavours of ice-cream she ate — so long as she got a lot of it — asked with transparently false brightness. 'Chiara, why don't you go with your brother and help him decide?'

Chiara pushed her chair back and got to her feet. 'How much?'

'Get the biggest container they have: we should begin the year with a bang, I think.' Then, to Raffi, 'Take the money from my purse. It's near the door.'

Before Brunetti could finish his dinner and in open defiance of family tradition, the children were out the door and pounding down the stairs.

Brunetti set his fork down, conscious in the silence of the sound it made as it tapped the wood of the table. 'And what was that all about, if I might ask?' he said.

'It's about not turning my children into spies,' Paola said heatedly. Then, before he could begin to defend himself, she added, 'And don't say you were just asking idle questions, making conversation over dinner. I know you too well to believe that, Guido. And I won't have it.'

Brunetti looked at his plate, suddenly wondering how he had managed to eat so much, for why else would he suddenly feel so uncomfortably full? He sipped the last of his wine and set the glass back on the table.

She was right. He knew that, but it angered him to have it pointed out to him so sharply. He looked at his plate again, picked up his fork and set it across the plate, then placed the knife in a neat parallel next to it.

'And, Guido, you wouldn't have it, either, not really,' she said in a far softer voice. 'I said I knew you too well.' There was a pause, and then she said, 'You wouldn't like it if you had done it.'

He pushed his chair back and got to his feet. He picked up his plate to carry it into the kitchen. Behind her chair he stopped and put his hand on her shoulder; hers covered his immediately.

'I hope they bring some chocolate,' he said, his appetite suddenly restored.

29

The next morning, Brunetti lay in bed long after Paola had got up and left to go to her early class. He considered his options, looking at the case of the Gypsy girl from a different perspective or what he thought was a different perspective. He had nothing, not really. The only tangible proof he had that the girl had not fallen to her death while leaving the scene of a robbery was the testimony of a child who claimed that his sister had been killed by the tiger man. As evidence of that, Brunetti had in his possession a single cuff link and a ring set with a piece of cheap red glass.

There were no signs of violence on the child's body other than that which would result from sliding down a terracotta roof, and the cause of death was drowning.

His judgement that the Fornaris had come into possession of some sort of guilty knowledge was entirely subjective. His original assessment — and Vianello's — had been that Fornari's wife had been genuinely surprised by the news of the robbery.

Fornari had seemed worried when Brunetti spoke to him, but he was a businessman working in Russia: well might he look worried. His wife had seemed nervous that time, as well. So what? Their daughter had seemed entirely untroubled to meet Brunetti. But then he remembered her coughing. It had begun when he had said he was about to leave and would get Vianello. 'Inspector' Vianello, he had said.

Even that was meaningless: people coughed all the time.

Brunetti shifted around under the covers, turned over on to his back and studied the ceiling until the growing light told him he could linger no more. The only thing for it was to talk to Patta and see if, just this once, the Vice-Questore would see the pattern that could be made from these events.

'Once again, you're letting yourself be carried away, Brunetti,' Patta said some hours later, just as Brunetti knew he would. Brunetti had not wasted time trying to predict his superior's exact words, but he had accurately predicted his superior's response. 'It's obvious that they had no idea what happened,' the Vice-Questore explained. 'She and her son probably came home and found the door to the terrace open: people forget about these things all the time. Unfortunately, the child had been in there while they were out.'

Patta, who had been pacing his office as he spelled out his judgement, turned suddenly and, much in the manner of the clever prosecution lawyer in American films, said, 'You said she was wearing a plastic shoe?'

'Yes.'

'Well, there you are,' Patta said, opening his hands in a gesture that suggested he had just revealed the final piece of evidence and there really was no need to waste more time in discussion.

'Where am I?' Brunetti risked saying.

Patta's expression made it clear that Brunetti was sailing too close to the wind. In a voice rich with sweet reason itself, the Vice-Questore went on. 'Plastic. On a slanted roof. A roof made from terracotta tiles.' He paused, then asked, 'I don't have to draw you a picture, do I, Commissario?' Patta's use of Brunetti's title was often an advance warning sign.

'No, Vice-Questore. I understand.'

'So this Signora Vivarini and her son, as I suggested, came home; she found the door to the terrace open and didn't give it a thought.' Patta paused long enough to smile in Brunetti's direction, now transformed into the charming defence attorney. 'There's no way they could be troubled by that, is there, Commissario?'

'No, sir.'

'You said you thought Signora Vivarini was surprised to learn of the robbery, didn't you?'

'Yes, sir.'

'Well, then, I'm not sure what all the fuss is about.'

'I told you about the daughter, coughing like that when I used Vianello's title.' As he heard himself saying it, Brunetti realized how limp, almost pathetic, it sounded. 'Before that, everything was entirely normal: she came in, introduced herself as Ludovica Fornari, shook my hand, but when I said —'

'What?' Patta interrupted, face suddenly alert.

'Excuse me?'

'What did you say the girl's name was?'

'Ludovica Fornari. Why?' And then he thought to add, 'sir.'

'You always talked about Signora Vivarini,' Patta said.

'It's in the report, sir. The husband's name.'

Patta waved that aside with a violent gesture, as if he were long past the point where he had to pay attention to written reports. 'Why didn't you tell me this before?' he demanded.

'I didn't think it important, sir.'

'Of course it's important,' Patta said, speaking as he would to a particularly dull pupil.

'May I ask why, sir?'

'You're Venetian, aren't you?' Patta asked, just short of sarcasm.

Surprised, the best Brunetti could do was say, 'Yes.'

'And you don't know who she is?'

Brunetti knew who her parents were, but from the way Patta spoke, Brunetti knew he knew nothing.

'No, sir, I don't.'

'She's the *fidanzata* of the son of the Minister of the Interior. That's who she is.'

Had this really been a cheap courtroom drama and Brunetti the lawyer whose only purpose in the scene was to be defeated utterly by the brilliant *coup de théâtre* of his opposite, then this was the point where he should have slapped his palm to his forehead and said out loud, 'I should have known,' or

'I had no idea.'

Instead, Brunetti remained silent, ostensibly to permit Patta to reveal more but actually to give himself time to fit it all together.

'I'm surprised at you, Brunetti, really I am,' Patta began. 'My son knows both children — he's in the same rowing club with the son — but I had no idea who you were talking about all this time. The Fornari girl. Of course.' Brunetti sat with a look of bright attention plastered across his face, as if still trapped in the conventions of this cheap film.

The Minister of the Interior. Among whose duties was the direction of the various forces of order, including the police. The scandal magazines loved his family: his wife one of the heiresses of a huge industrial fortune; the eldest son an anthropologist missing and believed dead in New Caledonia; a daughter famous for commuting between Rome and Los Angeles in pursuit of a film career that never quite managed to take off; another daughter married to a Spanish doctor and living quietly in Madrid; and the now-heir, a boy of unpredictable temper who had already been involved in more than one *discoteca* fracas and about whom rumours of more serious offences — always left unprosecuted — circulated widely among the police. The mother was Venetian, Brunetti knew, the Minister himself Roman.

'. . . idea is entirely untenable,' Patta said, approaching the end of his peroration. 'Thus the idea of even his most remote involvement with such a thing — which I hardly have to tell you is absolutely unthinkable — is not an idea we are going to consider.' The Vice-Questore waited for Brunetti to respond, but Brunetti was busy wondering how, and what, he could find out about the boy.

Brunetti nodded, as though he had been following every word his superior had said. He was curious about, among other things, who the 'his' and the 'we' in Patta's discourse were. The first could as easily be the Minister as his son; the 'we' most likely referred to the police, but could just as easily refer to the entire political establishment.

'Have I made myself sufficiently clear, Commissario?' Patta asked, this time infusing his voice with the heavy menace usually reserved for the villain of melodrama.

'Yes, sir,' Brunetti answered. He rose to his feet and said, 'I'm sure your analysis of the situation is correct, and we should be very careful about involving someone as important as this in our investigations without serious justification.'

'There is *no* justification,' Patta shot back, not attempting to hide his anger, 'serious or otherwise.'

'Of course,' Brunetti said, 'that's evident.' He took a few steps towards the door, waiting to see what sort of final warning Patta would choose to give him, but the Vice-Questore said nothing further. Brunetti wished his superior a polite good morning and left the office.

Outside, Signorina Elettra glanced at him as he emerged. 'Unpleasant, eh?' she asked.

'It seems that the Fornari girl is the *fidanzata* of the son of the Minister of the Interior,' he said. Her eyes widened, and he watched as she began to consider a new perspective on events. Then, should Lieutenant Scarpa perhaps be hiding behind the arras, he added, 'This, of course, means it is unthinkable that we make an attempt to find out the boy's past history or about any accusations that might have been made against him.'

She shook her head, dismissing such a course of action. 'If he's the son of a minister,' she said earnestly, 'then it's impossible that these inquiries would find anything, I'm sure.' As she spoke, her right hand reached aside to her keyboard: the mountain stream flowing across the face of her screen disappeared, replaced by a utilitarian panoply of programs. 'It would be a waste of time to pursue them,' she added, turning her chair to face the screen.

'I could not agree more strongly, Signorina,' Brunetti intoned and went upstairs to await the results of her search.

'*Mamma mia,*' she said as she entered his office two hours later. 'This is a busy boy.' She approached Brunetti's desk, some papers in her hand; she stopped and began to lift them one by one, only to let them flutter on to the surface, saying as they fell, 'Possession of drugs.' Flutter, flutter. 'Dismissed for insufficient evidence. Aggravated assault.' Flutter, flutter. 'Dismissed because the victim retracted his *denuncia.* Aggravated assault.' Flutter, flutter. 'Another retraction.' She held up one sheet a bit higher than the others and said, 'I put all four drunken driving arrests on one sheet. It didn't seem right to waste so much paper on him.' Flutter, flutter. 'Each time, he found compassionate judges who considered his age and his sincere desire to change himself, and so formal charges were never brought against him.'

Her smile was that of a doting aunt,

393

delighted that the forces of order joined her in seeing into the pure heart of this boy. Brunetti noticed that there were only two sheets of paper left. 'Assault on a police officer,' she said, placing one of them in front of Brunetti, perhaps to suggest that playtime was almost at an end.

'He got into an argument in a restaurant in Bergamo,' she explained. 'It started when one of those Tamils who sell roses came in. The minister's son — his name is Antonio — told him to get out, and when the Tamil didn't go, he started to shout at him. Someone at another table, this was the police officer, who was having dinner with his wife, went over and tried to quiet him down.'

'What happened?'

'According to the original report, the boy pulled a knife and stabbed at the Tamil, but he backed away in time. Then things got confused, but the boy ended up, handcuffed, on the floor.

'And then?'

'Then things get even more confused,' she said, setting the last paper on top of the others.

Brunetti looked at it: a government form he did not recognize. 'What is it?' he asked.

'An expulsion order. The Tamil was on a

plane to Colombo the next day.' Her voice was neutral. 'When they checked his papers, they discovered that he had been arrested a number of times before and told to leave the country.'

'But this time they helped him leave?' Brunetti asked unnecessarily.

'It seems.'

'And the police officer?'

'When he submitted his written report the following day, he remembered that the Tamil had been drunk and abusive and had threatened the girl.' When she saw Brunetti's expression, she added, 'Known for their violence, these Sri Lankans, aren't they?'

Brunetti restrained himself from comment and studied the surface of his desk. Finally he said, 'How lucky for the boy that the policeman remembered.'

Retrieving the last two pages, she glanced at them, though Brunetti knew this was more for show than from necessity. 'He also remembered that there had been no knife. He said it must have been one of the Tamil's roses.'

'He actually said that?' demanded an astonished Brunetti.

Waving the papers, she answered, 'Wrote it.' After a minimal pause, she went on, 'The police in Bergamo appear to have lost the original statement he gave when they got to the restaurant.'

'And the girl?' Brunetti asked. 'Did she remember that detail, about the rose, too?'

Signorina Elettra gave the shadow of a shrug and said, 'She said she was too frightened to remember.'

'I see.'

'How long has he known the Fornari girl?'

'From what the people I know said, it's only a few months.'

'He's the heir, isn't he?' Brunetti asked.

'Yes.'

'What actually happened to the older brother?'

'He was living with a tribe in New Caledonia, doing some sort of anthropological research. Living like them. And this tribe, or so the reports say, was attacked by the tribe living in the next valley and the boy disappeared during a raid.'

'Killed?' Brunetti asked.

She raised her shoulders and let them drop. 'No one knows for sure. He'd shaved his head and got all the tribal scars, so whoever raided might have thought he was one of them.'

Brunetti shook his head at the waste of it, and she added, 'The attack wasn't reported until months later, and by then there was no trace of him.'

'Which means?'

'From what I read, either the tribe he was living with would have buried him, or the others would have carried off his body after they killed him.'

Brunetti did not want to know more than that. He changed the subject by asking, 'So Antonio became the heir?'

'Yes.'

'Were they close?'

'Very. Or at least that's what the articles that appeared at the time said. "Brothers who were blood brothers," all those things the sentimental press loves.'

'Blood brothers?'

'Antonio went out there to visit him, it seems, and while he was with the tribe he went through some sort of ritual that made him a member, along with his brother.' She paused, trying to recall some of the things she had read and apparently not thought it necessary to copy. 'Learning how to hunt with a bow and arrow — all that Tarzan sort of thing that boys like,' she said. 'It was never clear if the brother who's missing — Claudio — got the ritual scars on his cheeks, but both of them did the tattoos and ate the honey-covered larvae.' She gave a delicate shiver at the thought of it, or at the thought of either.

'Tattoos?' Brunetti asked.

'You know the sort of thing. We have to look at them all summer. Those bands on the arms and legs: woven and geometric. You see them all over.'

Indeed. And in photos hanging on the walls of apartments. Reddish hair, all fluffed out and making his head look bigger, and tattoos on his arms that looked like stripes. 'Tiger man,' Brunetti said out loud.

'What?' she asked, and then more politely, 'I beg your pardon.'

'Are there any photos of him?'

'Too many,' she said tiredly.

'Go and print me some of them,' he said. 'Please, now.' He reached for the phone to call for a boat and a car and then for Vianello to go with him.

30

'So you think he's tiger man?' Vianello asked when Brunetti finished repeating what Signorina Elettra had told him. They were on one side of the deck of the police boat, heading towards Piazzale Roma, where Brunetti hoped the car he had called for would be waiting. Foa cut the boat suddenly to the left to avoid hitting a *sandalo* carrying four people and a dog that pulled too quickly in front of them. Foa sounded his horn twice and shouted something to the man at the helm, but he didn't even glance in their direction.

'And you think that's enough to let you go after him?' Vianello asked, his voice rising in volume as he neared the end of the sentence, almost shouting by the time he reached the last word. The Inspector threw both hands towards heaven, as if wanting to pass his question on to some higher authority than the man standing beside him.

Brunetti let his glance drift away from Vianello's face and toward the façade of the buildings on the left side of the canal. He noticed that the *palazzo* to the right of the Faliers' was finally being restored. He had been at school with the son of the former owners, remembered when the father had gambled the *palazzo* away in some private gambling club, after which the entire family had had to move. Though they'd been good friends, Brunetti had never heard from the boy again.

'Well?' Vianello called Brunetti's attention back by asking. When Brunetti did not respond, the Inspector went on, 'Even if what you say is true, and this boy he called the tiger man did do something to the Gypsy girl, we've got no chance of proving it. Do you hear me, Guido; no chance. Zero.'

Brunetti's attention started to wander to the buildings behind Vianello, but the Inspector called it back by placing his hand on Brunetti's arm. 'Guido, this is suicide for you. You go out there, and let's say you manage to convince this kid's parents to bring him in to talk about "tiger man".' To express his opinion of the probable conse-quences of this, Vianello closed his eyes, and Brunetti saw the muscles of his jaw draw tight.

'So you've got an under-age witness — and I'm sure the kid's family will have a long accumulation of arrests and convictions — and you're going to get this kid — and may I interject here what you told me, that the kid barely speaks Italian? — and you're going to get this kid to bring testimony against the son of the Minister of the Interior?'

The boat suddenly veered into a cross-wave, knocking both of them against the railing. Foa pulled the wheel back and turned his eyes forward again.

Brunetti opened his mouth to suggest they go down into the cabin before continuing this conversation, but Vianello rode right over him, 'And you think you'll find a prosecuting magistrate — whose career depends, as I hardly need to point out to you, upon that same Minister — and you think this prosecuting magistrate is going to work to get a conviction?' He pushed his face closer to Brunetti and added, 'On this testimony?' Then, as if that question were not sufficiently devastating, he added, 'On this *evidence?*'

Brunetti put his hand into the pocket of his jacket and fingered the cuff link and the ring. He had seen Fornari's nervousness, he had seen the rage in the small boy's face, the primitive lust for vengeance given full rein by the fact that his mother longed for it, too. This was evidence, but evidence that no court would credit, indeed, that no court would hear. In the halls of justice, where 'The law is equal for all', Brunetti's impressions were entirely without weight and entirely without merit. As he knew, and as Vianello had just reminded him, the law wanted evidence, not the opinion of a man who had run to ground a child half crazed with fear and then held him in the air until he told his story. Brunetti could imagine what any defence lawyer, let alone one who was defending the son of a cabinet minister, would do to a construction such as this.

'I want to be sure,' Brunetti said.

'Sure about what?'

'Sure that what the boy told me is true.'

Vianello lost all patience. 'Can't you understand that whether it's true or not doesn't matter, not in the least?' He grabbed Brunetti by the arm and pulled him down the three steps and into the cabin of the boat. When they were seated opposite one another, the Inspector went on. 'The kid could be telling the truth — for all I know, he is — but that doesn't make any difference, Guido. You've got the child of a Gypsy with a long criminal record bringing a charge against the son of the Minister of the Interior.'

'You've told me that three times already, Lorenzo,' Brunetti said tiredly.

'I'll tell you three more times if it will make you listen to me,' Vianello shot back. He paused for a long time and then, in a milder voice, went on, 'You might want to commit professional suicide, but I don't.'

'No one's asking you to.'

'I'm on my way out to this Gypsy camp with you, aren't I? I'm going out there with you while you talk to someone that Patta has told you not to talk to.'

'He never said that specifically,' Brunetti protested, splitting hairs.

'He didn't have to, for God's sake. He told you to leave this alone, and the first thing you do is run out there, without any authorization and in open defiance of your superior's orders — *our* superior's orders — to talk to people he's told you to leave alone.'

'The boy and the other sister were there that night. They saw what happened.'

'And you think their parents will let them talk to you, or to a judge?'

'The mother wants vengeance as much as the boy does. Probably more.'

'So now we're vigilantes, helping the Gypsies against the rest of the world?'

Vianello hid his exasperation by looking away from Brunetti, raising his head and closing his eyes for a moment, as if pleading with patience to return to him.

The boat began to slow and Brunetti saw that they had arrived at Piazzale Roma. He got to his feet and pushed open one side of the swinging doors. 'You can go back with Foa, then,' he said, then started up the steps to the deck.

As he got to the top, he heard Vianello coming up the steps behind him, 'Oh, for God's sake, stop being such a prima donna, Guido,' the Inspector said in his most disgruntled voice.

Today there was a new driver but, like the other, this one knew the way to the camp and remarked during the trip on how often he had taken people there. He chatted amiably on the way, and Vianello and Brunetti decided to accept the interlude his monologue offered rather than continue with their own conversation.

Brunetti had heard it all before, so he paid little attention, allowing himself the pleasure of watching the still-unfolding springtime that surrounded them once they left the city. Like most urban people, Brunetti romanticized the country and rural life. Once, when the family was eating roast chicken and Chiara, in one of her vegetarian phases, had asked him if he had ever killed a chicken, Brunetti had answered that he had never killed anything. He could not remember where the discussion had gone from there: to wherever most futile discussions went, he supposed.

The car turned, slowed, and stopped, and the driver got out to open the gate. Once inside, he got out again and closed it, then pulled around in a wide half-circle and parked facing the gate, as if eager to get all this taken care of so they could leave again.

'Wait here,' Brunetti said, leaning forward to touch him on the shoulder. He and Vianello got out of the car and closed the doors. No one was visible: no men sat on the steps of the caravans that day.

The blue Mercedes, Brunetti saw at once, was gone, as was the *roulotte* in which he had seen the female forms appear and disappear and into which Rocich had returned after every meeting. None of the towed cars had returned to their places in front of the *roulottes:* the unattached caravans remained in the back line like pieces on a chessboard upon which some of the pawns had been sacrificed.

Brunetti and Vianello walked over to the

leader's caravan. They stood in front of it. At that instant, as if it were a sudden eruption of birdcall, the varied tones of different *telefonini* could be heard from the row of *roulottes.* Brunetti distinguished four different calls, and then silence fell.

A few minutes passed, and then the door of the *roulotte* opened. From it came Tanovic. He gave an easy smile which made Brunetti uncomfortable.

'Ah, Mr Policeman,' the man said as he came down the steps. With a nod to Vianello, he added, 'And Mr Assistant Policeman.' He walked up to them, smiling, but he did not extend his hand, nor did the other two men.

'Why you come to visit us again?' He looked behind him and ran his eyes down the line of cars, turning in a full circle to study the entire line. 'To take more cars?' As he asked this, voice light and joking, Brunetti saw the rancour in his eyes that eliminated all humour.

'No, I've come to speak to Signor Rocich,' Brunetti said, then pointed to the place where the car and *roulotte* had been parked. 'But I see they're gone. Do you know where?'

The man smiled again. 'Ah, very difficult to tell, Mr Policeman.' He leaned forward and spread his smile upon Vianello, who remained stony-faced. 'My people are, what you call us — nomads — we go places, no one know where we go, when we go.' He smiled again, but his voice had turned sour. 'No one care.'

'I've got his licence plate number,' Brunetti said. 'Perhaps the road police could help me locate him.'

The man's smile grew stronger, but even less friendly. 'Old car. Old number. No help, I think.'

'What does that mean,' Brunetti asked. ' "Old car"?'

'Have new car, new number.'

'What kind of new car?'

'Good car. Not Italian shit car. Real car, German car.'

'What kind?'

The man raised a hand in the air to dismiss the very idea that a car could have a name. 'Big car, German car, new car.' Just as Brunetti was getting ready to speak, he added, 'New number.'

'I see,' Brunetti said. 'Then we'll have to check the vehicle registration office, won't we?'

'Ah, private sale. With friend. No change papers: car still belong friend. Hard to find, I think,' he said with another smile.

'What's the name of his friend?' Brunetti asked.

He shrugged eloquently. 'He no tell me. Just friend. But very big car. Very expensive.'

'Where did he get the money to buy this car?'

'Ah, he get money from other friend.'

'A Gy —' Brunetti began, but then remembered in time to ask, 'A friend here among the Rom?'

'You can say Gypsy to me, Mr Policeman,' the man said, no longer attempting to filter the venom in his voice.

'From a Gypsy friend, then?' Brunetti asked.

'No, from *gadje* man. He met man in Venice, and he ask him for money. Man very generous; he give much money. Buy car,' he concluded. He raised one hand in the air and waved it delicately back and forth, saying in English, 'Bye bye.'

'What man?' Brunetti asked.

'Man his son tell him.'

'And this man gave him the money for the car?'

A nod. A smile. 'And more.'

'Do you know how much more?'

'He no tell. Maybe afraid tell Gypsy because I steal, eh?' His smile had grown malevolent.

Brunetti turned away so quickly that he bumped into Vianello, who stepped back. 'Let's go,' Brunetti said, starting towards the car.

The man let them reach the car before he called after them, 'Mr Policeman, he gave me something for you.' The man's Italian flowed easily in this sentence, as if he had tired of playing the role of the bumbling Gypsy.

Brunetti, one hand on the handle of the door, looked back at the other man. The Gypsy slid his open hand into the pocket of his jacket and pulled it out a fist, which he extended towards Brunetti.

'I Gypsy, but I no steal this,' he said as he moved his closed hand from side to side. He and Brunetti faced one another across a distance of three metres. He held his fist up higher. 'You want?' he asked.

Brunetti walked towards him, fighting the sudden rigidity of his knees. He stopped close to the man and extended his hand, arm stiff and straight. For a moment he feared the man was going to tell him to say 'please', which Brunetti did not think he would be able to do.

Brunetti opened his hand and held it palm up.

The other man brought his fist above

Brunetti's and opened the index finger, then the next and then the next. Brunetti felt something drop into his palm. Before he could look, the man said, gesturing at Brunetti's hand. 'Man with money want that. Show boy was there, see all, see all what happen. But Rocich, he say give to you, Mister Policeman.' He let his hand fall to his side, turned and walked back to his *roulotte.* As he started to climb the steps, Brunetti allowed himself to tilt his palm so that he could see what the man had been told to give him.

The cuff link was identical to the other: silver border around a small piece of lapis.

A sharp noise caused Brunetti to flinch, but it was only the sound of the Gypsy slamming the door to his *roulotte.*

31

The lethargy into which Brunetti fell upon his return from the Gypsy encampment lasted three days before Paola asked him about it. They were seated on the terrace, after a dinner that Brunetti had barely touched and he was well into his second glass of grappa with the bottle on the table in the likely event that he wanted a third.

Gradually, as it grew darker and the evening chill settled in, he told her — all attempt at chronology or sequence ignored — what had happened. If there was any order in the story he told, it was perhaps the mounting importance of impression, the strongest saved for last, which meant the final stories he told described the mother's terrible wailing and the savage expression on the boy's face as he told Brunetti about 'tiger man'.

Even his final conversation with Fornari and his wife had not left as strong an impression. 'They didn't want to let me in,' Brunetti told her. 'But I told them I'd come back with a warrant.'

In response to the sudden tightening of her hand on his arm — it was too dark by now for him to distinguish her features, even a motion of her head — he said, 'That was nonsense, of course: no one would have given it to me. So far as we're concerned, so far as the entire *magistratura* is concerned, the case is closed: the girl died accidentally in a fall after robbing the Fornaris' apartment, and that is that.'

'But they did let you in?' she asked.

'Yes. You know how good a liar I am,' Brunetti said.

'You're not particularly good,' she said, a remark he took as a compliment. 'What happened?'

'She was nervous; so was he. At first I didn't think they'd have the courage to brazen it out.' And this, he realized, he meant as a compliment.

'What did you say?'

'That I'd spoken to one of the Gypsies at the camp, and he told me that Rocich claimed he had come into the city and spoken to them.' He recalled his pose during that conversation: the cool bureaucrat come in search of supporting testimony;

nothing more.

Brunetti was silent for some time. He sipped at his grappa, the Tignanello Paola had given him for his birthday. Fine as it was, the taste displeased him, and he set the glass back on the table.

'It didn't work,' he admitted. 'They said they had no idea who this Rocich was or why someone with that name would want to speak to them.' It had been the woman, Brunetti recalled, who was more vociferous in her protestations: Fornari had stood beside her, shaking his head, capable of speech only when Brunetti asked him a direct question.

Brunetti uncrossed his legs and stretched them out, then lifted his feet and rested them on the lower rung of the railing of the terrace. As he did so, he remembered how, as young parents, they had been so careful about keeping the door to the terrace locked and allowed the children on to it only when one of them was with them. Even now, after decades in the apartment, Brunetti still avoided peering over the edge and looking down at the ground, four floors below.

Paola allowed a long time to pass before she asked, 'What do you think happened?'

Brunetti had thought of little else during the last few days, had made and cancelled and remade the scenario of events, had imagined it this way and imagined it that way, always with the memory of the girl's face at the forefront of his mind. 'Their daughter was there,' he finally said. 'With the boyfriend, probably in her bedroom. They heard noises in the apartment.' He closed his eyes and tried to visualize it. 'Drugged or not drugged, the boy would still see it as his duty to go and find out what it was.'

'And the stripes?' Paola suddenly asked. 'How did the little boy see them?'

He turned to face the shadow of her head against the still-fading light. 'They weren't in her bedroom doing their calculus homework, Paola. Remember, her parents were out.'

He left it to her to imagine the scene as he had: the naked boy, roused from bed, wild stripes on his arms and legs, roaring at the Gypsy children. 'Tiger man,' Paola said.

'The parents' room has a door to the terrace,' Brunetti said. 'It's probably how they got in, so it's where they'd run to try to get out.'

'And then?' Paola asked.

Though Paola could not see Brunetti's shrug, she thought she heard it as his jacket rubbed against the back of his chair.

'That's anyone's guess,' he finally answered.

'But the brother said . . .' Paola began.

'The brother,' Brunetti cut her off to say, 'because he is a boy, was probably in charge of whatever they did. And he let his sister die.' Before Paola could protest, he went on, 'I know, I know, he didn't let anything happen. But I'm not talking about what actually happened, whatever that was, but about how he'd see it. She was with him, so anything that happened to her was his fault.'

He paused a long time after this, then said, 'But if she was thrown off the roof, then it's not his fault.' Before she could protest, he hurried on, 'I'm just trying to see it the way he would.' He stopped talking and the noise of the city flowed up to them: passing footsteps, a man's voice coming from one of the windows beneath them, a television in the distance.

'Then why are the Fornaris acting so guilty?' Paola finally asked.

'It might not be guilt,' Brunetti said.

'What else could it be?'

'Fear.'

'Of the Gypsies?' she asked in surprise. 'Some sort of vendetta?' Her tone revealed her refusal to believe this. 'But from what you said, no one except the mother and the brother seemed much to care about what happened to her.'

'Not of the Gypsies,' Brunetti said, wondering where she had been all these years.

'Then of what?' she asked, failing to see it.

'The state. The police. Being accused and being caught up in the mechanism of justice.' What greater fear stalked the average citizen? Being the victim of a robbery was nothing in comparison.

'But they didn't do anything. You said you checked their story, and they got home after the girl was already dead. And the father really was in Russia.'

'They aren't afraid for themselves,' Brunetti told her. 'For the daughter, for whatever she saw and didn't tell them and then didn't tell the police, or for whatever she might have seen her boyfriend do.' He decided to trust her with this, as well, and added, 'Or anything she might have done.'

He heard her sudden intake of breath. 'But the little boy talked about Tiger Man, not about a girl,' she said.

'He's just a kid, Paola. He probably ran the instant he saw someone come out of the bedroom. And left his sister there.' Brunetti got to his feet. 'It would be more reason for him to feel guilty and more reason for him

416

to say someone else was responsible.' He saw how unsatisfied this possibility left her but said only, 'I think I'd like to go to bed.'

'And leave it like that?' she asked, shocked.

'It's not one of your novels, where everything gets explained in the last chapter, with people sitting around in the library.'

'The books I read aren't like that,' she said indignantly.

'Neither is life,' Brunetti answered and extended his hand to help her to her feet.

Two days later, Ariana Rocich was buried on San Michele, her grave paid for by the *comune* di Venezia. No one was certain of the girl's religion, so officialdom decided that she be given Christian burial. Brunetti and Vianello attended, both of them having ordered large wreaths, the only flowers on her coffin.

The chaplain of the hospital, Padre Antonin Scallon, read the service over the coffin placed beside the open hole, the white skirt of his tunic invisible against the white roses of the wreaths. The ceremony took place in a different part of the cemetery from the one where Brunetti's mother had been buried, but the same trees stood here, as well.

The blossoms had disappeared, leaving no

trace on the grass. But green shoots, soon to be the first leaves of the season, covered the trees, and birds whizzed in and out among them, building and preparing.

When the priest finished the reading, he turned to the two men standing there: no one else attended. He raised his hand and made the sign of the cross over the empty grave, and then above the coffin, and then he raised his hand in benediction of the two men who were there with her that day. When the priest lowered his hand, the workers whose job it was to lower the box approached from the sides of the grave and lifted the ropes.

Vianello turned away and started down the path that led to the courtyard and the *portone* out to the boat landing. Padre Antonin closed his book, lifted his hand over the coffin which the men were now sliding towards the grave, and made a gesture that was half wave, half blessing. He turned away.

Brunetti stepped towards him and put his right hand on the priest's arm. 'Thank you, Padre,' he said and leaned forward to kiss the other man on both cheeks. Arm in arm, they turned from the grave and started back towards the city.

ABOUT THE AUTHOR

Donna Leon is the author of seventeen novels featuring Guido Brunetti — all of which have been highly acclaimed — and the winner of the CWA Silver Dagger Award. She has lived in Venice for twenty-five years.

We hope you have enjoyed this Large Print book. Other Thorndike, Wheeler, and Chivers Press Large Print books are available at your library or directly from the publishers.

For information about current and upcoming titles, please call or write, without obligation, to:

Publisher
Thorndike Press
295 Kennedy Memorial Drive
Waterville, ME 04901
Tel. (800) 223-1244

or visit our Web site at:

http://gale.cengage.com/thorndike

OR

Chivers Large Print
published by BBC Audiobooks Ltd
St James House, The Square
Lower Bristol Road
Bath BA2 3SB
England
Tel. +44(0) 800 136919
email: bbcaudiobooks@bbc.co.uk
www.bbcaudiobooks.co.uk

All our Large Print titles are designed for easy reading, and all our books are made to last.